Red Ink~ Bosses, Bullies, & Butterflies
by
Butterfly Brooks

About the Author
Butterfly Brooks is an author, musician, playwright, and educator.

Dedication
This work is dedicated to my children, Akilah, Jibril, Tigris, and Raphael. May you always be uncaged by your soul, enraged by the boldly unbold, and be a sage one million years old, just like a butterfly.

Acknowledgements
Eternal love and gratitude for all of those that love, support, and encourage creative fire. All of my mothers, fathers, children,

family, and friends, especially Gwendolyn Elizabeth, Dora Louise, Verta Elizabeth, Marji Jihada and Brenda Faye~ I love you, forever, for always.

Supreme Love and Gratitude to my pen sisters, Gina, Storm, Crystal, and Britt. Your Love and encouragement empower me in my creative experience~ I Love you! Faye Fite and Pamela Hunter are angels in the outfield~ I Love you too! xoxo

Chapter One
We Ain't Afraid of No Ghosts, Are We?

Friday 8:00 a.m.

"Deez bitches…" She couldn't help but pay attention. She had to monitor the action in cyberspace. She felt that she was the reporter, the necessary scribe, making detailed accounts of the demise of her people. It seemed nobody noticed that an entire institution was going down. Way down. Down into the doldrums of a sewer. This appeared to be the fate of African American fiction a.k.a. urban fiction. It had been an industry built from the pure grit and grind of hungry aspiring authors eager to share simple day to day life stories of everyday people, some ordinary, some extraordinary. Some famous, some infamous. The institution of African American fiction was being completely decimated by the new era of unthoughtful, poorly crafted, unedited uploading of rough drafts and meandering thought logs peddled as urban fiction books. African American fiction was going the way of music, it was a trap, loaded with trap books. And if there was nothing she could do to stop it, she was going to damn sure document the destruction. Maybe someone would come along after she was dead and gone and know that the beautiful, indigenous Black Americans were not always savages, thugs, plugs, pins, bullies, and bosses. They would know that we were once royalty, emperors, empresses, high priests, high priestesses, shamans, healers, and butterflies. But for now, here she was looking at her feed on Zing, tracking the latest frenzy in Latoya "Tea" Mitchell's Tea Thyme group, the largest Zing group dedicated to Black urban fiction. Tea was the best friend of Kendali Grace, Dominion Publishing's best-selling author and Tea Thyme was a great supporter of Kendali's books. The mayhem was about the latest post from Bree McDee, the number one author under Gutta Butta Books, founded by Maceo Grant, ex-con and bona fide go getter. Bree managed a large following in her Zing group, The Sauce Mobb.

Zing Post Tea Thyme Group
LaToya Tea Mitchell Post: Y'all read Bree's latest Sauce Mobb post? I know y'all have. I bet I know who she is talking about. 😀😑 What do you think? This is a tangy one. 👀
Reactions: 1,246 Comments: 2,403 Shares: 889

(Load previous comments)
Shanika J.: Fuck her! She ain't that great a writer anyways.
Katerra Johnson: After all that talk about being original and bashing other people for ghostwriting smdh
Diminka Johns: Who is her? Tag me in the post. What did she say?
   Shanika J: @Diminka Johns I tagged you.
   Diminka Johns: Ok. Thanks!
Geneen Matthews: Yeah. But y'all just assuming it's kendali. might not be her. could be anybody
Diana MacFadden: But you need to read the post. Sounds like she probably talking about Kendali.
Geneen Matthews: I read it. I still think yall assuming a lot

Felicia Stewart: Wonder what this will mean for her career. Can't be good.

Geneen Matthews: Not good? maybe. But doesn't matter to me. I love her books. I will still keep reading.

Amber Michelle: I'm a fan. She used a ghostwriter. So what. Who cares. Keep the stories coming.

Heather Dunwoody: Yeah, but she talked so much trash about people who use ghostwriters. Like real bad. And now, she uses a ghostwriter. Wow. She ain't shit. I'm deleting all her stuff from my kindle. It's one thing to use a ghostwriter, but then to say you don't and then bash people who do? HYPOCRITE! AND I HATE HYPOCRITES 😡

Paula Lelani: This is what I can't stand about this whole industry. This whole scene is so messy. Everybody has so much to say about Kendali, not even knowing it's her but what about Bree posting this bullshit. It's all too messy. And ridiculous. Just over it. All of it. I am going to start reading sci fi and fantasy. 😔

Jada Reynolds: Yeah. Throw the whole industry away. 😟

ZING-End Of Comments

Lesli leaned over her computer reading the heated thread. She decided to wash up and get her morning coffee before she sat down to decipher the madness. She took a quick shower, rinsed her braids thoroughly, pinned her hair up, wrapped her body in her favorite robe, and went to the kitchen to start her coffee machine. Her loft style townhome in the heart of Midtown afforded so many amenities, but the feature she loved most was the seven minute walk to the office. This was her best life and she was immensely thankful to Bradford Meade for giving her a second chance, resurrecting her from an all-consuming creative death in the urban fiction world. She had been signed to urban fiction's number one publisher, Dominion Publishing, releasing nine fairly well received titles under the imprint, using the pen name Butterfly Brooks. Ultimately, she learned that Dominion and others like it were essentially content mills. The publishers just wanted their small cadre of authors to continuously crank out material. The bottom line was quantity because quantity equaled money. Period. Point blank. No need for discussion. Lesli Lyn was a very gifted and talented storyteller, most interested in moving readers to a higher plateau, begging questions with her work and hoping her audience had answers. Dominion was not diametrically opposed to well rounded, well studied authors, motivated by the passion for the craft and writing as an art form, but they were not interested in nurturing said passions either. And so, the teaspoon of authors on the roster, like Lesli, were left to waste and wither on the proverbial vine, hoping for a bestseller, but usually just dropping little known, moderately successful books. She met Bradford one day at the local coffee hangout and he struck up a conversation.

"What are you working on?"

Lesli side-eyed him and continued typing. "Just a novel." She happened to have a paperback copy of *Redemption's Stepchild-Amel and Rico's Love Story Part Two*, sitting on the table next to her MacBook. She was ticking away on part three, her final book with Dominion as Butterfly Brooks.

"This novel?" he asked tapping the cover with his index finger.

"No. This one is already written," she answered flatly.

He laughed. "Stop being so tough, love."

She softened at his comment. She loved that he was chipping

away at her rigid presentation with his masculine charms. "I am working on part three." She smiled. "You're kinda interrupting my flow."

"Ahhh. A smile. And such a beautiful smile. I don't mean to interrupt. I just see you in here all the time. I've been curious about what you do. Today, I actually have time to stop and ask."

"Oh. Okay." She stopped to take him in. He was definitely taller than six feet she surmised. His caramel skin and same color eyes made for a handsome face. He was a lightweight doughboy, one hot dog away from fat, but he probably hit the gym just enough to keep him off the fat boy list. He was impeccably dressed, nice soft navy blue Kenneth Coles, sky blue, lavender, white, green argyle socks, Brooks Brothers light blue and white houndstooth oxford, medium blue jeans, not skinny, and a gleaming white Kangol and white linen blazer.

"Let me give you my card. Call me sometime. For anything. I always like to keep in touch with creative types."

She accepted his card, placing it on the table without reading it.

"Okay. Thanks so much. And I apologize. It's just that I really need to finish this up so that I can move on with my life. And I am a little frustrated."

"It's okay. I understand. You have my card. Call me. I will take you to dinner and we can celebrate when you finish."

"Okay. That sounds really nice."

"Alright. Get back to work. We'll talk soon."

"Okay. Have a good day."

"You too." He walked to the door and stopped about halfway. He looked over his shoulder and said, "Ms. Brooks."

"Yes."

"Don't let the grandmother die. Let her live." And he disappeared into the crowd outside the cafe.

She was puzzled, excited, and fluttering on the inside. *He read my books?! Oh wow!*

About a week later, she and Bradford enjoyed their celebratory dinner, talking, chatting, and exploring each other. She learned that he was *the* Bradford Meade, founder and CEO of Meade Communications, publisher of the number one urban lifestyle periodical, Mahogany Magazine, and owner of multiple historical Black newspapers and their archives. Unlike the vast majority of Black people, Bradford understood the value of historical Black newspapers' archives and artifacts. He had inherited his father's impressive collection of photographs. His father, Alistair Meade, served as a celebrated photographer for a variety of Black newspapers and magazines across the country including Jet, Ebony, and Essence. When Bradford found out that Bill Gates and Michael Ochs were buying up old Black newspapers, he jumped into the bidding wars and convinced most of them to sell to him instead of the others. He lost a few, but he won plenty. While enjoying their conversation, he learned that her birth name was Lesli Lyn Faulkner and she did not have a plan, post-Dominion. She had saved some money from her previous releases and secured a few editing gigs. Her father helped pay for her townhouse, which she got for a steal since he was well connected with the municipal networks in Seminole City. But she needed direction and more importantly inspiration. Her work with Dominion left her emotionally, mentally, and spiritually drained.

"Come work with us," Bradford had said.

"Really? What would I do? You all have it together. I don't think you need me."

"We actually could use a lifestyle editor of arts and culture. You can focus strictly on books, music, and film. Right now we have this area rotating amongst the other editors. You can take it, make it your own."

"Ya' think?"

"Yeah. You have already started your blog. The Kaleidoscope. I love it. With all the butterflies. You are so on it. You have a good following. Good people. Significant people."

"You've been following my blog?" She was amazed.

"Of course. I am always paying attention to the gifted and talented."

"Wow." She rubbed the gold butterfly diamond encrusted pendant dangling from her neck. Bradford watched her play with the charm and how it accentuated her double D cleavage so enticingly. It was the first time she noticed Bradford gazing at her breasts. Most men were ogling within the first ten seconds of looking at her. He lasted several hours and therefore, she categorized him as special from that day forward.

After her final release with Dominion, she rested for six weeks enjoying many lunches and dinners with Brad and finally accepting his offer to work with Meade. It was the best decision she had ever made in her life.

She returned to her desk while her coffee brewed to takes notes on the current industry episode. Latoya proved to be most aggravating. She was good for spilling tea without all the necessary ingredients. Generally, you had to depend on her eventually dropping the required information in the comments or a group member gathering and sharing the intel. Lesli loaded the page for Bree's Zing group, The Sauce Mobb, and read the post that Tea failed to include in her spillage:

♦ ♦ ♦

"This sauce is super supreme spicy-ALL HABAÑERO PEPPER based and everything! YOU ARE WARNED! So, I recently learned from a very, very reliable source that one of your all-time favorite authors who is notorious for talking about authors that use ghostwriters is, you guessed it! DA BITCH IS USING A GHOSTWRITER!!! And she been using a ghostwriter for years! Now, legally I cannot name the author. But you all know exactly who I am talking about. She is the favorite child of one of the top publishers and supposedly writes from her real life experiences. I will just say this, lights camera, action! And on that note-drip, drip bitches!!!"

♦ ♦ ♦

She sat and contemplated the post with disgust. Her blog was dedicated to honest book reviews and real publishing news for authors, readers, and publishers, but she had to address the dumb shit. There was no way around it. After reading the Tea Thyme post, the Turner Pages post (Tea Thyme's rival, managed by Shante Turner), several other reading group posts, comments, and memes, she wrote her analysis of the current scenario:

🦋Beloved Butterflies🦋

I greet you in silky, soft-winged peace. With regard to the recent sauce, dripping from The Sauce Mobb, first let me say, I have no issues with ghostwriters or people who employ them. Ghostwriting is a necessary trade. So, dragonfly to the butterfly~ if you use a ghostwriter, so be it. Some chefs have cooks. Some actors have stunt doubles. Rappers, singers, and musicians all use ghostwriters. They enjoy prosperous careers and their credibility and credentials remain intact. Now, butterfly to butterfly, if you call yourself an author, writer, pensmith or whatever lofty title you claim, and you are using a ghostwriter, you probably shouldn't be writing. We need *you*. Your readers need *you* to step up to your computer screen. We need *you* to raise your tablet. We need *you* to man your notebook and prove that *you* have earned the praise and accolades of your followers. Take off your sheets, boo, because we ain't afraid of no ghosts!

It's Double L. Silky, soft, and signing off. Float on.

She sent the piece to Bradford because every now and then, she liked to get his opinion of her posts and blog entries. She emailed the Mahogany Lifestyle team for final polishing, graphic design, and uploading to her blog, The Kaleidoscope. After the Mahogany upload, she would post in her Zing group.
She closed her laptop and went into the bathroom. Blinking her small slit eyes and admiring her narrow creamy brown face in the mirror, she enhanced her pretty countenance with a light dusting of bronze foundation. She dressed in a hot pink and white Adidas sweatsuit, shell heads to match, and headed to the office.

Kendali Grace, Dominion's starchild, rolled her juicy Amazon frame over the black satin sheets after she and Dre indulged their lackluster intimacy. She picked up her flashing phone to the tune of 120 Zing notifications and 32 text messages.
"Don't get over excited, Dali. 'Oh, Dre! You make me feel so good, baby. I love you, baby. Let's do it again.'" He imitated her voice. "You could say just a lil' sumpthin'. Let a nigga know you

feelin' him. Damn. Fake it. Shit."

"Dre, please don't start. My phone is on full tilt."

"Oh yeah. It's always about you. You and your lil' hard up, no-dick-gettin', lonely bitch fan club." He zipped his jeans and pulled his polo over his head of coal black waves.

"You not gonna, shower?"

"Naw. I'll shower later. I got a full day ahead. I still like having your yum-yum on me. Brings me good luck."

"Awww, Dre." She hated herself for falling out of love with him. Andre Walker had held her down from the rip, from way back when, but so much had changed. She had changed. Her life had changed. His life too, but he was just an average guy, making his way with his lawn care business and a few real estate investments. She, on the other hand, was delving into the semi-celebrity world of the urban fiction book publishing industry. They were growing apart and they both knew it, but the time between them formed an emotional glue. It was hard to let go.

"Yeah, yeah, yeah."

"Don't be like that, babes." She tossed her phone on the nightstand and kneeled in front of him, her voluptuous naked body inviting him to more intimacy. Kendali's bright yellow skin, big hips, juicy thighs, and C cup breasts made her appear as though, if you squeezed her, peach juice would begin to spurt from every pore of her luscious physique. She kissed him, stroked his twenty-four inch python arms, and hugged his strong neck tightly. He received her affection, flexing his buff chest muscles with joy, for he was still, very much in love with his peach. "Listen, Dre. I need you to have a very good day and let's plan on a very good night. Maybe a parking lot picnic?" He smiled. Parking lot picnics were one of their favorite things to do before Kendali's fame. They would get fried catfish sandwiches from Deucey's with a whole loaf of their homemade bread, hand tossed coleslaw, house recipe hot mambo sauce, sweet tea, and a whole chocolate cake. They would park by the water and eat, watch the people go by, and marvel at the calm of the bay.

"Deucey's?"

"Of course."

She mastered the art of bringing him down from his anger and frustration. He adored her power over him. No man can respect a woman who doesn't have the power to re-center him.

"Okay, Dali. I'm in." He cuddled her, smacked her ass, and continued his exit prep.

"Awesome!" she screeched. She returned to her morning cyberspace ritual of checking notifications, responding to messages, and planning her day. Toya's currently controversial Tea Thyme post halted her scroll.

"Oh my God! This bitch!" She opened her text app and her Zing messenger.

✦ Zing Messenger ✦

Kadaria Atkins: Yo! You need to call me, bih.

Hakeem Asim: Ma! Touch base with me. Damn. Toya trippin, huh? And Bree, fr fr. smh

Florence J: You okay, baby? I see what they are saying about you. I am here if you need to talk. Love you.

Bianca OhGee: You need me to beat dis bitch ass? Fuck Bree! And I thought Toya was ya' girl. wtf?!! Call me. If it's after 10 text me. Then I will call you back. Luv you. ♥

"Babe, what's going on?" Dre asked from the bathroom.

"Man, these hoes always hatin'."

"You already know that. But what's up now?"

"I will just let you read it for yourself. Go to Tea's Zing group. You will see."

"Alright. I will. I gotta jet right now."

"You can't look now?" she whined.

"Babe. I am going to look. I keep tellin' you to stay away from these hookahs. I already know, same ole dumb ass drama. Some made up bullshit about you or some other author."

"No, Dre. This is a lil' more serious."

"Alright. If you say so. I'ma look. I'll call you from the truck."

"Fine." She blew her breath upward through the bottom row of her laser treated teeth, strands of her light brown hair scattering around her face. Dre kissed her cheek and left.

Devastated, she studied the post again and read the comments. She texted Toya.

📱 Text Message 📱

Kendali: Tea, what's up? I am surprised you are posting this. Kinda disappointing. Why?

Toya: Hey girl. 😊 Don't worry about it. I am simply talking about what everyone is talking about. It wouldn't look right if I didn't post it. People already see my group as being biased toward you. Don't trip. It will blow over, just like everything else does.

Kendali: No. I don't think you see how serious this is. This is career damaging.

Toya: I think you are overreacting. Just like everyone else. If anything, you may have a libel suit against Bree. Besides, ultimately, you will probably gain more readers. But still,

15

nobody really knows it's you. I mean, is it?

Kendali: I don't know who she's talking about. But no, it cannot be me. But of course, everybody thinks it's me. And you are feeding the frenzy. I can't believe you. Dats some bullshit. You supposed to be my girl.

Toya: Whatever

Kendali: Whatever? Are you serious? wow

Toya: You taking it wrong. I am saying, it will blow over. Don't make it a big deal. Let them make it a big deal. You keep doing ya thing.

Kendali: Yeah. Okay, Toya. Whatever.

Toya: Girl. Bye.

Kendali: Fuck you fr fr. You just don't get it. But it's cool. Stay away from me. Don't text. Don't call. Be gone.

Toya: Yeah fuck you too, sis. Love you, girl.

Kendali furiously threw her phone on the carpeted floor. "That fuckin' bitch. Fuck Bree! Fuck Toya! Fuck 'em all!!" She jumped from the bed and stomped into the bathroom slamming the door behind her. After her tantrum of screaming and cursing, she bathed, styled her hair, and applied her makeup. She eased into a long heather gray short sleeve maxi dress and stepped into her gray Converse. A gray Michael Kors satchel polished off her ensemble. She hadn't planned to leave the house so early, but she needed to see Hiram. She hopped in her tricked out Hummer and sent him a text.

 Text Message

Kendali: GM. We need to meet.

Hiram: Hey sweet thing. What's up?

Kendali sent him the link to Toya's post. She waited. He

responded.

Hiram: I told you about these stupid bitches. Shit. You gotta give me some time.

Kendali: How much time?

Hiram: About an hour.

Kendali: Cool. Common Grounds. @ 10.

Hiram: See you there.

Hiram Rivers, Dominion's CEO and CFO, was kneading his wife, Georgette's pecan tan ass like dough, making biscuits from biscuits, ready to shoot his jam all over her perfect jiggly ass cheeks, so exotically odd for her long, lean dancer body. His six foot one baseball player physique kept a steady stroke in and out of her ass as she held onto the seafoam green marble top bathroom sink. His hands meandered up and down her slim torso and stopped on her perfectly round, barely B cup breasts.

"Sssssssssssss, aaah, baby. Ooooooooo, Hiram, honey. Aaaaaaah, baby. Ummmmmmm." Her orgasms exploded throughout her asshole rushing into her vagina and filling her entire vulva. Hiram was the only man she had ever allowed a blue light special.

"Yeah, baby. Yeah, Gee, baby. My sweet. You got the sweetest asshole, baby. Don't you know that? Don't you know how much I love this asshole, girl?" He pounded more and more forcefully with every word. Georgette was already weakened by her climax, just hanging on for Hiram to reach his peak. "Answer me, dammit!"

"Ooooooo, Hiram. Honey," she whimpered.

"Oh you can't answer? That's right, you can't. I done pummeled that ass into silence." He kept up the force, his dick hardening with every thrust. "Uh! Uh! Ah!" He spread her cheeks until he could see his meat shoving in and out of her. He was excited at the sight of the pinkness and the power of his slender fingers, massaging her ass. He admired their reflection in the mirror, especially his long, sinewy arms and tight gut. "Yeah, that's it! That's it. Here I come, dammitt! Fuuuuuuck! Here I come, baby. You sweet ass bitch!" He watched his semen pour from her asshole and drip onto the white and green marble floor which made him cum even more. He stumbled backward onto the edge of their gold fixture jacuzzi tub, still holding her by her ass. She collapsed, her butt cheeks spreading across his lap. They slid into the tub and turned on the water. Georgette sprinkled bath salts under the jet streams and added a peppermint bath bomb. They sat and soaked in the sparkling water, him caressing her crown of very low cut blonde waves, and her, rubbing his buttery soft goatee. They still enjoyed their bath ritual after 10 years of marriage. Georgette was a well-known author when she met Hiram, who was eight years her senior. He was a hustler, establishing a new hustle and Georgette fit into his plan. He had made several fortunes in real estate, beauty salons, concert promotions, software companies, and money laundering. He was ready for a new fortune, but did not expect marriage to come with his newfound treasure chest. Even so, matrimony made sense at that point in his life. He convinced Gee to leave her publisher and let him start their own firm, combining her creative ability and publishing experience with his business acumen. Dominion Publishing was the eventual result and they were the number one publisher of Black fiction books; all other African American companies, while successful in their own right, were far behind Dominion. For the past 3 years, Muse.com, the online publishing monster corporation that controlled 85% of the book making market, sent Hiram a request every week for a partnership. He consistently declined their offers. He and Georgette enjoyed each other and the life they built together, two delightful children- a son, Hendrix and a daughter Harlem, several beautiful homes, a country farm, nice cars, frequent travel, a dog, a cat, and a housekeeper. Life was divine.

"So, baby. What are we gonna do about Kendali and the Bree blog post?"

"So, you know about it?"

"Of course I do." Georgette swam to the other side of the tub to face her husband.

"I don't know. I am going to meet with her this morning. She texted me about it."

"I'm sure."

"What do you think?"

"I think we should be concerned. We don't know how far Bree is going to take this. She seems to think her evidence is factual. Now the question for you, my loving husband, is this true?"

"Awww, c'mon Gee. You know Kendali can't write."

"Yeah, but she has talked up her creative expertise over the years and bashed a lotta people for using ghostwriters."

"That's why I have been telling her for years to shut her fuckin' mouth."

"Well, we know she can't do that." Georgette turned the Jacuzzi jet up a notch.

"Yeah. We know." Hiram immersed himself under water and emerged from the spa. "You really think we should be concerned?"

"Yeah. A lil' bit. This can be very damaging. But hopefully she will gain as many readers as she may lose. You see what I mean?"

"Yeah, I do."

"We will see. But you definitely need to work your PR magic. Wait a few days and you will know what to do." Georgette played with her nipples.

"I am so sick of these cut rate bitches. I need to find me some real fuckin' women to write."

"Yeah. But these cut rate bitches sell books."

"True dat. Aaaaaaargh!" Hiram balled his fists and punched the air. "Let me get goin' cuz I see you tryin' to recruit me for round two." He licked her right nipple. She giggled. He scrubbed his body with body wash and a loofah, then hosed off with the hand held sprayer. He kissed his wife.

"I will catch up with you later, Gee. I love you."

"Love you too." She sucked his earlobe. "Tell baby sis, I said hey. And I love her. And everything will be alright."

"Will do."

Chapter Two
Restless Natives

Friday 10:10 a.m.

"Hey, sweets." Hiram bent down and kissed Kendali's forehead. She was impatiently waiting for him while torturing herself scrolling through the thousands of comments about the anti-ghostwriter writer. He sat across from her in the booth, his black coffee cooling for him to taste.

"They only had the Jamaican Blue. They're out of your favorite House Blend Trois."

"This is fine. It's cool." He sipped the black liquid crack. "Okay. I'm going to listen to you."

"What do you mean you're gonna listen to me. *I* need to hear *you*."

"Since when? You ain't never listened to me before."

"That is not true."

"It's mostly true, Kenni. I told you to stop fuckin' around with these hoes. I told you to stop talkin' smack. I told you to shut your mouth. Keep it all about business. You didn't do that. You still fuck wit' Toya. You go on rants with people on Zing. You bash ghostwriting. I mean, c'mon. But you listen to *me*?" Kendali rolled her eyes. "Yeah, right. Okay."

"Well, fine. But what are we gonna do, Hiram?"

"Nothin'. We are gonna just see where it goes."

"See where it goes? Really?"

"Yeah, really. First we need to see if she is going to reveal more of her sources. If she will reveal the author's name that she's draggin'. You see? Truly, we don't know if she is talking about you."

"Sweet Jesus. Are you kidding? Everybody knows she's talking about me. How in the hell did she find out?"

"Now see. That right there. You can never talk like that in public. And I mean *never*. You are admitting guilt. Damn, Kenni. Shit."

"Well, what the fuck? Everybody knows now. And they are gonna assume it's true." She leaned down close to the table top and whispered, "Because it is true."

"Dammit, girl! You so damn hard headed."

"Shit, Hiram. I'm asking you for guidance and you tellin' me just wait and see. Meanwhile, my zinger and my texts, my phone is blowin' the fuck up. I'm not supposed to say anything? Do anything?"

"Oh, we gonna draw up a nice simple post to make everybody shut up while we get to the bottom of this."

"Okay good." She stirred her coffee and bit into her danish. "You think lil' Miss Muffet told?"

"No. Not her style." He peered around the restaurant. "I'd rather we not discuss this in public. You never know who's listening."

"Fine. But I hate to think I will have to fuck her up for trying to ruin my career."

"I don't think she is like that."

"But she is the only other person who knows, right? Not even Gee knows, true?"

"True," he fibbed. "Georgette doesn't know."

"I'm not gonna worry. If you're not worried, I'm not worried. Fuck it."

"Good. I will have our people send you a post and a series of talking points. Meanwhile, shut your mouth. And learn to say, 'No comment' and 'Can't we all just get along'. It may be best for you to deactivate your Zing account for a while."

"Fine." She slouched down in the seat, stretched her arms out to her sides, and pressed her palms into the vinyl upholstery.

"Okay. I have work to do. You comin' in today?" He gulped his warm coffee.

"I doubt it. I think I need to go to the spa."

"Cool. I will catch up with you later." He extended his hand across the table. She placed hers atop his. He squeezed. "Everything's gonna be alright."

"Okay." She sighed, feeling comforted. He rose from the booth, kissed her on her head, and left Common Grounds. She finished her coffee and headed to the spa.

Mustafa read his morning paper, indulging a late breakfast with his wife, Aminah. He had the hardcopy newspaper delivered to his door five days a week to remind him of his grandfather's teachings- "Son, a man should always read the morning paper, especially the local paper. The local section is most important. We need to know what's going on around us." They lived in a modest seven bedroom colonial style home, remodeled to their liking, nestled in the city's historically affluent Black middle class neighborhood, Cheyenne. Aminah prepared a hearty breakfast of homemade waffles, fresh fruit, veggie sausages, and cheese grits. She made their plates and sat down in her usual chair on the sun porch next to the kitchen. Mustafa blessed their food.

"Damn, this is so good, Meena Weena," he said at the first forkful of grits. "Mmmm. I musta really put that thing on you last night, huh?"

Aminah chuckled. "Mustafa, stop." She shifted her eyes side to side. He smiled at her. She paused, and then waved her spoon in the air. "But yeah you did. You *did*," she admitted, shaking her head affirmatively in a rapid motion.

"Aaaaah, I know. I know. Might put that girl up in you." Mustafa slapped the air imitating slapping Aminah's butt cheeks.

"Maaaaan. I done told you this shop is closed. Our two boys are plenty."

"Yeah, but how you gonna tell me you proud of me when I make this next big move, huh? C'mon, Meena. You gotta give it up."

"Well, make the move and we will see." She swirled a piece of her waffle in the syrup. "Mmmm. That is good."

"Girl, you know you da bomb chef."

As founder and president of BlackOut Media, Mustafa used Zing as part of his advertising and marketing strategy for his mostly non-fiction Black studies titles. His company had a small, but impressive urban fiction catalogue containing the magnum opus of its bestselling author, Thaddeus Kane, who wrote *The Street Chronicles: Black Blood Gang*. The book was a moderately successful mini-series on BlackTV Network, the premier all Black cable television channel. Thaddeus Kane used to write for Dominion, but left because he felt he didn't have enough creative control. Since Thaddeus' television success, Hiram shunned Mustafa in their movement throughout the industry. Even though Hiram reigned supreme in urban fiction, BlackOut helmed the Black Studies genre, a place where Hiram had little influence. Ultimately, BlackOut didn't suffer much from Hiram's professional snubs, but Mustafa suspected Hiram's sphere of influence hindered the success of the Black Blood Gang TV show.

He and Aminah ate the last of their breakfast and Mustafa checked his phone for Zing updates. Two hundred messages and notifications were significantly more than usual. One message from his number one selling author and friend, Thaddeus, read:

"What's up, big homey? I know you going in on these bitches on this one. Where you at? HMU"

He was repulsed by the overall information that the notifications illustrated. More of the disgusting madness in the Black urban fiction publishing world permeated the internet waves. More Black sistas fighting, backbiting, and gossiping, tearing each other up and down. He despised them. He abhorred them with every proton, neutron, and electron of his being. "Deez bitches…"

Aminah rose from the table and collected their plates. "What is it now?"

"Man. I'm so sicka deez whores. I swear."

"Mustafa!"

"Meena, a hoe is a hoe is a hoe. You act like, talk like, walk like, write like a hoe, I'm calling you a hoe. Period."

"I just hate when you do that. I keep telling you. They are still our sisters. You degrade them, you degrade me, you degrade yourself."

"And that is where we respectfully disagree, my love. Maybe they were my sisters. They are, no more. Do I have to give it to you, right here?"

Aminah rolled her eyes, rapidly batting her eyelids. "You're gonna give it anyway, whether I say yes or no."

"Sho ya right." Mustafa laughed and gave it to her. He quoted, "Flesh of my flesh…"

She recited with him sarcastically as she washed the dishes. "…blood of my blood…"

"They are strangers unto me. I know them not!"

She inhaled deep inside her belly, and exhaled very slowly. "Yes, Mustafa. But please…"

"Love, I hear you. But I call spades, spades."

"Fine. Can you just, at least for today, refrain from all the extra. Don't do a Zing Live. Pleeeeze."

"Meena. Get yourself ready for work. You have customers to attend to. They need their Goddess Garments," he said, referring to Aminah's boutique. She was a women's clothing designer, tailor, and seamstress. "Don't worry about me. I got dis."

"Mustafa." She put her hand on her hip and tapped her foot on the kitchen floor. Mustafa stood in front of her, sticking his chest out, looking off into the distance, his arms outstretched, assuming a royal posture.

"I am the king of this pride, woman. You do as I command." He waved his hand across the air, dismissing her from their palaver.

She burst into laughter. "Maaaaaan."

As she started walking away, he spoke, still in formation, "Give me my sugah, woman!"

She laughed heartily, kissing him all over his face. "That's what I'm talkin' 'bout." He hugged her and humped her body.

She laughed louder. "Boy, go 'head. You heard what I said."

He kissed her neck and released her from his comedic embrace. "I told you. I got this, girl." He danced out of the kitchen into his office. He turned on his computer, opened his Zing app, and pressed the live button.

Zing Live-Mustafa Speaking From His Office
"Peace, love, and blessings, Black family. I aint gon' be long cuz y'all already know the wife shut me down before I even got started. Y'all need to kiss her ring when you see her because she saves y'all from the real tongue lashing. Trust! Y'all get the fat-free version. Believe that!

Real quick. You already know why I'm on here. And once again, I'ma say the same thing: you low life, back bitin', self hatin', hate mongerin', non writin', wanna be authors and publishers need to stop worrying about dumb shit. For real, Black family! Get back to bein' Black!
Two points.

One. You don't know if Bree is talkin' about Kendali and if she is, who the fuck cares who she's talkin' about. One non writin' chick talkin' about a half-ass writin' chick. So. So what.

Two. Instead of worrying about all this dumb shit- who's ghostwritin'. Who's not. Who's bashin' who about ghostwritin', ALL OF Y'ALL asses need to take some writing classes or better yet, take ya' asses back to the strip club-PERIOD!

And as always, Business over Bullshit.
Zing Live End

Reactions: 432 Comments: 168 Shares: 271
(Load previous comments)

Pamela Hunter: Did this dude just say, back to the strip club? Tsk tsk. Some folks gon' be big mad about that one!

Forest Not Whitaker: Yeah but he is right. Get back on that pole. Non-writing bitches. Keep it 💯 G!

29

Octavia Denai: Really? I can't believe he said that. Everyone is entitled to pursue their dreams.

Wendy Latimer: Dreams, yeah. But a lotta these chicks ain't never thought about writing until technology made it most accessible. Now they doin the most with this garbage ass writing.

Vanessa Peyton: I have to confess. I used to read a lot of the popular urban fiction, street lit. But then I started reading other less popular authors and indie authors who write the same or similar stories, and I felt like I had been duped. I been reading this bad writing for years. When I started reading better books, I felt refreshed. Like a whole new world opened up. So, I see his point. I read Black Blood Gang. It's street lit but it's well written. It's a really good series. I hated to see it end. So I get it. I love Thaddeus Kane! 🐾🐾

Janaya Reade: Shiiiit! Mustafa be quiet. You probably hang out in the strip club.

Charlie Swagg: Naw I met his wife. She ain't goin' for that. lol.

Zing End Of Comments

Friday 11:00 a.m.

Bree's text notification buzzed.

Mace: You finish your spin class?

Bree: Yes. And GM to you 😶

Mace: Yeah. GM. Meet me in the parking lot. I'm finishing up.

Bree: Cool

Bree tightened her scarf on her head and wiped the rest of the sweat from her neck. She put her bag on her shoulder and exited Bomb Body Fitness. She relaxed in her car, waiting for Maceo to come out and preparing her mind for his tongue lashing lecture. She reviewed her Zing alerts and responded to messages while she waited.

Zing Message
Mz. Shay Shay: bih, fr fr. you burnt up the internet. That's all I gotta say

Bree: Who? Me? What I do?

Mz. Shay Shay: You definitely get the crown! #queenpetty

Bree: 😂

Zing Message
Devina Dee: Bitch why? I mean damn. smh. You telling who it is or what?

Bree: I told it. We all know who it is.

Devina Dee: Bitch, bye!

Bree: 😑

"Open up," Maceo shouted, knocking on the window of Bree's Lexus coupe.

Bree dropped her phone in the passenger seat and exited her car. She and Maceo embraced. "Hey, boss."

"Yeah, hey." He put his gym bag on the ground next to his feet and leaned his six foot two inch body down so that he could look at Bree, right in her eyes, since she was barely five foot three. "I am so fuckin' fed up with you and that gotdamn group." His salt and pepper beard and shiny bald head were still damp with sweat from his workout.

"Mace, look…" She narrowed her round bright eyes and straightened her chocolate brown face with sternness.

"No, you look. You are an author. A writer. And I know we use social media to create buzz, and our readership is a ratchet crowd, but you don't have to overfeed them the bullshit, Bree." He stepped back two paces, giving her room to reflect.

She huffed. "Mace, all I'm sayin' is, from my perspective, bitches need to be put on blast when they outta order. Talkin' shit about other people. Other authors. Lookin' down on us because they think they betta than us, but ain't even half as good

32

as we are."

"Aubrey Nicole McDaniels. Why does any of that even matter, yo? Why?"

She despised when he called her by her full birth name. "It matters because..." She paused. Maceo widened his eyes and rocked his head side to side, waving his hands and moving his chunky muscular body like a magician in a "ta-da" motion. She grimaced at his sarcasm. "...because it just does," she finished.

"Yeah right. Aight. It's whatever you say. But you ain't sayin' nothin'. You see that, don't you?"

"Mace, I hear you. But I don't care. A bitch need to be blasted, then I'm blastin'. Period."

"Who are you talking about anyway? And where did you get this info?"

"I-"

Maceo interrupted, "You know what? Wait. I don't wanna know. Just tell me you have real proof. Real tangible evidence."

"I do."

"You are never gonna reveal who it is, right?"

"I don't know. We'll see. If a bitch keep fuckin' wit' me and runnin' her mouth, I don't know." Bree shrugged and smiled a girly innocent smile.

"Bree, this shit ain't funny, ma. I'm tellin' you- you playin' with fire. Fuckin' wit' people's careers, but more than that. You fuckin' wit' dey money. Kendali is Dominion's cash cow."

She looked away from him, across the highway, blocking out the truth he spoke to her. "Bree, I am telling you. I know Hiram. I know his kind. Don't let dem suits and college degrees fool you. The nigga is shiesty, shady, and savage. I ain't fuckin' around wit' none of y'all bullshit and wind up back in prison. No fuckin' way."

"Mace, c'mon. You goin' too far with this. It ain't that serious."

"No. I'm not going too far, mami. And it *is* that serious. I am tellin' you. Dead this thing. Leave it alone. Stop playin' with fire." He leaned down again, his eyes piercing her pupils with razor sharp urgency. "You fuckin' millennial wanna be cyber gangsters. You don't wanna find out what real street niggas do. What real street broads do. Y'all don't get it. Ya' poppin' ya gums all up and down that internet highway and I'm tellin' you, you don't wanna real muthafucka to pull up on ya ass."

"Aight. I gotchu."

"Aight. I'm onto my next move." They hugged and Maceo jumped in his Escalade.

Bree pulled off burning rubber, thinking out loud, "Whatever! Fuck deez hoes, especially Kendali Grace."

34

Lesli Lyn drove into the parking lot of Meade Communications, which had been the home of The Heritage News, Seminole City's first Black newspaper, for over 100 years. Bradford Meade bought the paper, its edifice and its archives about 8 years ago. He redesigned the building, which had been a Black owned two story inn. He had the main edifice remodeled with a Chinese pagoda theme, the trimmings and moldings were carved with black, gold, red, and silver Chinese symbols, animal emblems, and I Ching motifs along the edges of the windows and the two gargantuan handmade doors of the main entrance. Gold dragon handles greeted Meade Comm family and guests as they crossed the threshold into the lobby decorated with Asian lanterns. In the rear, he added a courtyard with four pagodas enclosing an open space with a skywell, and a meditation fountain at the center. Bradford was compelled to remind Black people of their Asian roots. Lesli walked to the courtyard and sat on one of the meditation benches, praying silently. After she was satisfied with her talk with God, she entered the main building.

"Good morning, Lesli Lyn-Lyn." Samara greeted her cheerfully with her thick southern drawl, sitting pretty at her desk. She was cute, smart, charming, brown sugar bubbly, the perfect receptionist for Meade Comm.

"Good morning, Sam! Always bright-eyed and bushy tailed."

"That's me!" Sam giggled. "I read your blog this morning, of course. And as always, you give it to them, right between the eyes." She pressed her finger on the center of her forehead, then turned the same finger into a gun and pulled the trigger, raising her arm from the imaginary kickback.

"I do what I gotta. That's all. The antennas stay ready. I aim; I shoot. One shot, one kill." Lesli moved her work bag from her shoulder to her wrist. "I'm sure you have a thought on the controversy. Let's hear it."

"All I can say is, I read Kendali's books. And they're okay, some written better than others. I just like getting the inside scoop on the hip hop industry and trying to guess who are the real life characters." Samara smiled. "But honestly I don't care if she has a ghostwriter."

"Even after she bashed so many people for using ghostwriters?"

"Welllll...hmmm... I can see why her fans are disappointed. But I think they should just forgive her and move on."

"I dunno. We shall see." Lesli removed her pink sun shades. "Folks are not so forgiving. And they are always ready to see a fall. A failure."

"That's true. But we don't even know if it's her, do we?"

"Oh, yeah, we do. It's her."

"How do you know? You got the inside scoop? I bet you do. You worked at Dominion, so you must know. Yeah?" Samara leaned toward Lesli, her forearms flat on her desk.

"Ha, uh~hmmm…" Lesli harmonized in a teasing tone.

"Aw, c'mon. You can tell me, L-Double."

"Uh-huh. Ah-huh, ah ah hah" she sang. "Have a good day, Sammie Poo." She blew her a kiss.

"Aw, Les!"

"Trust your gut, girl," she advised stepping onto the elevator.

Sam bounced back in her chair, defeated.

Once at her desk, Lesli checked her emails and thumbed through her snail mail. She tapped her pink polished nails on her white lacquer desk as an email alert popped onto her screen. It was Bradford.

From: Bradford Meade

To: L. Lyn Faulkner

Subject: The Kaleidoscope 🦋

"Lyn! You go in! 😊 You always break it down, all the way down. To the least common denominator. I am so glad… "you're miiine" 😊 🎵 I'll be over to talk in a few.

Regards,

Bradford Meade

She laughed out loud. Whenever he was giving her kudos, he always sang "...you're mine." from The Temptations song, *Nobody But You*. His sense of humor was the icing on his beefcake good looks, Mr. Caramel Eyes, same color as his skin. She continued her morning mail ritual and reviewed her checklist for the day's agenda. Bradford arrived at her office about an hour later. He tapped on her open door. Everyone had their own office with a door at Meade; even Samara had a small office on the first floor where she could sit, study, or nap as needed.

"Hey Brad. Good morning. C'mon in." She waved him toward her. He gave her a quick hug, stood back, looked her up and down, then raised his arm, stretching it far around his back. Lesli prepared for the extra dramatic dap. He brought his arm around his body slowly, landing his hand in her open palm with a loud smack.

"Sssssssss," he hissed. "Sis, you know you breaks them down, don't you?" He locked his fingers with hers, tickled her palm, wiggled his fingers, and released her hand. She received his love and gave it back with a hug. They sat. "You are so gifted. We are gonna have to do a book and a tour for you, or something." He crossed his leg, man style, revealing his baby blue and yellow argyle socks and his soft white Ugo Vasare slip-on's. He relaxed in the cushy oversized white chair facing Lesli, modeling his white linen slacks and custom made baby blue and yellow

38

pinstripe oxford with dapper perfection.

"A book?"

"Yeah. You need to be on some kind of women's empowerment circuit. Using your Kaleidoscope platform. Spiritual enlightenment and self-development. We can call you the break 'em down butterfly."

"Ya' think?"

"I know. But that's about a year away from now. Just keep building. Trust. I got plans for you."

"Oh you do, do you?" Lesli rested her feet on her foot stool and pressed her weight on the back of her chair, her double D's saluting the atmosphere.

"You know this."

"So, what do you think about the madness?"

"Just more in-fighting, cat scratching destruction that we don't need. But they don't care. It's like the reality TV shows. Drama, fighting, sex-it all sells. Sad state of affairs. We just need to keep doing our part to be sure that we preserve our legacy, in spite of the attacks on our culture."

"Yes, definitely. We must do our part." She toyed with her big silver hoop earring as she thought about the controversy. "I used to be soooo angry. Especially when I first started at Dominion and a while after I left. But now, I just feel a deep sadness and despair."

"Yeah." Bradford massaged his beard and goatee, a few salty strands were growing in at the corners of his mouth, maturing his regal presence. "We know this is Bree attacking Kendali. She may retaliate. Inevitably, the fans will start fighting. They will battle for a few days. Then, it will fade to black. Same ole dumb shit soup. But this soup has a different flavor because Kendali is their star child. So, it will be interesting to see where this goes."

"Where do you think it will go?"

"Don't know."

"Hmmm. All of this is surely dumb shit soup. Too typical. Hmmm. But a different flavor, you say. Hmmm. We shall see. But do you think it's true, that she uses a ghostwriter?" Lesli twirled her braided tendrils.

"Hell yeah!!!"

"For real?"

"You were at Dominion. You should know."
"But I really don't. There were rumors about several authors using ghostwriters. Rumblings about stealing royalties, cooking the books, paying for reviews. Rumors about affairs, especially Hiram and Kendali. But just rumors and rumblings."
"And you don't know nuffin'?"

"Too busy pruning my own wings. Building my brand." She tapped her temple. "But what do *you* think, B?"

"Lyn, you know Kendali. She ain't no dummy, but she ain't no writer. You gotta go back, way back, and read her very first novels. Before Hiram fashioned her."

"I have. And you're right. I got it. Thanks for reminding me. I guess...I just think, damn. You need a ghostwriter to write what she writes? Really? It ain't no Pulitzer prize winning literature."

"Riiight. But she ain't no writer. She is a theme writer. A storyteller. A tale spinner. Which used to be a paid profession. People were paid to come up with the ideas. They call them producers, creators, conceptualists. But they couldn't write worth a damn. Look at your TV show and movie credits. Everybody has their role. Their lane. You get it. But now, they are allowing these so called writers to believe they are writers when really, they may be conceptualists. If they are even that. Most of them just saw the opportunity, thanks to modern internet technology, to make a quick buck. They have no care or concern about the art."

"Yes. You know I have perfect understanding on these points. We agree all day long. I guess I was still holding out hope that maybe there was just one in the bunch that was 'bout it. You know what I mean?" Lesli put her feet on the floor.

"As ole boy said in Fight Club, 'Losing all hope is true freedom'. Free yourself, Butterfly."

Lesli laughed. "My favorite quotist."

Bradford grinned. "I do what I can. But really. They did not need to present Kendali as a writer in that way. She has good stories to tell and Hiram should have teamed her with the ghostwriter. Made them co-authors or gave her an anonymous identity. Or made her keep her mouth shut, which is probably impossible. My opinion- anonymity would have been best."

"Definitely. Like Zane."

"Like Zane," Bradford agreed. "Well, I am going to get some work done. Gotta get out of here early to have dinner with the wife. I know you will continue to follow the soup."

"Surely, I will. And tell Charlene I said hello."

"Will do. Make it a great day, sis."

"You too, brother."

🦋🦋🦋

Friday 7:00 p.m.

Monique Ellis, CAO of Dominion Publishing and Hiram's right hand and Shante Turner went way back. They knew each other as children, attending the same day care center. Their mothers were chummy. They had lunch about once a month to catch up on the latest in their lives. Tonight, they were dining at everyone's favorite spot, KD's Supper Club, home of the city's beloved internationally acclaimed, homegrown jazz soul funk fusion ensemble, Indigenous Soul. KD's boasted a sophisticated, earthy design- mahogany floors and walls, complemented by Native American artifacts displayed throughout, Native American designed metallic fabric ceiling drapes, and Native American sculpture decorating its 200 person dining room. At its center, a lighted square bar made of hand blown glass illuminated the club. Modern and contemporary art from mostly local artists adorned the walls depicting various dedications to the history of Black American music including portraits of Miles Davis, Aretha Franklin, Ella Fitzgerald, The Ohio Players, and many others. On Friday nights, they served an all-night buffet showcasing the best dishes from different chefs around the city, allowing select culinary craftsmen the opportunity to get new customers from KD's patronage.

Monique placed her hustle gear on the seat in the booth where Shante had her jacket and work bag. Shante approached with her buffet plate loaded with delicious goodies from Nina's Kitchen, The Loving Spoon, The Land Of Kush, and Teavolve.

"Ayyyyyyyyyye, chica chica!" She was delighted to see Monique. They squeezed each other a long time, lingering in their sisterly embrace.

"Girl, you look good!" Monique said admiring Shante's silver butterfly earrings, necklace, ring, anklet, and broach accessories. Her dress was a black A-line rayon blend with white butterflies imprinted on the fabric hugging her overweight figure eight curvature. She was the consummate bubbly, chubby pretty dough girl.

"I'm keepin' up with you, ma."

"Girl, please. You know you always a hitta with your swag." Monique ran her hands down her chunky frame, smoothing out her cap sleeved denim dress, and then tucking her extra-long bone straight silk pressed hair behind her ear.

"And you always a hitta with the hair! My lil' chocolate Native American Wind Rose." Shante settled herself in the booth. "Your hair has grown another four inches since I saw you last month."

"Girrrrrl." Monique smiled at her friend. "I'm gonna go to the ladies room, get my plate, and I'll be right back."

"Okay. Take your time. I have all night." Monique left for the bathroom and Shante examined her Zing group, The Turner Pages. She read some of the new comments about her anti-ghostwriter writer post regarding Bree McDee's latest gossip from her Sauce Mobb group.

Zing Post – The Turner Pages

Shante Turner: So, what do you think about Bree McDee's sauce? Does using a ghostwriter make an author less of a writer? Using a ghostwriter depletes their artistic quality? Ghostwriting- does it matter? Who do you think Bree is talking about? Tell me what you think, Page Turners!

Reactions: 3,672 Comments: 654 Shares: 1175

Callie Cee: I do not see the point in using a ghostwriter if you are a writer. Why don't the ghostwriters just write and publish the damn books? 😳 I thought ghostwriters were for famous people writing memoirs or something like that.

Wendy Woo: Who cares? NEXT! 😊

Niemah Wilkes: I prefer people write their own stuff.

Yolanda Sykes: I am just tired of all the rivalries and bickering in this genre. Maybe this happens with other genres. But it is out of control here. I wish we talked more about books. 😤

Felicia Jones: I think it's all made up. It's all a publicity stunt. I think a lot of these battles are created to sell books. Because that is the bottomline, the bottom dollar. $$$$$$$$
Zing End Of Comments

Monique returned to the table with her plate.

They paused to say grace. "Okay, so what's been going on?" Monique swigged her lemon water.

"You tell me. I know you know who Bree is talking about."

"I know everybody is saying it's Kendali, but there are other folks it could be."

"Mo, tell me the truth. Kendali uses a ghostwriter?"

"Not for me to say, Shante."

"You know you can tell me." Shante twirled alfredo pasta on her fork.

"Girl, stop."

"Mo, you gotta confirm."

"No. Seriously. I can think of three other authors off the top of my head that she could be talking about."

"Like who?"

"Princess J, Wendi Kincaid, and Amber Alise."

"Really?" Shante stopped eating, miffed by Monique's information.

"Yes, really. People just want the post to be about Kendali because it feeds the rivalry between her and Bree. But it's not necessarily Kendali she's talking about. So when you say confirm, I can't. Only Bree can do that."

"Hmmm. I see." Shante tasted her sautéed cabbage. "Oh my gawd. This is sooooo good."

"I know, right. Nina over there puttin' crack in her cabbage."

"Yaaaaaas." Shante swallowed her veggies. "What about the Platinum Quill award? Kendali is up for it. You think they still gonna give it to her?"

"I don't know. Only Toni can answer that. She has her rules and I don't recall any rules about ghostwriting."

"Yeah. I don't either."

"But Toni is particular. My guess is, she ain't feelin' no ghostwriter writer getting her Platinum Quill. At least not knowingly." Monique savored her moscato chicken wing, licking sauce from her fingers.

"Yeah, you right. Probably not. Toni's hardcore."

"Yep." Monique wiped her hands. "So, what's goin' on with you?"

"Oh you know me- no life. The store, work, home, read, review, Zing. That's it."

"How are things at the store?"

"Really good. I think they are going to force me to take a regional manager job." Shante was the manager of the largest Dress Barn store in the city.

"Whaaat? Can they do that?"

"They have ways."

"Oh yeah. That's corporate America."

"Exactly."

"No new bae?" Monique desired love for Shante, someone to take care of her. She had not been so lucky in love lately, even though she was a helluva catch.

"Nah. Keepin' my kitty to myself. I've decided to wait on the Lord."

"Good strategy."

"How about you? How is hubby? The kids? Dominion?"

"Family is blessed. I thank God. Dominion is... interesting."

"What do you mean?"

"The natives are restless." Monique stretched her big round eyes and wrinkled her long straight nose. Her deep cocoa brown skin glistened under the soft lights of the club.

"You a native?"

"Somewhat."

"Mmm. This will be something. We know what happens when you get restless." Shante batted her eyelashes and curled her lips playfully, the flickering candlelight spotlighting her freckled face.

Monique winked. "Yeah. We do, don't we."

Chapter Three
Flowers Wanted: Dead, Alive or Digital

Wednesday 9:00 a.m.

Meade Comm was beginning its day, as folks milled about getting their coffee, tea, and breakfast snacks. Lesli was typing diligently at her work station when her phone buzzed.

Toni: GM. You at work?

Lesli: Hey Toni. GM. I am. What's up?

Toni: Let's talk soon

Lesli: Let's

Toni: I will call you in about an hour.

Lesli: I am looking forward

Toni: 😎

Antoinette 'Toni 'Griffin worked in media relations for several major publishing houses before she quit corporate America to start her own thing, The Platinum Quill Book Expo. Her Platinum Quill Expo, or PQ as everyone called it, was the ultimate book exposition for Black authors and readers of all genres. The first PQ event was held in a small hotel meeting room with about 100 attendees. The festival grew exponentially over the past decade playing host to hundreds of authors and tens of thousands of readers from all over the nation and around the world. Every year one author in select genres- urban fiction, street lit, romance, suspense thriller, crime drama, sci-fi, fantasy, memoir, history, science, and non-fiction- was given the Platinum Quill Award for Literary Excellence. No other book event for African American writers and their fans compared to The PQ.

Bradford peeked in her office as Lesli was adjusting her red sports bra under her red and white Puma sweat suit.

"Good morning, sis."

"Hey, Brad."

"No word from the defamed?" he asked referring to Kendali's quiet disappearance from Zing. After the weekend craziness, Kendali deactivated her account.

"No. Not yet. But I am sure she will reappear soon. Poised. Rehearsed. And ready to reclaim her following."

"Okay."

"You know, you can get on Zing and find these things out for yourself," Lesli said with a sarcastic smirk.

Bradford despised social media and made a concentrated effort to avoid it at all costs.

"Why? That's what I have you for." Those creamy caramels glimmered and his bearded grin warmed her spirit.

"I guess so." She giggled and continued typing. Bradford double tapped her door and walked back to his office.

Her phone chimed. It was Toni.

"Toni Toni Toni!"

"Hey, ma. What's goin' on, baby girl?"

"Ain't nothin' much. Tryin' to keep my wings outta trouble."

"Yeah, sis. You speakin' the impossible." Toni chuckled.

"Not the impossible?"

"Yeah, sis. The impossible. You a bad girl butterfly. The only butterfly I know that stings like a bee."

Lesli laughed. "That would make me a butterbee. Bzzzzzz. Like Bree's character in her 'City' series."

"Absolutely. That's what you are."

"How are you, Toni Tone?"

"I'm good. You know I have one role, one purpose in life. My only focus."

"Yes. The PQ."

"The PQ, baby."

"You know I am here to help."

"Oh, Lesli Lyn. Don'tcha worry. You know I will be calling you soon. Your assistance is invaluable, ma. You have helped me grow this thing more than anyone else."

"Awwww, T. I'm gettin' misty."

"Well, it's true." Lesli Lyn had assisted Toni with ideas, publicity, and logistics for the PQ over the last five years. "So, you can draw up your invoice sooner than later, babe."

"Yes. I am looking forward."

"So look, L-Double. This Kendali thing. What's up? Whatcha know?"

"Honestly, I don't know jack shit. I just know what I have read on Zing. I haven't investigated. I try to stay out of the gossip shit. I get enough hate mail from writing book reviews. So, I try to steer clear of the high drama. But *that* is the impossible."

"I know right. But I read your post and as always, you da bullseye butterfly."

"I try to keep the people on point."

"And you doin' it, ma. But you know I am rethinking this award. We have Kendali slated as the urban fiction winner, but this ghostwriting mess-I don't know. You know PQ has a certain standard."

"Yes. I know. And you need to maintain that standard. No wavering."

"You know I can't compromise our brand. I haven't had to address this kind of situation. We have assumed that all of our awardees are authentic in the craft, but maybe not. Even so, their business wasn't out in the open. Bree has put Kendali right out on front street. I hit 'em up, but I ain't heard from either one of dem bitches."

"You probably won't hear from them for a minute."

"They betta reach back to me."

"We'll, see. It's one thing to spew all that bullshit on Zing, but a whole 'nuther thing to talk voice to voice or face to face with a real deal business woman. Datz dat grown up shit."

"On the real."

"And we are assuming a lot to say Bree is talking about Kendali. She could be talking about several other authors at Dominion."

"For real? Like who?" Toni asked.

"Could be Princess J. She comes to mind. I am sure there are others. I can't recall right now, but yeah."

"Yeahhh, but we know that it's a ninety percent probability that it's Kendali."

"No doubt. But hey, who knows." Lesli kicked off her red suede Puma sneakers and admired her heart covered socks.

"Yeah. Well, I don't know that I want my award mixed up in this mess. The PQ board will decide."

"That is best. And we definitely don't want that drama at the PQ."

"She gon' be mad about dem 20 g's," Toni remarked, referring to the cash prize that accompanied the PQ for urban fiction.

"Yeah, I would be boiling."

"Well, we gon' let the board work it out. Let me know if you learn anything."

"I will. Have a good day, sis."

"You too, ma. Peace."

Lesli returned to her typing. An hour passed and Samara waltzed into her office with a long white flower box.

"Somebody's got flowers," she hummed. She placed the box on Lesli's white lacquer round table in her meeting area. "You must got dat good-good, girl." She did a little shake dance twerk.

"Samara, you are crazy with a capital 'C'."

"I'm just sayin'."

"Thanks, Sam." She continued tapping her keyboard, cranking out her novel.

"You ain't gonna open 'em?"

"You so nosey," Lesli replied, rising from her chair. She opened the box. There were about two dozen dead roses lying lifeless on a bed of fresh white tissue paper. She gasped. Samara's mouth dropped silently. They froze.

"Oh my god." Samara broke the silence. She pulled the card off the box top and read the note in amazement. *'Yeah, keep poppin' them wings, butterfly bitch. You gon' end up like these flowers.'*
"Sam, this is between us for now. Got it?
Samara pulled the imaginary zipper across her lips with her thumb and forefinger. "Lips sealed, L-Double."
"Good." She put the card back in the envelope and gave Sam the box. "Dispose, please."
"Of course." Sam took the box and left the office.
Lesli fell into her chair wearily. "I guess I am a butterfly that stings."
🦋 🐝 🦋

Wednesday 11:00 a.m.

Tiyanna typed her final instruction on her IPad as Georgette dictated her itinerary for the next several days. They both sat facing the city skyline view from Georgette's office windows on the thirteenth floor of the illuminous, skyscraping Cartwright building in the heart of downtown Seminole City.

"I think I've covered everything," Georgette said.

"Okay, good. You will see this in your calendar shortly."

"Awesome. I don't know what I'd do without you, Tiy."

Tiyanna smiled and her eyes zoomed in on Georgette's screensaver- a big, blue rose, brushed with midnight dew and a quote, by author/ educator, Srikumar Rao, *'When the flower blossoms, the bee will come.'*
"Nice screensaver," Tiyanna said.

"Thanks!" Georgette turned toward her computer screen, away from Tiyanna.

"Okay. I will get back to work."

"Yes. Thanks again."

Tiyanna plopped down in her desk chair and opened her Zing app on her phone. She started texting her sister.

Zing Message

Tiyanna: Darla, wyd?

Darla: shit. what's up? you at work?

Tiyanna: Yeah. This bitch is at it again. I mean I know it's just little stuff, but that's what makes it so creepy.

Darla: What was it this time?

Tiya: Copying my screensaver.

Darla: smh

Tiyanna: Not exactly copying, but copying. Her rose is blue. Mine is pink. She used a different quote about flowers, but my thing is, she never said, oh that's a nice screensaver, I think I want one like it. No. I just happened to see it while we were working. Remember the perfume? And the dress?

Darla: Yeah. Monkey see, monkey do.

Tiyanna: Everybody, well a lotta folks think she is soooooo sweet. Yeah right. Undercover hater

Darla: Yes. You know the type. Want all the shine for themselves. Hate to see anybody else shining MORE than them. So she fine and sweet and loving as long as you less than her. FOH!

Tiyanna: Eggszacklee!!!!!!!!! Aight. I'm out.

Darla: ard
🌸🌸🌸

Kendali gazed at her computer screen analyzing the outline for her tenth and final installment of her monumentally successful series, *The Vixen Notebook*, which fictionalized her experiences as a video vixen. She thought of Dre who had been such a stabilizing force for her. They attended the same high school, but only knew of each other. They casually dated while she was in college and then drifted apart after she left school to pursue a modeling career. They reconnected at a photo shoot; he was hanging out with some of his hip-hop comrades on the set. They were industry guys; he was a working stiff, but he was so fine and gentlemanly. They were inseparable thereafter. He worked while she returned to college to finish her degree in psychology. He started his lawn care service while she began a writing career. Even though they enjoyed a nice life, she was ready to end their relationship. She lacked the courage to break his heart and now, with the ghostwriting controversy, she was unsure of her career status. At this point, she may need Dre. She ceased her reflections and refocused on her computer screen, reviewing her outline and editing a few chapters. Of course, as soon as she got into a groove, there was an interruption.

Tap, tap, tap! on her open office door. "Kendali, these just came for you." Rica, the receptionist/ secretary placed a humongous arrangement of orchids and a box of chocolate covered strawberries on her desk.

"Wow." Her face blushed bright red as she leaped from her chair.

"From Dre?" Rica asked with a quizzical grimace.

"I am thinking not. Dre isn't the floral arrangements kind of guy." Kendali responded.

"Hmmm. Somebody's messin' around, huh, Kendali?" Rica stood next to her as they both admired the love token.

"Girl, no," she lied, elbowing Rica on her shoulder.

"Hmmm, hmmph. If you say so," she remarked, sashaying back to her desk.

Kendali rolled her eyes, guessing in her mind about the sender's identity. She read the card:

'For The Amazing One...With Grace, The Loving One'

She couldn't stop smiling. She felt the petals and inhaled their fragrance. She opened her chocolate strawberries and bit into one, its juice trickled down her chin. Hiram entered.

"Whoa! Somebody has an admirer."

"Yeah, I do, don't I?" She rubbed the strawberry seductively across her lips. Hiram looked around her office and up and down the hallway. No one was looking. Everyone was busy working.

He mouthed, "It wasn't me."

Kendali whispered, "It wasn't?"

"No," he replied aloud.

"You serious?"

"Yeah, I am." His face tightened, jealousy oozing from his aura. He folded his arms and huffed. "So, what's up?"

"I don't know." She was dumbfounded.

"You don't know who they are from?"

"I don't." She reread the card silently. Hiram snatched it from her grasp and read it.

"The Loving One?" He raised an eyebrow. "And you don't know who it is?" he asked in an accusatory tone.

"I am telling you. I don't. I really don't." She fell back in her chair. Hiram saw her sincere befuddlement.

"Okay. Well, I just came to tell you to stay offline a few more days. Go back in on Friday. All your social media PR is in its final tweaking stages, so you will be well armed for your return."

"Good!"

"Maybe you will learn to lay low from now on."

"Yeah. Maybe."

"You think you may have a stalker?"

"A stalker?"
"Yes, a stalker."

"Why can't it just be a secret admirer?"

"You a celebrity, Kenni. It's a stalker. Secret admirers are for school kids and everyday people."

"Oh." She dropped her shoulders, confused, disappointed, and sad. She was so certain the flowers were from Hiram. And she liked the idea of a secret admirer, but of course, Hiram knew precisely how to rip a girl from her fantasy world. A stalker? She thought about the car that had been following her from time to time over the past couple months. It wasn't every day or even every week, but about every 10 days, she felt like somebody was watching her from the same nondescript black vehicle. She hadn't told anyone. Now, Hiram saying the word out loud, *stalker*, coupled with The Loving One's flowers, she recalculated the possibilities.

"We may need to get you some security," Hiram suggested.

"Hiram. Really?"

"Yes, really. I am not playing around with your safety. We will start with an investigator. Find out who sent these flowers."

"Okay fine."

"Alright. I need to finish up a few things before I leave for this meeting. We'll talk later."

"Okay. Have a good one."

"You too."

She leaned over the bouquet again and took a long deep breath, the aroma soothing her troubled soul. Whoever he was, he knew how to pick flowers. Orchids were her favorite and she didn't care; it was the first time in many days that she felt uplifted.

"Thank you, Loving One," she said into the atmosphere, hoping he would hear.

Chapter Four
Fantasies

Wednesday 2:00 p.m.

Back in the day, Nikki Pearl Pennington was the around the way filet that everybody wanted. She was the standard dope hustler girlfriend, 5 foot 3, pretty round face, chocolate brown skin, small waist, fat ass, thick thighs, round perky dark chocolate nipple breasts, and thick calves. She was the short stack heart attack, a fine dime from a clan of fine dimes. When she blossomed at age 16, the hustlers started lining up, bidding for her affection. She accepted various bids, loving the lavish gifts bestowed upon her, the most luxurious cars, an abundance of money, and the finest fashions. She would date one at a time, for six months to a year, and then, she would go on to the next one.

But it was Maceo Grant, the city's top kingpin turned owner/CEO of Gutta Butta Books, that captured her heart. He did more than shower her with material things, he nurtured her dreams. At the time she met Maceo, she had just finished cosmetology school and desperately wanted to open her own shop. "That ain't a thing, Nikki. I got dat for you," Maceo had said. She didn't believe him, but he proved her very wrong. She worked for six months at Hair Etc and one day Maceo picked her up after work, gave her a set of keys, and drove her to her brand new shop, The Black Pearl. She was awestruck; Maceo had the shop designed in her favorite colors, red, black, and gold, according to the sketches of the name, layout, and logo that she kept in her planner. The Black Pearl became the ultimate salon experience in Seminole City; everyone wanted to be a stylist, a patron, or employee of her shop. After his powerful gesture of love, she had to say yes when he asked for her hand in marriage. They enjoyed a lavish life, had two sons, and founded themselves as a power couple in the city.

Life had been delicious for The Grants until the police came knocking. They charged Maceo with the classic kingpin bundle, drug possession, conspiracy, illegal guns, and second degree murder. His arrest had a silver lining: because the local authorities had such a hard-on for shutting him down, the feds extracted Maceo from a RICO case they were building. Talk about a horseshoe up a nigga's ass?! That same lucky horseshoe worked its magic for a release on a technicality, eight years later. Nikki held him down for five years and then walked away from their union. Her final visit to the prison was worse than the day he was arrested:

"What do you mean, Nik?"

"Mace, all I am saying is, I need to live a little. I have to live some of this life."

"Boo. I get it. I know it's not easy. But I'm tellin' you. I am gonna get outta here."

"Maceo, they making you do a mandatory twenty. Do you understand that?"

"I know what's on paper, but I am working on it. I am telling you. I'm gonna get out."

"Babe, listen. I will still be here for you. Money on your books. Making sure your sons write to you. Making sure they talk to you. All of that. But I have to move on."

"Well, I am not giving you a divorce," he affirmed.

"I'm not asking you for one."

"Fine. Fuck it." He jumped up from the table, yelling, "Cee-ohhh!" The visiting room guard turned toward him.

"Hey, bruh. You still got thirty-five minutes. Your visit ain't over, man. "

"Yeah, it is," he murmured, his eyes filling with tears.

Nikki left the prison weeping profusely. When she arrived at her car, she sat and cried for an hour before leaving. She kept her word to him, making sure he had money, especially since it was his money, and maintaining a letter writing schedule for their children. He called them once a week, never talking to her except the one time she begged him to listen to the new money making opportunity she was researching.

"Maceo?"

He didn't respond. The background noise of the inmates and guards interactions let her know he was on the line.

"I know you don't talk to me, but I gotta tell you something. Really ask you. Please talk to me."

He remained silent.

"Please, Mace."

He didn't speak.

"Okay, I'm gonna talk anyway. I know you hear me. We can make some good honest money publishing books. The internet has made this thing real easy. And it's good money."

"Aight. I'm listening." He finally joined the one-woman conversation.

Nikki told him everything he needed to do, from start to finish. Maceo took notes, did his own investigation, and shortly thereafter, with the help of his sister, Violet, Gutta Butta Books was born.

The only day worse than the day she walked away from Maceo, was the day she learned he was coming home.

"Daddy's coming home!" Her sons, Cameron and Canaan danced around the living room tossing the cordless phone between them like a football.

"Huhhh?" Nikki jumped from the buttery soft black leather couch throwing its accompanying red silk throw pillows onto the carpet in the process.

"Whoooo~whooomp!" Cameron shouted.

"Wait. Is he still on the phone?" she asked. The pre-teen boys continued their festive dance towering over their mother.

"Canaan!"

He stopped. "Yeah, ma."

"Is your father on the phone?"

"Yeah, I think so." He put the phone to his ear. "Dad?"

"Yeah, I'm here." Maceo's grin spread to the top of his ears.

Nikki snatched the phone. "Mace? You gettin' out?"

"Yeah. I am."

"Wow." Her eyes glazed over in shock.

"Yeah, wow. Don't worry about it, Nik. I know you laid up wit' dat nigga Isaac. But you still *my* wife. And you gon' be the first to get this eight year build up."

"Huh? What?" She listened to his mandates in disbelief.

"Yeah. That's still *my* pussy. You betrayed me, Nik and I'ma take it out on that ass."

"M-mace. Y-you comin' here?"

"Hell naw. I know you got dat nigga there. I got my own shit. You just get ready to slide through tomorrow. Soak dat pussy, and get dat ass ready. I will send you the address."

"Well, who pickin' you up?"

67

"Don't worry about that." He had made arrangements with Violet for his pick up and his apartment lease.
"Oh. Okay," she replied nervously.
"Yeah, daddy's home, girl. To stay."

Isaac never knew about their release month sexcapades, though he had his suspicions. She lied to Isaac, saying that she was going to take care of her aunt in Tubman City, about 2 hours away. Meanwhile, Maceo fucked the lining clean out her coochie for 30 days straight. They never stopped loving each other but they would never be a couple again. Their relationship revolved around caring for their children. They lived their lives, Maceo with whomever he wished, and Nikki with Isaac.

"Babe, this thing with Bree and Kendali is stupid. Now, you can't even find Kendali on Zing," Isaac said to Nikki.
"Why you lookin' for her?" she asked with a tinge of jealousy. Her insecurity had nothing to do with Isaac, but everything to do with her eternal flame of love burning for Maceo.
"What? I look for everybody. I am being social." She grimaced.
"Babe, are you serious? It's for the books. I got all the juice I need." He licked his lips at her lustfully. He sat at his computer while she sat on the floor sorting paperback copies of their recent Black Pearl Publications releases. Nikki had established a solid roster of forty authors, Isaac being one of them. Over the years, since Maceo's release, she fantasized about rekindling their marriage, managing a publishing house together and giving Dominion a real run for their money. But that was just a fantasy.
"All the juice you need, huh?" she asked jiggling her butt cheeks. She was a plus size dime these days. After two children and five years of celibacy, while Maceo was incarcerated, ice cream and

fried chicken were her comfort. The pounds piled on. Isaac helped her lose a few, so she was a firmer, tighter, curvier plus size short stack. And she always wore dresses that fell gracefully over her figure and Isaac loved it.

"Yep," Isaac reassured.

"Well, the thing with Kendali and Bree will blow over. She'll be back. She has to return. Her final installment of *The Vixen Notebook* comes out soon. So…"

"True. Yeah. I wish they would get it together. It's plenty for everybody. That's what I used to tell your ex-husband back in the gap."

"We're still married." Nikki rolled her eyes.

"Fuck dat. You *my* wife." He shifted in his chair. "And when are you gonna divorce him anyway?"

"Soon enough. He refused before."

"Yeah, but if you really want a divorce you can get it."

"I know. I just don't feel like fighting with Maceo."

"Yeah, well. You need to feel like it."

"We'll see." She stacked a few more books, creating piles alphabetically by author's name. "Let's just focus on our books," she retorted, visions of her and Maceo dancing in her head.

Wednesday 4:00 p.m.

Hiram's office boasted the L-shaped east corner of the Cartwright building's thirteenth floor, sitting diagonally opposite to Georgette's work hub. They worked together, so having offices on opposite sides of the floor gave them some space and allowed them a bird's eye view of Dominion's rank and file, nestled in a maze of cubicles between them. Everything was black lacquer and black leather in his office- his desk, his chairs, his planning table, his roundtable, his picture frames, and the figurines placed throughout. Hints of silver chrome accessories including an old fashioned radio, a coat rack, and an umbrella stand gave the room just enough decorative contrast to emanate a contemporary vibe. He reclined in his chair, listening to his right hand, Monique, talk about the Kendali controversy.

"She just couldn't keep her damn mouth shut," she said crossing one big juicy thigh over the other. Her light blue denim skirt sprinkled with a silver dust design was the perfect match with her steel starched, church white tuxedo top, lighting up her cocoa brown face. "I am so sick of these authors and their foolishness. What are we doing to squash this?"

"I have AJ on it. She is making a damage control package. We will be fine."

"You sure? Kendali is about one third of our profits, Hiram."

"Mo, I *do* know this. Everything is going to work out just fine. AJ is an expert writer, persuader, manipulator. Her pen is blessed."

"True enough. But are we sure she isn't Bree's source?"

"Kendali asked me that too." Hiram stroked his goatee and flashed his Larenz Tate smile.

"Well, Hiram? And is something funny?"

"No. Nothing is funny. And no. I don't think AJ is on that type of time."

"Well how in the hell did Bree find out?"

"I don't know, but I have investigators looking into that."

"Is this whole thing a result of the beef with you and Maceo?"

"I have no beef with Maceo."

She uncrossed her legs and sat straight up in the black leather armchair. "Hiram. You talkin' to me."

"I *don't* have beef with Maceo. *Mace* has beef with *me*. He is still my brother. I love Maceo."

"Yeah, but does *he* know that? And you gotta admit. You didn't do him all the way right."

"Mo, I really don't feel like the olive branch conversation. That shit happened years ago. He should be over that. Right now, we need to focus on our number one cha-chinger."

"Hiram, all of this goes together. And I don't care what you don't feel like. Maceo probably just wants you to acknowledge that you took off with your own thing and didn't even attempt to join forces with him when he asked. He *did* give you the idea while you all were in prison."

"But I don't owe Maceo anything. I built Dominion with my own money. My own blood. My own sweat. My own tears."

"Jeezus! You can be such an asshole!"

"Why am I the asshole?" he asked, flashing his smile cavalierly.

"Because your money and blood, sweat, and tears have nothing to do with this. This is about a mutual love and respect. Brother to brother. He gave you the publishing game and asked you to help him build a bigger empire from what he started *while* incarcerated. You watched him and learned from him. And then you built your own company, never looking back. And never saying a word. C'mon, Hiram."

"Yeah, but that was between me and him."

"Yeah, but no. Everybody knows what's up. The streets talk and the streets know. Especially our authors and our employees. That shit carries over to them, whether y'all wanna believe it or not. You need to acknowledge him and apologize. You need to clear the air and show some brotherly love. Be a man about it."

Silence filled the room for one long reflective minute.

"Be a man about it, you say?"

"Yep."

"Okay. You are probably right."

"You know I'm right." She pulled her vibrating phone from her pocket. Her husband, Vaughn, was texting a reminder to ask Hiram about her own publishing house. "Now, about my publishing subsidiary..."

"Mo, I know you wanna go your own way, but I don't think you're ready. We have discussed this."

"Not ready?"

"No. I don't think so."

"You cannot be serious. While your money, your blood, your sweat, and your tears built Dominion, my hands, my feet, my mind, and my heart furnished and nurtured what you built. "

"You do not need to tell me about your feet and hands. I know you are an integral part of Dominion. And your generous paycheck reminds you every week that we know this."

"We?"

"Yes, we. Me and Georgette."

"Is she behind the hold up with my subsidiary?"

"No, she isn't." He rearranged some papers on his desk. Monique rolled her eyes. "I mean, she doesn't wanna lose you, but she doesn't wanna hold you back either."

Monique heard her grandmother's voice in her head, *You oughta know a lie when you hear one.* "Yeah. Okay, Hiram." She envisioned herself smacking Hiram's goatee off of his face, the hairy bundle bouncing off of the skyscraper window and landing on the floor and him grabbing his bald face in shock. She was ready to leave his office. "So, back to Kendali."

Hiram loosened his tie. "I am going to check in with Kendali and AJ when you and I finish up."

"Okay. Good. We do have other Dominion business. Let's move on."

"Yes. Let's."

Andrea Jenner, pen name AJ West, was a nerdy Jada Pinkett, petite frame, cute face, light copper skin, and thick glasses. She was a brilliant mind and a helluva writer. She graduated from Wellington College, located in the Deep South, with degrees in chemistry and English. Writing was her true passion and her father who was a scientist hated that she chose her passion as her profession. She wrote several moderately successful novels for Dominion in the urban fiction romance and sci-fi genres. As the social media manager she served as the administrator for all of Dominion's social media accounts, monitoring the profiles, pages, and groups of all Dominion authors.

Unbeknownst to the masses, she was the ghostwriter for Kendali's *The Vixen Notebook* series. The Dominion team intended that the series would be written in the typical three book installments, the standard for the industry. After book three, the readers seemed to think it a savory appetizer for a much more delicious entree. So, as the song says, you got to give the people, give the people what they want. And Dominion was delighted to oblige the hungry readership. The people gobbled up the saga, book after book, page after page, word after word. The executive decision was made to finally end the collection at number ten simply because there were no more stories to tell, Kendali desired to explore other topics, and everyone was ready to write the next big thing. Dominion staff, especially AJ, had been focused on the final book's completion and its promotional campaign, but then Bree decided to share the ghostwriting truth, retaliating against Kendali for a snide remark she made about Bree's last release, among other things. Kendali could be a real bitch on Zing, negatively criticizing other authors, and over complimenting her own work and the work of her Dominion pen siblings. Many times her social media presence seemed self-absorbed and egomaniacal. At the same time, she did post a plethora of positive, uplifting, inspirational memes and photos.

AJ despised Kendali and her kind, mediocre storytellers with subpar writing skills and no respect for the craft. Hiram begged her to rewrite Kendali's initial *The Vixen Notebook* that she had published independently with little success. Initially, AJ flat out declined, but Hiram made her an offer she couldn't refuse. He increased her managerial salary by thirty-three percent and gave her a percentage point of Kendali's sales. She hated herself for the ghostwriting deal, but she planned to pay off her parents' house and her own little plantation, a small farm house on 40 acres in the countryside. She was very close to fulfilling her real estate goals.

She sat at her desk polishing the final book of Kendali' bestselling series, *The Vixen Notebook 10: Age Is More Than A Number*. Her phone buzzed. She glanced at the screen. Lesli Lyn was texting. Her spirit elevated.

 Text Message

Lesli: Hey Butterfly 🦋

AJ: Hey Butterfly 🦋 I miss you so much. You just left me here 😐

Lesli: Never leaving you 😊 Always here for you. You can walk away whenever you wish. You choose to stay.

AJ: Well I have a plan. I will exit shortly.

Lesli: Whenever you're ready, you know Brad would love to have you here.

AJ: Is he ever gonna publish books?

Lesli: I think so. He brought it up to me a few days ago.

AJ: I hope so. That would be dope! 😃

Lesli: Lol. 😁 Yes, dope.

AJ: Are you laughing at me?

Lesli: You know it 😁 You are too cute using urban lingo.

AJ: 😊 How are you?

Lesli: I'm good mostly.

AJ: Mostly?

Lesli: Yeah. Got a death threat delivered to me at the office. It was unnerving.

AJ: Whaaaaaat?! OMGEEEEEEE!! 😠😠

Lesli: Yeah 😠😒😠 Box of dead flowers

AJ: Wowwwwww. See. That just makes me so mad. I know it's probably some of those idiot fans of these idiot authors. Mad about your book reviews or something. Arrrrgh! 😠😠😠

Lesli: Probably. They never understand that we all just looking to be better. We can't be mediocre. We have to be excellent! Because we are! 😃

AJ: Eggszacklee! 😊 😊 😊 You be careful out here. Did you tell Brad? You call the police?

Lesli: No, not yet.

AJ: Lesli Lyn! Why not?!!! Jeez!

Lesli: I know. I will. Relax. I told Titus. I will be fine.

AJ: Well at least you told Titus. 😊 Cuz we know he will handle the situation. I like Titus. Why don't you marry him? 😊

Lesli: Okay. That's my queue!

AJ: 😁 Okay. Let's have tea soon ☕

Lesli: Yes! We are overdue.

AJ: I love you, Butterfly 🦋

Lesli: Love you too 😊

She silenced her phone and tossed it in her purse. She refocused her attention on the book and typed for about an hour when Hiram double tapped on her cubicle wall. AJ had the largest cubicle space in the farthest corner of their thirteenth floor set up, away from everyone.

"Got a minute?"

"Yes, Hiram?" She thought Hiram a sleaze ball but he cut those checks regularly and did not skimp on the zeros.

"How is our collateral damage package?"

"All done. I emailed you yesterday. You didn't get it?"

"Hmmm. I don't think so."

"I will send it again. There are several hard copies there in my out basket." She pointed to her rectangular cherry wood work table. He picked up the hard copies and skimmed through the document.

"Wow! Looks good. Of course. I don't expect anything less than stellar from you."

"I'm glad you're pleased." She wanted to like Hiram, especially since she understood his money motivations, but he was so sheisty and egotistical. Everything was about him and his money. He created a facade of humble generosity but deep down, AJ knew he wasn't genuine.

"Okay. I'm going to go back to my office and review this. I will email you in a few minutes."

"Cool."

She went back to her writing.

Hiram kicked off his shoes and stretched his body, bending over touching his toes, then arching his back. He sat in his chair and reviewed the Zing posts that AJ wrote, the press releases, and the pre-release book promo tour schedule. Hiram grinned like a Cheshire cat when he read over the pre-release tour section. "She's so brilliant. You know how to pick 'em, bruh," he said to himself aloud, greasing his ego. He inhaled and exhaled slowly and deeply for four counts. Relief felt divine. Hiram sent Kendali a text instructing her to come to his office.

He cherished Kendali, for he had meticulously fashioned her into one of the best-selling urban fiction writers of the modern era. He reminisced on their first meeting. He had established Dominion with Georgette and they were always building their author roster. He would travel to author workshops and self-publishing seminars to recruit writers. He learned early on that these venues were gold mines bursting with raw creative talent. Her tall thick body, well maintained, bone-straight weave, and bright round eyes caught his attention. She perused the books in the makeshift book store of the self-publishing convention. Hiram approached her.

"Hey, how is everything?"

"Everything is everything," she replied, sipping from her water bottle. She had no interest in talking to the old dude.

"Have you learned anything?"

"Yeah. I need to step my game up."

"Well that's good information," he said as he watched her thumbing through a sci-fi novel. "You like sci-fi?"

"Sometimes."

"I take it you're a writer?"

"Yes."

"Have you published anything?"

"Yes."

"You are self-publishing?"

She blew her breath impatiently, annoyed by his questions. "Uh, yeah."

"What's the name of your book?"

"The Vixen Notebook."

"Hmmm. That sounds real interesting."

"It is."

"Well, how are your sales?"

"Okay."

He was exhausted with her indifferent attitude. No wonder her sales were 'okay'. "Here's my card. When you ready to sell some books, hit me up."

She took the card reluctantly and he left.

A few days later he searched for her book on Muse.com and skimmed the sample. His dick got hard thinking about the potential of what he read. It was the fictionalized account of the life of a hip hop video vixen. He wanted to find her but he knew she would find him once she realized who he was. He definitely wasn't chasing after no cut rate writer with a nasty disposition. And sure enough a few days after he sampled her book, she called. He didn't answer. She left a voicemail, then a text, then an email. He let her do three rounds of voicemails, texts, and emails before he responded. They arranged a lunch date, talked, shared life stories, plans, and visions. By the end of that week, Kendali signed on the dotted line and was on her way to millionaire status.

"Hey, Hiram. What's going on?"
"Ready to return to your fans?" He admired her style, long lime green wrap around dress, kelly green converse, kelly green and lime silk scarf tied around her bone straight auburn weave, and green eyeshadow on her light bright skin. He envisioned her bouncing up and down on his rock hard rod. Her voice snatched him from his fantasy.
"It's about time!" She sat her fat booty on the edge of his desk. He watched her femininity spread across his desk like butter on a hot roll. He licked his lips and she bit her bottom lip seductively.
"Y'all bitches addicted to damn Zing. It's worse than crack. Zing is definitely the new kingpin, reigning supreme out in these cyber streets."
"Whatever." She flipped him off with a wave of her hand. "What I gotta do?"
"Here's your hard copy." He pushed the document toward her hip resting on his black lacquer desk. She thumbed through the pages. "I will have AJ email you a soft copy."
"Okay, great!"

"You follow every instruction to the letter. She will update you on the pre-release tour. All the dates are tentative."

"Okay." She turned to the tour schedule and scanned the short list of media outlets. "The Myesha Morgan show???!!!" She jumped up from the desk.

"Aw hell. Here we go." Hiram pushed back from his desk revealing his blue, white, and purple checkered socks, his light gray slacks, and his purple pinstripe oxford. Kendali was turned on by his pop color conservative style, but not enough to quell her anger.

"Yo! Hiram! She will rip me to shreds! Are you fuckin' serious? And we never do this level of pre-release promo. Why you got me doin' it?"

"AJ has planned this for you, very methodically. She has studied marketing. Self-taught, but she is an extraordinary mind. Just trust us on this."

"I don't give a fuck about her extraordinary mind. Myesha Morgan is the loch ness monster of media! Oh my god." She shook her head slowly, holding her chin in her hand. Her face was on fire with fear, anger, and frustration. "I feel like this is a setup. We still don't know if she isn't the one who leaked the info to Bree."

"I am tellin' you. It ain't her." Kendali sighed and crossed her arms calling Hiram's attention to her C cup cleavage peeking thru the V-neckline of her dress. She saw his nature rise. She blushed and rolled her eyes, still disgusted with the comeback plan.

"How do you know?"

"I just know. And on Myesha Morgan, trust. She knows how to treat you."

"What does that mean?"

"She is not going to get out of line with you."

"How can you be so sure? She is a gossip terrorist, Hiram."

"If you must know, I got so much dirt on Myesha Morgan, she don't wanna cross me. Believe that."

Her pussy purred and her clit throbbed with erotic excitement thinking about Hiram's power in the industry.

"Okay." Her spirit calmed and her body relaxed. She dropped her hands to her sides.

"I gotchu, love."

"I know." She blew him a kiss.

🌀🌀🌀

Friday 10:00 a.m.

Zing Post

Kendali Grace (Post): I have missed you all these past several days. I deactivated my account to sit in my quietude and contemplate the controversy started by my sister of the pen, Bree McDee. Yes, in spite of what she said to me and what I've said to her, she is still my sister and I will always embrace her. I write my books, period. These are MY stories. I crafted the tales from the soul of my experiences. She says I use a ghostwriter. The truth is there is A WHOLE TEAM OF DOMINION FAMILY that writes, rewrites, edits, re-edits, tweaks, works, toils, struggles, and pours over my manuscripts, from start to finish. From the first idea spark, to the synopsis, to the chapter outline, to the writing, to the editing, to the cover design, to the layout, to the upload, to the printing, to the promotional campaign. We do work as a family here at Dominion. There are no ghosts. There are FAMILY MEMBERS working together for a common goal in the spirit of love.

I ask forgiveness for all of the negative speech, hate talk, derogatory comments, and ugly words, that I have posted in the past. I am a work in progress, intending to be a better writer, a better person, a better woman.

I pray we move forward in Love and Positivity. I love you

Reactions: 4,345 Comments: 269 Shares: 6,589
(Load previous comments)

Amber Alise: Datz my pen sissy We are FAMILY FOREVER!

   Kendali Grace: I love you, babe

Princess J: Datz right! DOMINION RULES

Ray Austin: Datz love

Samantha Cole: Wow. Your readers still love you, Kendali

Melissa Jaye: Hmmm.

   Deena Deen: @Melissa Jaye What are you saying?

   Melissa Jaye: Nothing. Just listening. Good PR spin

   Deena Deen: Gurl, bye! @Kendali Grace you need to block this bitch!

Carla Rae: Back to love people. Welcome back, Kendali!

   Kendali Grace: Thanks, sweets

Kathy Kay: Awww, I actually teared up on this. I love you, Kendali

   Kendali Grace: And I love you too

Calvin Spriggs: That's what's up

Kendali Grace: Hey, Calvin 😏

Zenobia Zee: I'm glad you're back! Can't wait for the finale of The Vixen Notebook 😄 📓

Kendali Grace: Awww, thanks, babe. Coming soon. Can I tag you? 📓 😄

Zenobia Zee: Yaaaaaaaaaaas! 😃

☄ Zing End Of Comments ⭐

There were a few negative comments, some people saying she still did not address if she was using a ghostwriter, others who just didn't want to forgive, and some who just refused to allow the drama to end. Even so, for now, she planned to stick to the instructions in AJ's PR plan- posting ONLY positive thoughts and information, ABSOLUTELY no responding to negativity or blocking the negative people or deleting their comments, and shifting ALL focus to the final book of *The Vixen Notebook* series. She loved the positive vibrations. She felt fantastical, like a fairy queen sprinkling magic dust all around her queendom. Life felt good again.

☄ ☄ ☄

Chapter Five
Situations & Confrontations

Saturday 12 noon

Aminah made two lunch boxes each for her family of four while Mustafa talked business on a phone call and their boys, Garvey and Biko, watched the latest Black Sands cartoons. She made tuna salad, a fruit salad teeming with berries, and fresh homemade wheat bread. She added granola bars, various chip snacks and trail mixes to complete their lunches for the beach.

She went into her husband's office. "Mustafa. Excuse me, babe." "Hold on for one second, baba." He muted the call. "Yes, Meena."
"I have to go to the shop for a pickup and I will be right back."
"Okay. Then we are off to the beach?"
"Yes. Be right back." She blew him a kiss. He caught it and rubbed his cheek with her love.
"Okay, baba. I'm back." Mustafa was talking with one of the elders in the community, Brother Nati, president and founder of Every World Africa, LLC, the number one distributor of rare and new books, mostly non-fiction, about Black life from around the world. He had single handedly amassed and maintained the most thorough catalogue of Black history, research, academic, and culture books on an international scale. Nati was guiding Mustafa on BlackOut Media's expansion venture- gathering all of the distributors like Nati and creating an online print and video streaming service of Black non=fiction books, documentaries, and lecture presentations. It was a daunting task, but Mustafa was built for the challenge.

"Alright, baba. I appreciate you setting up the meeting."
"That's what I'm here for. We need you to take it to the next level."
"And that's what *I'm* here for." Mustafa smiled. "I love you, baba."
"I love you too, youngblood. Peace and love."
"Peace."
Mustafa looked at the time and calculated that he could quickly do a Zing Live. He had to respond to Kendali's comeback.

Zing Live - Mustafa
Peace, Love and Blessings, Fam.

I gotta give it to the homegirls and the homeboys at Dominion. They know how to work their handle. They kept the ghostwriting question vague, which of course gives us our answer that Kendali probably uses a ghostwriter. But they turned us toward love. And I am always for the love. Always! Because y'all don't write about love enough. Y'all say these are love stories, but I don't see the love conveyed. You want a good love. A good man. But you keep writing and reading about savages, bullies, and monsters. What the fuck you think you gonna attract if you readin' and writin' about savages?!? A fuckin' savage! You get it? No, you don't get it. But try to get this: you are what you read, people. Stop bein' a dumb, miserable broad, hangin' with a buncha dumb miserable broads that want savages, bullies, thugs, monsters, and animals as mates. Kendali and her Dominion people got that part right- "I pray we move forward in love and positivity." So, let's move forward in love, Black family. Now, I'm off to the beach with my tribe. And as always, business over bullshit! Deuces!"

The weekends at Dominion's thirteenth floor office were always mildly abuzz with authors who had nine to five day jobs. They came on weekends to congregate, write, and motivate one another's writing endeavors. Many times the group would coordinate a potluck lunch or breakfast. Sometimes Hiram would have KD's prepare a simple buffet including KD's signature cheesecake explosion for dessert. This particular Saturday, there were fewer folks than usual, maybe fifteen authors were working. AJ was there every weekend and Kendali was rarely present, but in light of the recent social media madness, she felt the need to be close to Dominion headquarters and even closer to AJ, monitoring the progress of *The Vixen Notebook* finale.

"So how is everything going?" Kendali made herself comfortable at AJ's work table. AJ had the largest cubicle of any staffer; of course, Kendali's workspace was huge too. They were Dominion's favorite daughters.

"It's goin'. This will be an awesome finale."
"Well, I didn't just mean the book. How are things with you?" Kendali asked.
"Oh, no. You just meant the book. It's okay though."
"I'm just making conversation, AJ."
"No need to do that. But you already know this."
"Why are you always so cold to me?"
"Not cold. Just business. That's all." AJ wiped her glasses.
Kendali straightened her posture and placed her arms on the table. "AJ, I'm not trying to be besties or anything. You have been crucial to my success. And I'm thankful for everything you have done for me. I just want us to be cool."

AJ slid her glasses onto her face and spun around in her chair, looking Kendali dead in her eyes. "Is there something on your mind, Kendali? You have something you wanna say?"

"Well, maybe I do."

"Feel free. What is it?"

Kendali performed a quick mental inventory of her conversations with Hiram, Dre, and Monique. While she trusted Hiram implicitly, she needed to see AJ's reaction to the question. "Did you leak the ghostwriting story to Bree?"

AJ removed her glasses again. "No. I did not. I leave all that craziness to y'all."

Kendali was surprised that she believed her. She felt AJ was sincere. "AJ." She rolled her chair closer to the ghostwriting genius. "I know you don't feel like I deserve my success, but I had a story to tell. And I needed to tell it. That's all I wanted to do. I'm just a woman...with a story. That's all."

"Kendali, I don't begrudge you your success. I despise the machine that promotes and pushes mediocrity and dismisses brilliance as if it's some thorn in the side of creativity. As if skilled writers are the gnat on the ass of the literary arts."

They stared at each other in silence, each convicted in their perspectives.

Kendali spoke. "AJ, call me with updates from time to time."

"I will shoot you an email soon so you can review the next three completed chapters."

"Good enough. Thanks." She rose from her chair and returned to her work area.

Hiram and Georgette rarely enjoyed an absolutely lazy Saturday, but this Saturday was one of those rare occasions. They slept late, ate a big breakfast with their babies, played video games on the Xbox and watched AfroMan movies. As the afternoon heat fell upon them they decided to indulge in a poolside barbeque. Georgette patted some turkey burgers, made veggie salad with mandarin oranges, and assembled a few shrimp kabobs. Hiram pulled some Hebrew National hot dogs from their meat locker and fired up the grill. Georgette dressed Harlem, their daughter, age six and Hendrix, their son, age four, for the pool.

"Mama, I love my bathing suit," Harlem said spinning around in her yellow flowered one piece.

"You do look pretty." Georgette smiled at her six year old carbon copy.

"Mommy?"

"Yes, Hendrix." Georgette responded admiring Hiram's mini-me.

"Can we get the super soakers?" She melted at his impishly handsome face.

"Ooooo, yeah! Mama, can we?" Harlem joined the plea.

"Yes, get the super soakers!" Georgette pumped her fists in the air, cheering on her little ones' excitement.

"Yay!" they screeched and made a beeline for the garage to get the water sprayers.

"I'm right behind you," she sang as she tidied up Harlem's bedroom, putting away her myriad of Dr. Seuss books, fifty piece puzzles, and Curly Fro dolls. Her overstuffed toy chest prompted Georgette to make a mental note to buy a bigger fun box for Harlem. After she repositioned the collection of her baby girl's Cabbage Patch Kids, she headed to the garage. She recalled the prelude to their existence, a sweet, simple invitation from Hiram and a smooth, easy acceptance from her at a popular local book store, The Lotus Leaf.

"I love your work."

Georgette raised her big bubbly eyes from the autograph she penned for a fan to behold the masculine beauty waiting to get his signed copy of *Hood Love Story: Luke and Loni On The Run*, her latest release.

"Thank you." His dashing smile and piercing gaze warmed her spirit unnervingly. She rejoiced that she was seated because she was paralyzed by the magnificent stranger. "Have you read the whole book?"

"Definitely. I loved everything about it."

"Wow! That makes me feel so good." She blushed. "Tell me your name."

"Rivers. Hiram Rivers."

"Okay. *Hiram,*" she repeated as she inscribed a note in his book. Though sensuously unsettled, she pushed past his calculated gaze and asked, "Will you stick around for our book chat?"

"Of course. I'm here for all of it."

"Good." She prayed her anxiety didn't show.

"I was hoping you would be open to having a late night snack with me after the book discussion."

A wave of heat scorched through her body and her brain. Erotic thoughts and visions liquefied her gray matter. She imagined herself showering in a cool waterfall to calm her down.

"That would be lovely."

"Good. I'm going to grab a seat."

"Okay. Cool."

After the book chat, she followed him to Chey's Bar and Grill about fifteen minutes from The Lotus Leaf. They ate, drank, and talked until the bar closed. She learned that he had studied her career, read her books, examined her publisher and followed her fan base through a variety of media content including news articles, blog stories, radio broadcasts, and social media platforms. Hiram impressed upon her that she was undoubtedly better than her colleagues, a better storyteller and a better commander of the English language. He told her that Write Way Books had to prepare itself to release her because Hiram had to have her. And Hiram Rivers always got what he wanted. And just when she thought the whole escapade was just a sales pitch, he said, "Your pictures do you absolutely no justice."

She breathed a sigh of relief. Hiram wasn't the first to attempt luring her away from Write Way, but he was unequivocally the finest. "You think so?"

"I know so. And you draggin' that wagon too. Woo!"

She laughed uproariously, celebrating the new attraction and the potential love affair.

"Mommy, you gonna get a super soaker too?" Hendrix asked bringing his mother back to present day.

"Oh yes, baby." She selected a blue and orange water toy for herself.

"I'll get one for daddy," Harlem announced.

"Yes, one for daddy," Georgette agreed. "Okay, troops. To the pool!"

The warm, sunny day pampered the Rivers family as they relished the grilled vittles Hiram prepared, played water games in the pool, and relaxed on the brick-laden patio. After they were satiated by the backyard barbeque delights, Hiram and Georgette mellowed out with jazz tunes serenading their quietude while the children played board games on the grass. Hiram answered his cell for the first time during their lazy Saturday festivities.

"Yo, yo!"

"My man." It was Crispus Adams, Hiram's hired fixer. He called upon him to do the dirty work, clean ups, and fixes that managing a million dollar corporation required.

"Whatcha got for me?" Hiram crossed his legs sinking deeper into the peach colored cushion of the chaise lounge chair.

"Truly, bruh. I don't have much but I need to check in with you."

"Alright. Gimme whatcha got."

"On Bree, nothing. Nothing out of the ordinary happening with her. I've followed her, monitored her calls. Nothing strange yet. But I am just starting the investigation. We *will* uncover her source."

"Well you do what you do. I got some things I am gonna survey on the Bree matter."

"Alright. Good." He flipped through a few papers in a manila folder while sitting in his old black Chevy Tahoe watching a house for another case. "Now for the stalker. The flower shop manager allowed me to look at the store camera footage. It was an elderly woman who ordered the flowers. She paid cash of course. They say they had never seen her before. Don't know who she is. I don't have much right now, but you know I will get to the bottom of this."

"This I know, bro! We definitely need to know what's going on with the stalker."

"She have security detail?" Crispus inquired.

"Yep. I got somebody shadowing her. She don't know it."

"Okay. That's good. I will be in touch with you again. Real soon."

"That's what's up. I appreciate you, man."

"Just doin' my job."

"Yeah, yeah. Have a good day."

"You too."

Georgette had been ear hustling the conversation. She asked, "A stalker? Who has a stalker?"

"Kendali."

"You didn't tell me. Oh my god. Seriously?"

"Yeah. She got some flowers delivered with an anonymous cryptic note attached. Then she tells me later on, after she got the flowers, that she thinks she's being followed."

"Followed? How so?"

"She thinks she sees this black car popping up every now and then. Just lurking."

"Hmmm. Well. It does happen. Celebrity status brings the crazies."

"True enough. I got Crispus on it."

"If Crispus is on it, we know we gonna find out *exactly* what's going on," Georgette said adjusting her bikini top.

"Word!" Hiram aroused, eyeing her perky breasts and flat belly with faint stretch marks that reminded him of his favorite creations. Harlem and Hendrix made him whole; he never imagined that fatherhood would be so fulfilling. "I'ma need to see you tonight." He touched her thigh and gritted his teeth, shifting her restful position on the lounge chair next to him.

"See me? Oh yeah?" She shivered, thinking of Hiram's hands exploring her body. There was magic in his fingertips.

"Oh yes."

"You say that until you get home, tired. You have KD's tonight, right?"

"Yes, I do." At least twice a month, Hiram visited KD's Supper Club, owned by Khai Draper, his frat brother, and college roommate. He gave KD the seed money for the supper club and he liked to check in with his friend. Because of their busy schedules, they committed at least two days a month to seeing each other face to face. The restaurant was the ideal spot for their mano a manos. "I'm gonna start preparing to leave soon. But not before I have…" He increased the volume of his voice bellowing, "…one last swim with my royal court!" He ran toward the children and they gave chase, screaming with delight.

"Aaaaaaaaaahhhhh!" Harlem and Hendrix ran around the lawn screeching and laughing, "Daaaadddy! Ha ha ha haaaa!"

He scooped them up, one under each arm and headed to the pool. "Hiram, be careful with our babies please!" Georgette shouted jumping from her chair.

He stood them on the pool's edge on each side of him, holding their little hands.

"One, two, threeeeee!!! Aaaaaaaaaaaahhhhhh!" the three yelled as they jumped in the pool.

Hendrix swam to the top first while Harlem lingered underwater, practicing holding her breath. She emerged, saying, "Daddy! That was fun! Let's do it again!"

"Yeah, Daddy!" Hendrix exclaimed.

"Okay." And they played together until sunset.

❋ ❋ ❋

Saturday 9:00 p.m.

Indigenous Soul was closing their first set when Hiram arrived all decked out in his white linen suit, a cobalt blue t-shirt with lime green art deco design, and his lime green and white Nike Air Max. He ordered his usual Don Julio tequila, gave all the bar staff greetings, and walked to Khai's VIP lounge, tucked away in the furthest southeast corner of the venue on its own secluded mezzanine. He stood at the threshold, tapped his fingers on the brass bars of the balcony, savored his drink, and bobbed his head to the genius rhythms of the band. KD's was packed every weekend because its house band was a multigenerational, multicultural ensemble, attracting young Black professionals, ages twenty to fifty. It was the only place in town with a robust cross cultural patronage and a dessert menu serving a variety of homemade baked goods-vanilla pound cake, birthday cake, strawberry shortcake, banana pudding, sweet potato pie, peach cobbler, chocolate chip cookies, and various flavors of KD's signature cheesecake explosion. Hiram relished his meet ups with KD; he found great comfort in spending time with his friend.

"My man!" KD snuck up behind Hiram and bear hugged him, startling his friend ever so slightly, for he had lost himself in the music and libation.

Hiram turned around quickly to face Khai, returned the hug, and topped off their greeting with lingering dap. "I miss you, bro. So much to catch up on."

"Good to see you, bruh. Always dapper. Fly guy number one." KD was a snazzy colorful dresser, more daring than Hiram choosing a rainbow of patterns and fabrics for his six foot, cream skinned frame, topped with a head full of sandy brown curls.

"You already know." KD flashed his toothy grin and spun around, showing off a sky blue and peach printed jacket, traditional khakis, and sky blue docksiders.

"Man, you a fool with it." They dapped each other again and turned their attention to the crowd.

"How are things turning out with Miss Numero Uno?" KD asked referring to Kendali.

"I think the tide has turned in our favor. AJ is a brilliant marketing manager. She is the duchess of smooth."

"She is. She has certainly masterminded Dominion's success," KD asserted.

"No doubt. Dominion is the house that she and Kenni built."

"For real, for real."

"We are anticipating an unprecedented blockbuster with her final *Vixen Notebook*. It's a heavy finale," Hiram informed.

"I know it will be."

"So what's happening with you?" Hiram swallowed his liquor, watching the crowd as the band left the stage for a break.

"You know me, the club and the honeys. That's it." KD opened his arms, over the crowd, showcasing his empire.

"Yes. I do know you," Hiram stated, nudging his friend's arm.

"What we eatin' tonight?"

"Oh, you know. All good stuff. It's a diner theme tonight. Traditional diner eats- meatloaf, mashed potatoes, fried chicken, waffles, pancakes, coffee cocktails, fruit salad, chef salad. I think that's about it."

"Man! Y'all keep that menu on one hunnit!"

"Gotta do that." KD remembered Dominion's Saturday lunch was earlier. "Oh! Did the family like their lunch today?"

"Maaan, you know they licked the pans clean. Didn't leave a crumb."

"That's what I wanna hear."

They chatted, reminisced, and updated each other from their last texts and talks over the past couple of days. The wait staff set up a buffet for them and any more VIP's that might stroll to the lounge throughout the night. They enjoyed their vittles and more soul shaking sounds from Indigenous Soul. Eventually, the two friends left the lounge and joined the main floor crowd, walking around talking with the patrons, ensuring everyone was having a good time. KD noticed Maceo and a female companion nursing

95

margaritas at the bar. "Yo, Ram!" Hiram looked at KD and KD pointed in Maceo's direction. Hiram glanced at his alleged rival and did a double take. Maceo saw Hiram's surprise, nodded his head, and raised his glass. Hiram acknowledged his gesture with a peace sign. KD cut his conversation short with a honey to talk to Hiram. "Yo, this is a good time to bury that hatchet."

"What hatchet? And what is he doing here?"

"You know what hatchet and Maceo is a regular, rarely on a Saturday though."

"You never told me that," Hiram said, making scissor motions with his fingers.

"There was nothing to tell. Why don't y'all go outside on the patio and handle this once and for all."

Hiram hesitated. It was a serendipitous occasion because he planned to call Maceo to get to Bree. He needed her source and it was best to get it from the horse's mouth. He failed to feel apologetic, but if a truce was a requirement to obtain the intel, he would oblige.

"Yo, bro!" KD beckoned Hiram's attention.

"Yeah, yeah, man. Okay. Okay."

Hiram walked to the bar, its lights flashing blue, green, and purple through the glass. "Bobby, their drinks..." he pointed to Maceo and his arm candy. He continued, "On my tab." Bobby nodded.

Maceo's bald head rippled at the gesture. "Thanks, bruh."

"Let's go outside and talk."

"I'll be right back, boo," Maceo said to his date. She smiled.

"Bobby!" Hiram shouted for the bar manager's attention.

"Yo!" Bobby looked at Hiram.

"Give her anything she wants."

"Sho' ya' right," he responded.

Maceo followed Hiram onto the torchlit patio where KD's customers were enjoying the evening breeze and the supper club's outdoor ambiance. They settled in a quiet corner away from the party goers.

"What's up, man?" Maceo asked.

"I need to talk to Bree. I need to know her source."

"Why you tellin' me? You need to talk to her, so talk to her."

"Well, I am asking you about her first, as a professional courtesy."

"Professional courtesy? Ha ha ha ha ha haaa!" Maceo's laughter floated on the air drawing some attention from the patrons. Hiram sighed and crossed his arms. "Man, listen. I know how you feel."

"You don't know jack shit about how I feel, Hiram." Maceo popped his upper body, flexing in Hiram's direction rippling the fabric of his all white Middle Eastern tunic.

"Ease up, bruh. I am apologizing, Mace. I should have been straight up with you."

"You only apologizin' cuz you want Bree's intel. That's all this is."

"For real, for real. If I want to talk to Bree, I can just go talk to her. I-"

"Whoa. You tryin' me, man?" Maceo stepped closer to Hiram, face to face and eye to eye.

"Maaan. Look. All I'm sayin' is this. I am talking to you. I am asking you about your people to be better about how I handle my business and better with you."

"Uh-huh. Yeah, right." Maceo stepped back, away from Hiram. "Stay away from Bree."

"What? Are you serious? Bro. I am trying to put an end to all the bullshit. And some of the bullshit stems from the ill vibe between us. We need to squash all of this and move forward."

"Yeah, I hear you, Hiram. But stay away-"

"Oh, uh-huh, bitch! Not today!" a screeching female voice interrupted their palaver.

"Whatchu gon' do?! We right here, right now! I'm sicka all y'all Kendallites. Fuck all y'all, whores," an opposing catfighter screamed. Each contender was flanked by her posse of two women each.

"Whores? Bitch, who you callin' a whore?" The screecher grabbed the whore caller's hair and the fight commenced. The scufflers were some of Bree's and Kendali's fans. Through the back and forth exchange, the onlookers learned that the beef started in one of the Zing readers groups and that these two women only knew each other through the group. They became rivals, having an ongoing difference of opinion about books, authors, publishers, and urban fiction in general. Hiram and Maceo rushed to the fight, picking the women up off the ground, pulling them apart. Seconds later, KD and his security team arrived, quickly restoring order. Maceo and Hiram escorted the fighters to the exit making sure they went their separate ways, speaking words of calming wisdom to each crew. The two men recentered themselves smoothing out their clothes and breathing deeply, resting on the patio gates. Hiram looked at Maceo and asked, "You still don't want me talking to Bree?"

❧❧❧

Chapter Six
You Been Schooled

Monday 10:00 a.m.

"So, how was your weekend?" Monique asked running her fingers through her bone straight silk pressed hair. She admired the sunshiny view from Hiram's office windows. The Cartwright building definitely offered the best panorama of the city skyline, not too high, not too low. Hiram stopped tapping his keyboard. "Really good. The best I have had in a long time. Me, Gee, the kids, the pool, the grill. Perfect lazy Saturday. Sunday. Church. Brunch. Sports. Work."

"Awesome. Glad you had some family time."

"How 'bout you, Mo? How was your weekend?"

"Nice. We actually had a spa weekend in Tubman City. Left the kids to fend for themselves. Ha ha ha ha."

"Seriously?"

"Hell yeah. Y'all work it out. They know better. They don't want me blackin' out on they asses. They know how to act."

"Heh heh heh," Hiram laughed. "Mo, you crazy. I guess I have that to look forward too. We still got babies."

"Yeah. But enjoy this time. They grow up so fast."

"True enough."

"I have been trolling our social media platforms. Looks like Kendali is okay. Of course some people can't let shit go."

"You know you always have those types. They just can't do it." Monique sat in the soft black leather guest chair with chrome armrests in front of Hiram's desk, her cream colored and chambray patchwork skirt rising slightly. Hiram observed

Monique's thickness with a raised eyebrow. "Vaughn know you out here like that?"

"Hiram. Don't even try to distract me," she retorted.

"You the one distracting witcha big legs bustin' out."

"You need to stop," she chuckled. "But you are not distracting me. I know how you work. You forget that sometimes."

"Mo, I know-"

"Hold up," she interrupted his anti-Monique, the publisher spiel. "Just let me talk. I am going to start my own house. I was hoping I would have your support, but if I don't, it is okay. I mean really okay." She breathed deeply. "I definitely have sad, angry, and disappointed feelings about it, but I will get over it."

"Monique, publishing is a big step. And while you are incredibly skilled and talented, there is so much more to this industry."

"Hiram! You have got to be kidding me! Sweet Jesus! You are disgusting!" She leapt from her chair, flinging her arms with dramatic abandon.

"Monique, you need to calm down." He sat up.

"Dammit! You calm down!" she screamed. "I built this damn company. While your ego pumps you up to believe otherwise, *I* signed 80 percent of the authors! I hired the graphics design team, the editing team AND your precious AJ and made her the PR director." She exhaled a grand sigh. "I'm the one who told you to make Kendali and her Vixen Notebook more than a book series. I told you to fashion her and her book into a brand that is now responsible for more than a third of this company's revenue!"

He leaned back in his seat, smiling cavalierly. "Monique, I know these things. You are yelling and shouting unnecessarily. All I am saying-"

"I don't give a fuck what you're sayin'! I'm outta here." She turned abruptly, her bone straight locks slapping the air.

Hiram felt nervous and nauseous. He stood up behind his desk. "Wait. You leavin' us? You quittin'?"

"Not yet," she snarled looking back at him over her shoulder.

"Monique, just gimme some time. Just a lil' time."

"Whatever, nigga," she spat and slammed the door behind her. There were several employees milling about Hiram's reception area pretending to be busy, acting as if they didn't hear the argument. They heard Monique's screaming muffled by the heavy walls of the skyscraper's architecture. They could not decipher details of the heated debate, but it was clear that their CAO was very displeased. The natives were way past restless. Hiram plopped onto his leather sofa and bent over until his head was between his legs. He felt his heart beating like a ticking time bomb. He had to figure a way to keep Monique happy and Dominion thriving. There was too much to do. He still had to get to the bottom of Bree and Kendali and the stalker. *Strategy, brother, strategy*, he thought to himself.

🪨🪨🪨

"Girl, she ain't tell me nothin'. She didn't even confirm that you were talking about Kendali." Shante updated Bree on her conversation with Monique as they walked the treadmills at Bomb Body Fitness. Her machine was set at a slower speed than Bree's since Bree was more athletic than Shante's doughy figure eight.

"My goodness. Monique needs to quit it. For real, for real. I know she knows." Bree's slim hips and thick thighs kept a nice brisk pace on the treadmill while Shante's freckles began sweating.

"I think so too. But she suggested it could be somebody else. *And* Monique may be leaving Dominion." Shante and Bree had agreed on Zing messenger when Bree first posted her Kendali ghostwriting sauce that they would discuss the matter face to face only. No texts, no DM's, and no phone conversations.

"Somebody else? Like who? And Monique is leaving Hiram? I can't believe that. "

"Amber Alise, for one. She named two others, but I don't recall right now. And yes, leaving Hiram, not for sure. She dropped a hint of the possibility."

"Damn! Amber Alise? They do and say anything to protect this slut."

"Well, she *is* their golden girl."

"Whatever! Fuck her." Bree increased the speed of her stride.

"And Monique leaving Dominion, we'll see. I will believe it when it happens."

"Well, you were referencing Kendali, true?"

"You know it," Bree confirmed.

"How did you find out? Who told you?"

"I don't know."

"Huh?"

"I don't know."

"Now, you talkin' like Monique- *you dont know?*" Shante scoffed at Bree's response.

"I am telling you. I really don't know." Shante frowned at Bree, her confused expression dripping perspiration. "I will explain everything. Let's finish up. We will talk outside."

"Okay." Shante picked up her speed to a light jog. "Gotta keep the figure eight straight!"

After they left the gym, they stood on the parking lot and talked for about an hour. Bree revealed to Shante that someone slipped a plain unmarked envelope under her apartment door. The contents were a stack of emails, communications among Kendali, Hiram, and AJ, clearly indicating that AJ was ghostwriting for Kendali.

Shante questioned Bree. "And you have no idea who delivered the envelope?"

"None. The envelope was just sitting there when I got home from an event."

Shante, still doubtful, inquired, "You sure the emails are real?"

"Judging from the content, the style of the email, the conversations, I am ninety-nine percent sure they're real."

"Wow."

"Yeah, wow," Bree said.

The two sister friends stood quietly.

Bree reflected on how she arrived at her current space discussing the anonymous informant with Shante, how she and Shante met at her first book signing and became fast friends, and how the urban fiction rivalries had spiraled out of control. She heard Maceo's voice in her head, *"You are a writer, an author. Why does any of this even matter?"*

Monday 2:00 p.m.

Rica searched high and low around Dominion's reception area. She had asked almost every member of the staff, except the executive team; they were out at a conference. *Where was her butterfly paper clip?!* Lesli Lyn, pen name, Butterfly Brooks gave her the clip before she left Dominion. Rica loved the paper clip for two reasons- one, she absolutely adored the giver and two, its exquisite design. It was about six inches long, 24 karat gold plated antique brushed finish, a two inch wide butterfly on top with little Swarovski crystals on the wings and antennae. "Aaaaaargh!" she shouted. "Where the hell is my damn paper clip?!" She tossed stuff around her desk for the third time, rummaging through drawers, and shuffling things about in the cabinets of her domain.

"Hmmm. The first thing you may want to do is calm down." Tiyanna observed Rica's hurricane, exiting the elevator into the reception hall of Dominion's thirteenth floor. She was returning from a late lunch.

"I can't calm down. I love that paper clip. It's special. It's one of a kind." Rica paused her search and faced her co-worker. "You just gettin' back?"

"Hmm…hmmph. Yeah. Nobody's here checkin' for me. So, hey. " Rica continued looking, slowing her pace on the fourth round of her inspection. Tiyanna put her hand on her hip and gazed thoughtfully at the ceiling. "I bet I know where it is."

Rica spun around creating a breeze with the force of her excitement. "You do?!"

"Not sure, but let's go see." Tiyanna led Rica to Georgette's office.

"Hold on. Wait. Why are we going to Georgette's office?"

"Because this is where you will find your paper clip," Tiyanna replied, rifling through Georgette's desk.

Rica stopped in the doorway watching Tiyanna conduct her shake down. She felt uneasy about being in the boss' office without her present.

"Ha-ha! Found it!"

"Whaaat?" Rica was shocked. "Why would Georgette have my paper clip?"

"Girrrrrrrl." She gave Rica the prized possession, admiring the craftsmanship. "It is a nice clip. I see why you were searching like a savage."

"Yes. Isn't it lovely?" Rica beamed with happy relief, holding the treasure against her heart. "But why would Georgette have it?"

Tiyanna straightened the desk and walked out of the office toward her cubicle. Rica trailed behind her.

"Sis. Our boss is a lil' off." Tiyanna tossed her workbag in a chair and sat at her desk.

"Off?"

"Yes. Just watch. You will see if you pay attention. She is a lightweight 'thief'." Tiyanna made air quotes.

"Really?" Rica was astonished.

"Really. It's little stuff. She is probably more covetous than thieving. She covets." Tiyanna saw Rica's confused expression. "Like one time I wore this dress to work. And I mean the dress izzzz bangin'. Well, about two weeks later, she shows up in the dress at one of our release events."

"Wow."

"Yeah, but the point is, she never complimented me on my dress. Never said anything. See how that's a lil' creepy?"

"Yeah. I do."

"So, she probably doesn't see, taking your paper clip as stealing. You see? She just scooped it up and started using it."

"Hmmm. Like she is entitled?"

"See? I think you're gettin' it," Tiyanna said.

"Yeah. Sounds like ego- *I see it. I want it. I take it,*" Rica deduced.

"You got it!"

"Georgette gon' fuck around and have me come outta character on her ass."

"Don't do it. Just watch. You been schooled."
"I have. Thanks, Tiyanna."

Monday 5:30 p.m.

The Goddess Garments boutique was in the Main Street historic district of Seminole City. Aminah picked a simple colorful bright open air design for her shop. Three snow white walls with one wall a mural of ancient America the way she imagined- lush green forest, pyramid castles with a huge mothership parked out front, small flying aircraft manned by beautifully dressed copper, bronze, black, and blue black people floating hither and thither, and an open valley at the center with its citizens dancing, laughing, loving, and building. Light oak hardwood floors captured the sunlight beaming through the oversized picture windows. Georgette Rivers was definitely one of her top five customers, of course since she was a social butterfly, a community icon with a plethora of events to attend, and she had money to burn. It helped that they knew each other in high school. During their teen years at City High, Georgette had a crew of flunky wanna be's swarming in the atmosphere of her popularity, a popularity earned being one of the smartest and prettiest girls in the school. Aminah was popular in her own right as president of the dance and fashion clubs, serving as executive producer of the City High Fashion Extravaganza the last three years of her matriculation. Everybody in the city, from eight to eighty, blind, crippled, or crazy attended City High's legendary fashion shows. Georgette steered clear of other girls who possessed their own power, but she seemed to evolve in her older years, at least in that she diligently patronized Aminah's designs and sent her countless clients.

Georgette arrived at Goddess Garments, fumbling through her purse, waving her phone, and alarming her BMW M6 coupe. "Girl, I am so sorry I'm late. We had the most boring conference to attend. And I do mean boring." She sashayed toward Aminah who was finishing a sale with a customer at the multi colored stain glass register station centered in the middle of the store. "Hey, Georgette. I'll be with you in just a few moments." Aminah forced a smile, annoyed by Georgette's interruption.

"Oh girl. I'm sorry." She looked at the customer. "I apologize." She looked at Aminah. "Please forgive me, girl. I'm gonna shop while you take care of your customer."

"It's okay. I am finishing up shortly," Aminah reassured.

"Okay." Georgette browsed Aminah's handbag section. She admired her craftsmanship, picking up a purse shaped like a mermaid, fully bedazzled with only the best variety of crystals. Aminah had blessed hands, especially with handbags and purses. Georgette never, not one time left without a purse. She remembered her last time in the shop about a month ago; she bought one of her specialty cigar box purses covered with magazine covers of famous Black women models and actresses. She chuckled to herself thinking of all the sisters who tried to con her out of that purse.

"Hey sis!" Aminah opened her arms to hug.

Georgette turned around and embraced her. "It's good to see you." They released each other.

"Come on. Follow me," Aminah instructed

"Yes. Yes. I can't wait to see the dress."

The two women relaxed in the workroom of the shop. Georgette was exceedingly pleased with Aminah's creation, a medium blue denim dress with handkerchief hem and black marabou feathers sewn into the hem's creases and the wrist of its goddess sleeves. She made her a set of feather shoe clips to match.

"You always outdo yourself. I absolutely love it." Georgette modeled her new dress in the mirror, turning, spinning, and vogueing.

"I aim to please, sister. I'm so glad you love it."

"I do," Georgette confirmed, taking one last spin and admiring her reflection. She slipped off the dress and hung it in a garment bag. "How are things with you?"

Aminah organized her work table, replacing scissors in their containers and sweeping shreds of material onto the floor. "All is well, give thanks to the Creator. How bout you?"

"Pretty good. Terribly busy. Stressed. But we are moving through."

"Yes. A multimillion dollar empire has its challenges."

"You betta know it." Georgette put on her work skirt. "I am so thankful for our team. They make everything work." She wrapped her blouse around her body and tied it on the side. "But we may be losing the quarterback."

"The quarterback?" Aminah stopped her clean-up.

"Yeah. Monique may be leaving us."

"Really?" Aminah couldn't wait to tell Mustafa to gain his insight.

"Yeah. She wants to go out on her own. She needs our help. Our support. But we have encouraged her to wait, declining her proposal. Postponing our support, but now, I think she is ready to go it alone. Do or die."

"Well, why don't you help her?"

"We don't think she's ready."

"Hmmm. Or she is too valuable to you and you don't want to release her?" Aminah questioned.

"I mean...well...she is valuable, really irreplaceable. But we don't wanna hold her back."

"You sure?"

"I'm sure."

"Ohhhhh-kay," Aminah replied reluctantly.

"I'm sure," Georgette insisted.

"Alright." Aminah dismissed the conversation, certain that Georgette got the message.

Georgette was ready to go. "Let's ring me up. My dress. The mermaid purse. And one of the *This Love Thang* t-shirts."

"Let's ring, cha-ching, Madame Big Spender!" Aminah did her happy dance all the way to the customer service station as Dwele serenaded them from the ceiling speakers.

Georgette giggled at her graceful movements; she was still a great dancer. "Girl, you a mess."

"And you're the best!" Aminah replied excitedly, thinking of the $4,500 that Georgette was spending. She looked forward to sharing the Dominion status with Mustafa. She had mixed emotions and she knew he would too. On the one hand, she hoped the disturbance at Dominion would make them change their agenda and creative motivations. So what if they crumbled? Good riddance! On the other hand, she felt sad because even though she disliked their books, their authors, and the overwhelming trap nature of their catalogue, she understood that deep down they were just trying to find their way back to love.

♥♥♥

Chapter Seven
Hulks, Henrys, and Heartaches

Wednesday 2:00 p.m.

Crispus Adams was a former military intelligence officer. Upon retirement, he worked briefly in the civilian world as a special investigator for cold cases with Seminole City's police department, and then turned his attention to private investigation. Working as a private investigator for some of Seminole City's top law firms proved most lucrative for him, which is how he met Hiram. Hiram had retained Schwiner, Smith, and Rosenberg as his legal team when he was charged with fraud, money laundering, and conspiracy to commit murder in a big RICO case. Ultimately, as a result of Crispus' investigative work, Hiram's parents' municipal connections, and the prominence of the law firm, he wound up serving three years for mail fraud at Avondale Correctional Institute, where he met and befriended Maceo. Hiram had Crispus on retainer as a 'Special Assignment Coordinator'. His current task was finding Kendali's stalker and so, he started following her, checking her movements, and hoping the stalker would be in the mood to stalk. He had debriefed her and Hiram about his plan, showed her his face and his car so that she would understand that he was her protective shadow and not the stalker.

He sat in his car about a half of a block away from the spa where Kendali was having her beauty treatments surveying Mondawmin Street, the cars, the shops, the people, the traffic lights, and the surveillance cameras. Her bodyguard, hired by Hiram, emerged from a black bulletproof Suburban and stood under the cranberry canopy draping the entrance of Epi-Spah.

Kendali stepped outside while the bodyguard held the door, his six foot seven inch hulk body towering over her. He walked closely to his client, opened the truck door, and helped her settle into the back seat. He took his place behind the wheel and they eased away from the curb. Crispus admitted to himself that the bodyguard was a scary looking dude, about a solid three hundred pounds, black as ten thousand midnights down in a cypress swamp, to quote Langston Hughes, and long black dreadlocks. Hiram knew how to pick what was required in any situation. He had been following Kendali for several days without event or episode. Tailing her had become a lesson in how to conquer the boredom of investigative surveillance. Crispus kept his eyes peeled, watching the truck in front of him and maintaining a conservative two car length distance from them. They sat at the end of the block at a traffic light, when the light turned green, the hulk drove slowly crossing the light, increasing his speed gently. A nondescript black car pulled up to the red light on the cross street and made a dangerous turn on red in front of the green light traffic. Crispus' spidey senses turned on high and intense when he saw the car. He continued to trail his subjects for another five blocks. Kendali and the hulk entered the interstate, the nondescript suspect followed. Crispus' adrenaline surged. He dialed their car via bluetooth.

"Yo! I need you to get off at the next exit," Crispus commanded. "Already," the hulk agreed. Kendali was listening to a podcast with her earbuds, oblivious to the goings-on around her.

"Stay on the line, bruh," Crispus ordered.

"Alright. I gotchu." The hulk bodyguard exited the highway. Just as Crispus suspected, the probable stalker exited too.

"Yeah. This is him. I'm sure. Y'all are being followed."

"Well, he can come get this, if he wanna," the hulk stated confidently.

"I didn't catch your name, youngblood."

"Just call me Black."

"Cool," Crispus replied. "Alright. Keep driving easy and toward your destination, but don't get on the highway."

"Got it."

"I am gonna call you back in a few."

"Alright, my man."

Crispus disconnected the call and dialed his Department Of Motor Vehicles connect.

"Myra James. How can I help you?"

"Myra! My love. My joy!"

"Crispus Adams! What's goin' on, babes?! Haven't heard from you in a while."

"Same shit. Different day."

"I know whatcha mean. What am I lookin' up?"

"Okay. Plate number, 056SMZ."

"Alright." Myra keyed in the numbers and waited for her computer to generate the data. Her screen read, *No results for your search*. "Hmmm. Gimme the plate again, babe."

"056SMZ."

"Okay," she mumbled with curious suspicion. Her machine gave the same response. She typed it a third time to be sure and still no results. "I think you gotta fake plate, Cris."

"A fake plate?"

"Yep. I get no results. I entered the numbers three times."

"A fake plate. Mmmm. The plot thickens."

"Whatchu workin' on? Big corporate lawsuit? C'mon and tell me a few juicy details."

"No. This is much more basic. At least I thought so. I don't even have anything to tell you because, now, since you telling me I got a fake plate, I don't know what the hell is goin' on. But I will have some answers within the next forty eight hours."

"I know you will."

"Alright, Myra. Good lookin' out. I owe you another lunch."

"Yes, you do," she chuckled.

"Just keep track of my tab. I'll make good on it real soon."

"Take care, babe."

"You do the same. Bye now."

Crispus made a series of mental notes, his mind racing with possibilities. This supposed stalker situation was more than he imagined; clearly this dude wasn't your average everyday crazy. About five minutes had passed and they were less than two miles from Kendali's house. He called Black again.

"Bruh. When you get to the shopping plaza, right before Kendali's community, pull in and park away from most of the cars. Stay on the phone."

"Alright. Gotcha." Black followed his instructions and turned into the Featherstone Town Center. Kendali had closed her eyes, resting in the back seat, listening to her favorite podcast, Chit Chat Chicks. The truck's turn into the lot got her attention.

"Black, where we goin'?"

"Nowhere, Ms. Grace."

"Black, please stop calling me, Ms. Grace. It's Kendali."

"Okay. Ms. Kendali."

"Black!" she bellowed, annoyed with his formality.

"Ma'am. It's protocol. I have to use a title of respect for all clients. You don't want me to lose my job, do you?"

"Of course not." She sighed. "Why are we here?"

"Everything is okay, ma'am. We are just taking a lil' extra precaution."

"At the mall?" She moved closer to the window to analyze her surroundings and the extra precaution situation. Everything seemed normal. She reinserted the earbuds and bounced back on the headrest, tired and ready to go home.

Just as Crispus suspected, the shadow car pulled into the lot and parked two rows behind Kendali and Black. Crispus backed into a space perpendicular to his subject and his target so he could see everything. The stalker car was an old black Toyota Camry with dark tinted windows and black rims. He was tempted to approach, but thought it would be better to wait and observe. They waited about five minutes.

"Y'all okay?" Crispus asked.

"We're good. Kendali is ready to go home."

"Yeah. You can leave. Take the usual route."

"Okay." Black drove toward the Town Center exit. Thirty seconds and two cars later, the shadow followed. Crispus inched out of his space after two cars went past him. They drove for another mile straight down Featherstone Boulevard. Arriving at the traffic signal for the right turn into Kendali's Featherstone Commons, they were the only three cars in the turning lane. Black made the right turn; shadow Camry followed; and lastly Crispus turned into the commons. About five hundred feet down the road, the shadow Camry stopped suddenly, made a U-turn and sped toward Featherstone Boulevard.

"Shiiiiiiit!" Crispus shouted.

"What's up, my man?" Black asked slamming on his brakes.

"You take Kendali home. Stay close to her. I think I've been made. The muthafucka is on the run!" Crispus yelled, weaving in between cars. "Get outta the way! Get outta the way!"

"Man, you al-"

"Don't worry about me! Just stay with Kendali! I'm gone!" He slapped his bluetooth disconnect button and increased his speed through the traffic. "Out of the way!" he yelled, honking his horn. He still had the Camry in sight. From the adjacent lane, a city bus inched in front of him and he swerved to avoid a crash. "Aaaaaaargh!" He maneuvered past two slow moving eighteen wheelers and a series of other cars. He ran two red lights veering around the greenlight traffic, the drivers cursing and yelling at him. After running the second red light, he was right behind the stalker dude. "I gotchu now. You son of a bitch!" He stayed right on his tail as the subject ran through red lights and switched lanes erratically. Suddenly the Camry careened into a left turn lane, peeled out in front of oncoming cars and nearly hit a woman pushing a baby stroller across the street.

"Fuuuuuuuuuuuuuck!" Crispus banged his steering wheel in frustration and defeat, sitting in the left turn lane and watching the suspect disappear down Eutaw Street. He zoned out in anger for a few seconds, jolted back to reality as cars were honking for him to get out of the way. He cruised Eutaw Street peeping around the houses and shops that lined the street, hoping that he would see the shadow car, but he knew it was long gone.

Wednesday 4:00 p.m.

Hiram had Rica act as his semi assistant. Georgette had been telling him for years to hire a personal secretary, but he felt he had enough capable women handling his needs. Rica filled in the blanks, performing tasks like opening mail, running errands, and arranging his calendar. She opened and sorted most of his correspondence, except for items addressed directly to him; he handled those. The plain brown nine by twelve envelope with no return address sitting on his desk was such an item. He pushed the pile to the side, reviewed his calendar, and called Bree.

"Aubrey McDaniels?"

"Yes?"

"This is Hiram. Hiram Rivers. At Dominion Publishing."

Bree rolled her eyes, putting the last flexi rod in her freshly tightened weave. "Yes, Hiram. Mace told me you were going to call."

"Good. Getting straight to the point."

"Yes. That's how I like it." She pushed back, away from her brightly lit vanity, and sashayed into her kitchen to get a fruit bowl and make sure her children's snacks were prepared. It was almost time to pick them up from school.

"Yes. To the point. Who or what is your source?"

"Like I tried to tell Maceo, I don't know. I came home to an envelope someone slipped under my door."

"An envelope? Under your door?"

"Yeah. Just a plain brown envelope. A big one. With a stack of emails printed out. Emails between you, Kendali, and AJ. Y'all talkin' about Kendali's books and AJ writin' 'em."

Hiram was blown away. "What?"

"Yeah. That was it." Bree popped a pineapple in her mouth.

"Bree, I need those documents."

"You *need* them?"

"Yeah, I do."

"Hmmm."

Hiram's adrenaline was bursting as beads of sweat formed on his brow. His whole body became an inferno. "We need to meet."

"How much are they worth to you?" she asked.

"You mean money? Are you fuckin' for real?"

"Well, you said you *need* them."

"Bree, those emails are not yours anyway."

"Yeah, they are. The envelope was given to *me*." She sucked on a strawberry. She couldn't stand Hiram, nor Kendali, nor Georgette. None of them.

Hiram was livid, a fever fermenting with evil thoughts burned in his belly. He allowed the heat of his anger to calm him like a warm blanket. "Okay, Bree. What do you want?"

"Twenty G's."

"Fine. I will setup the exchange. I will text you the details."

"Good."

Hiram hung up. Crispus called. He answered on the first ring. "Whatcha got for me?" he inquired smoothing out the wrinkles of his own brown envelope. He sliced it open with his chrome plated opener.

"We need a meeting. Me, you, and Kendali. This dude that's stalkin' aintcha garden variety coo-coo." He had pulled over on Eutaw Street and was rearranging his Kendali dossier, scattered in the passenger seat.

"Yeah, we definitely do. Definitely. I have something else for you. I need you to make an exchange. Money for a package and a lil' dirty work."

"How dirty?"

"Not muddy. Just a lil' dusty," Hiram described.

"Alright. Let's touch bases later."

"Cool." They ended their conversation. Hiram leaned back in his chrome chair, squeezing the leather armrests with sickening anger. Bree was a simple task but the contents of his big brown envelope required the strength of a John Henry lumberjack.

⚒⚒⚒

Ha! Did they honestly think a bodyguard would stop me? Pure insanity. I will have her. She is for me. His thoughts churned like butter, bitter, salty oozing from his brain, forming snot in his nose and tears in his eyes. He walked around his sparsely furnished house, a bungalow he inherited from an uncle, his mother's brother who had no children. He kneeled on the prie dieu that he had especially made for the shrine honoring the love of his life, Her Majestic Grace, Kendali. He prayed that she would stop doing things to make him hurt her. *I swear I didn't wanna send the stuff to Bree. You made me do it. How could you be with him? How could you be with a low life like him? You know you love me.* He pleaded with the life size poster of Kendali Grace pinned to his wall. He folded his hands as the teardrops fell onto his fingers.

He recounted in his mind the day he followed her to the Shawnee Hotel, located an hour away from Seminole City. He marveled at the way her all white sundress flowed over her strong, firm Amazon body. The thought of her thighs pressed against his waist as he pushed inside her sweet, lush divinity made him swoon. She baptized him and he became a faithful follower. He pondered the possibilities of her presence at the hotel. A conference maybe? Visiting a relative? Three hours later his curiosity was assuaged in the most betraying manner when he saw Hiram paying the valet, sliding into his powder blue Jaguar XJ. He balled his fists and pressed them into his thighs, trying to control his rage. About twenty minutes later, Kendali sauntered through the hotel doors and an attendant helped her get into her Hummer. *Why, Kendali, why?*

Folks in the industry had their suspicions about an affair between the two, just because of who they were. Ultimately, there was nothing about their interactions that concluded an affair. They were always extremely professional. They were never seen together looking like lovers. Whether nighttime or daytime, their engagement was always meetings, conferences, and business soirées. Hiram seemed to be up Georgette's ass and Kendali was with her precious Dre. He tailed her back into the city and watched her disappear into her condo. He returned to his humble abode and printed the ghostwriting emails he collected from his hack of Dominion's servers. He had organized all pertinent communications with accompanying photos from the phones he had cloned. She left him no choice; he had to bring her down a peg or two, but he made a promise to himself and to Kendali that he would make up for his transgression. Meanwhile, he had to plan a new strategy for following her. He prayed for guidance, still kneeling before the altar decorated with Kendali's favorites- vanilla scented candles burning, purple sashes, gold handkerchiefs, chocolate chip cookies from the DoubleTree Hotels, purple ink pens, swedish fish, lavender oils, strawberry incense, a copy of Terry McMillan's *Mama*, and a copy of Tina McElroy Ansa's *The Hand I Fan With*. He prayed for a minute and then ended his prayer, in the same way he always did, *In time, you will be mine. With Grace.*

Wednesday 8:00 p.m.

Hiram had texted Kendali before leaving Dominion headquarters, telling her that they needed to meet with Crispus. She suggested they come to her apartment because she didn't feel like going out and Dre was at his place finishing his daily administrative stuff for his business. She seldom felt like going out anymore since Hiram forced her to have the big black babysitter. Her intrigue with his Egyptian god body, tender smile, and kind manner wore off after two days. She needed her freedom; *fuck the damn stalker!* She piddled around her townhouse, cleaning up her living room and wiping down her kitchen. She dusted her purple leather sofa and gold colored coffee table. Taking a quick inventory of her refrigerator inspired her to prepare a wine punch and a snack platter for her guests. As she sliced cheeses and various salamis and pepperonis, she prepared her answers for Crispus, knowing that he disliked the results of his previous interrogation.

"Kendali, you can't think of anybody, nobody who would come after you like this?" he had asked

"No. Not right off hand," she lied. There were numerous possibilities. She had done a lot of dirt in her vixen days. Sleeping with too many husbands and boyfriends, there were infinite lovers scorned.

This time, she had to give up some names and some clues to Crispus or she would have to answer to Hiram, the only man to whom she relinquished any iota of control over her. She finished arranging her tray with cheeses, meats, breads, crackers, and fruits and decided to drop some leftover meatballs that Dre had cooked into the crockpot. She lay out in front of the coffee table on the snow white carpet, stretched her arms and legs and made sweeping motions across the plush fibers, forming 'angels in the snow'. Kendali dozed off, wishing she had an angel that could take her away from everything. The door knocker woke her. A quick glance at her phone displayed three missed calls from Hiram. She opened the door to his beautiful smile.

"Damn girl! We been callin' you."

"I'm sorry. I drifted off." Hiram and Crispus stepped inside.

"Good evening, Kendali."

"Hey, Cris."

She closed the door behind them. They sat on the sofa. She brought out her vittles and turned the coffee table into a welcome spread, making several trips to kitchen.

"Even though I had dinner, I must partake. This looks so good," Hiram said.

"Well, I didn't have dinner. And I am hungry," Crispus growled putting food on a purple paper plate. "This was so on time, Kendali."

"Good." She smiled. "So, what's up?"

"You have to give my man here more to go on. This guy following you ain't no average crazy." Hiram gulped his punch.

"What do you mean?" Kendali asked nervously.

"He means that the guy is smart. Very smart. He knows how to move in stealth." Crispus gobbled several pieces of Jarlsberg cheese. "So smart that my first question to you is, are you a CIA operative?"

Kendali laughed heartily, the melody shaking the air. She realized she hadn't laughed in many days. "Bruh. Stop. That's too funny."

"Are you? Or not?" Crispus stopped chewing.

"Dang! That serious?" She shifted her disposition and straightened her posture, sitting Indian style.

"Yes. So, are you?"

"Of course not. I'm just a book writer."

"Okay. Next question. You have to give me some names. Some people who would want to disrupt your life. Who have you had trouble with? I don't care if you gotta go all the way back to the little boy who pulled your braids. I really don't think it's a woman behind these shenanigans. But I know there are some dudes out here tripping over you. Concentrate on the men in your life. So, I am listening."

She exhaled. There was a long pause, amid the silence of her thinking and the men munching the goodies she had prepared.

"Kendali?" Hiram urged her to answer.

"Okay, if I had to think of the top three. Tasir Samaan."

"The record guy?" Hiram wanted to know.

"Yes. The record guy," she confirmed.

"You used to fuck around with him?" Hiram quizzed.

"No. And that was the problem. I didn't want to. He is as crazy as they come. Savage. Into S and M. Whips. Chains. Horror games. A real monster. Likes to disfigure women. I heard he was into snuff films. I know he was keeping tabs on me at one time. Couldn't handle the rejection because *no one* is supposed to refuse Tasir Samaan."

"Hmmm, now we gettin' somewhere," Crispus said pulling out his phone to take notes.

"There was that dude. Ummm. What was his name, Hiram?" Kendali asked.

"Who?"

"The one you fired. He had gotten completely outta hand."

"Oh yeah. Dat crazy muthafucka. Emory Parker."

"That's him!"

"Yeah, I fired his ass. No sexual harassment lawsuits at Dominion!"

"Okay. Anyone else?" Crispus used his stylus to write details in his note app.

"Hmmm. I hate to even bring him up. But Isaac Cole."

"Not the author? Nikki Pearl's sidekick?"

"Sidekick? I can't believe you called him a sidekick." Kendali shook her head.

"That's what he is," Hiram attested. "I don't think she divorced Maceo. And she probably won't. So, that makes him a sidekick. Nigga crazy. Beta male, all the way. You used to fuck with him?"

"Yeah. Briefly. During my vixen days. He wanted more. I didn't. He melted down. Just got crazy. Callin' and callin' me. Textin' me. I would block him. He would buy a burner or call me from other people's phones. It was nuts."

"Okay. I got my notes. This is good. Your top three, right?"

"Yeah. As far as I can see. As best as I can remember." She rubbed her knees. Hiram's dick throbbed, thinking about her being on those thick, strong knees, bouncing her fat ass all over him. He licked his lips and swigged his punch.

"Okay, good. I got what I need."

"Alright. We all good?" Hiram stood. He was ready to leave. He planned to thrust his lust upon his wife.

"Yeah, let's roll." Crispus put some more food on his plate and wrapped it with a napkin. "I'm a single man and I don't cook."

"Take as much as you want, love." Kendali giggled as Crispus piled even more food on his plate.

Hiram smirked. "Maaan." He looked at Kendali. "Aight, ma. We out."

"Goodnight, y'all."

"Goodnight."

123

Hiram and Crispus sat in Crispus' car talking. Hiram gave him the update on Bree's source.

"She said she just got an envelope under her door."

"Hmmm. And the envelope had copies of your emails?"

"Yeah."

"Mmmm-ummm. I think you have been hacked. That's why I am saying, the source and the stalker are the same. Smart guy. Knows how to hack. Knows how to hide. Now, this list she gave me, we will see. But keep thinking of possible suspects. Remember, he might be fuckin' with you *through* her."

"Well, you know my enemy list is way too long."

"Yeah, but you gotta top three too."

"A top three? I don't know. I think it's a jumble, cuz everybody vying for number one." Hiram laughed at his half joke.

"Maaaaan, you crazy."

Hiram moved to the next topic. "Okay. This exchange I need you to do with Bree. It's twenty G's." He gave him a black envelope. "Now, I need you to get my money back. Bitch, ain't got no business with my money."

"I gotchu. Consider the mission complete."

"My man."

"No problem. Quick question, bruh."

"Yeah, what is it?"

"Does Georgette know you and Kendali fuckin'?"

Hiram's face turned stoic. Crispus was the best in the business. "Everybody wants to believe we are, just because of the relationship, the investment. But there is no evidence. No traces at all. So, the rumors ceased about six months after we signed her."

"So, again. My question, does Georgette know?"

"Naw. I don't think so." Hiram sighed. "Nobody does. What tipped you off?"

"You let your guard down, just for a split second. I might have missed it if I was a bit hungrier, but I caught the lip licking between bites."

"Hmmm."

"Y'all good though. She doesn't give off anything. Nothing. She acts indifferent toward you. The average everyday Joe would not catch it. People are just assuming, but they don't know."

"No. They don't."

"It's cool. I will keep that close to my vest."

"I appreciate that, bruh. I'm out."

Hiram dapped Crispus and walked to his Jaguar. Crispus pulled off. Hiram left shortly thereafter anticipating fucking his wife, long, strong, and slow.

Kendali cleaned up the table and made a plate for Dre. While she was washing dishes, he entered the house.

"I'm here, baby," he shouted from the entry hall.

"I'm in the kitchen," she replied.

He dropped his duffel bag in the living room and met her in the kitchen. He hugged her tightly from behind, squeezed her breasts, and kissed her neck.

"Mmmm. You smell so good. That lavender." He inhaled slowly and kissed her again. She rubbed the back of his head and they melted into a lingering embrace.

"I made you a plate. Meatballs are in the crockpot."

He released her. "Yes! Cuz I am starving." He danced toward the crockpot and peeped through the glass top. "I put my foot in these."

"Yes, you did."

"How did your homeboy like 'em?"

"Huh?"

"Your homeboy? I saw Hiram leaving."

"Oh, yeah. He was here with the investigator. Crispus. He wanted to ask me some questions. Give him some suspects for this stalker situation."

"Yeah. I see we still got the babysitters parked outside. They got one out back still?"

"Yep."

"Well, Hiram is a businessman. He has to protect his biggest investment." Sarcasm laced his comment. She ignored him. Dre thumbed through the mail on the kitchen counter while Kendali finished her chores.

"Baby, when you been to the Shoshonee Day Spa at the Tatanka in Tubman City?"

"What's that?"

"I am looking at the *Thank you for visiting our establishment* postcard. We went there?"

"Hmmm. Lemme see." She read the thank you note. "I don't know," she lied. The Tatanka was one of her and Hiram's getaway spots, remote, secluded, and relaxing. The resort was just how they liked it and just how they needed it.

"You don't know? You playin' dumb?"

"Playin' dumb? Dre, quit it. Seriously."

"Ain't no 'Dre, quit it.' You think I'm dumb. I know you fuck around, Kendali."

"Here we go." She blew a long exasperated breath into the air.

"Naw. No 'here we go'. Here I go. I'm out." He left the kitchen and started for the front door.

"Dre, wait." She grabbed his arm. They stood in the living room. "I don't know about the spa. Me and Tea probably went there some time ago."

"Yeah right, Kendali. You fuckin' somebody. I think I know who. But fuck it. It doesn't matter. I am sick of guessing. I'm sick of being suspicious." He snatched his arm away from her. "Fuck it! I am gone!" He grabbed his bag and left the house. She followed behind him. The second shift bodyguard watched the heated exchange taking place in front of Dre's work truck.

"Kendali. You just a hoe bitch. It ain't even your fault. And I ain't even mad about it."

"Please stop it, Dre! I hate you for that!"

"It's true. Once a video vixen, always a video vixen. I should've just fucked you and rolled on. But no! I put on my cape. Captain Save-A-Ho! Dumb mistake. And that's on me. Not you."

"Dre. I keep tellin' you. You have nothing to worry about. *You* are my man. Period!"

"Yeah. Whatever, Kendali. I have been taking notes on your movement. You slick wit' it. That's for sure. But I do *know* you. And I *know* who you are. And *what* you are. It's cool. I'm out."

"Fine, Dre. Fuck it. Shit. And fuck you!" Her soul sunk under his truth, conjuring tears of weariness grown from a love strong and loyal, but stale and stagnant.

She returned to her house and slammed the door. He jumped in his truck, his heart breaking loudly in his ears. He backed out of the parking space and drove off into the night. He felt so sad, tempted to call her and go back to her place. He resisted the urge. *A man knows what he knows.*

127

Chapter Eight
Power Squandering

Friday 11:00 a.m.

It was quiet at Meade Comm. Most of the staff was attending the Souled Out Media Expo, the biggest Black journalism conference in the country. Lesli Lyn opted out this year. She focused on helping Toni with The Platinum Quill and her writing. She hadn't released a book in a while and she had two manuscripts to complete. Bradford was serious about delving into book publishing, adding to the magazines, newspapers, and their archives. She had to have something to publish when he pushed the 'on' switch, hence her focus on her job and her craft. She checked her email spam folder after reading, sorting, classifying, and responding to correspondence in her main inbox. It was mostly junk, fan, and hate mail. Even with all the cyber security filters, some pesky angry readers and authors managed to get through. One email caught her attention with the subject line, "3 stars'. The sender was Ebony Webb, an author of street lit. Most of her books had the word, "Trap" in the title. Lesli actually categorized her as a good writer, much better than many. The email read:

Hi, Butterfly.
I hope this note finds you well. With regards to your recent three star review of my book, I read the review and I am thoroughly confused. You wrote all these nice compliments and then gave it three stars. Why?

Curious and Perturbed

Lesli rested her face in her palms, and sucked in three deep yogi breaths. "Now see," she thought, "deez some unappreciative bitches." She responded:

Hi, Ebony!
I am glad to hear from you.
First, a three star review is a good review.
Review Muse's Star rating guide. I use this as a rule when reviewing books on my blog and Mahogany Magazine. Four and five star reviews are books that readers see as highly impactful; books they would read over and over again, or books they would want to see made into movies, or not. Some diehard bibliophiles see movie adaptations as sacrilegious.
Your book, I thought, was good. A good book. A simple, easy read. Good plot. Good characters. Good. I would not read it over and over again. It was not highly impactful for me. My thoughts are neutral about movie adaptations for your title. And that brings us back to three star good.
I hope I answered your question.
Keep up the good work!

"Bih," Lesli said aloud after reading the last line she typed. She proofread her message and clicked 'send'. Then she wrote her blog post and sent it to Mahogany's edit team:

🦋Beloved Butterflies🦋
I greet you in silky, soft-winged peace.

I tell you that the madness never ends. 1 star. 2 star. 3 star. 5 star. Super star. Death star. Rock star. Starr Jones. I don't know, but y'all gotta stop tripping over these Muse reviews. Really. Let me say this and be as light-winged as a butterfly in the blue sky can be. I wish that some of you would be glad that people even read your books AND miraculously take the time to leave a review. Purge yourself of the notion that EVERYONE that reads YOUR work is going to absolutely love it...or hate it. Some readers may feel neutral.

And quite honestly, a 3 star review is not a bad review. As a matter of fact, for some of you with these kindergarten-style written novels, it is an intervention from God. And so, on that note, give honor to God with a double tithe this Sunday and thank me on Monday.

PS. Here is the inspiration for this post-an email from disgruntled author, Ebony Webb of Gutta Butta, dismayed by my 3 star review of her book:

Hi, Butterfly.

I hope this note finds you well. With regards to your recent three star review of my book, I read the review and I am thoroughly confused. You wrote all these nice compliments and then gave it three stars. Why?

Curious and Perturbed

My response:

Hi, Ebony!

I am glad to hear from you.
First, a three star review is a good review.
Review Muse's Star rating guide. I use this as a rule when reviewing books on my blog and Mahogany Magazine. Four and five star reviews are books that readers see as highly impactful; books they would read over and over again, or books they would want to see made into movies, or not. Some diehard bibliophiles see movie adaptations as sacrilegious.
Your book, I thought, was good. A good book. A simple, easy read. Good plot. Good characters. Good. I would not read it over and over again. It was not highly impactful for me. My thoughts are neutral about movie adaptations for your title. And that brings us back to three star good.
I hope I answered your question.
Keep up the good work!

It's Double~L, Silky, Soft, and Signing Off...Float On

She kicked off her green Adidas shell toes and started walking around her office stretching and bending her body to get her blood circulating. She had been sitting, typing nonstop for three hours. After about ten minutes she returned to her chair. Her phone buzzed. It was Toni.

🔲 Text Message 🔲
Toni: Double L 🦋
Lesli: Toni Toni So Toni!
Toni: Hey chica. What are you doing later?
Lesli: Nothing in particular. Uber-focused on my writing now and later. What's up?

Toni: Let's meet up. Go over some PQ stuff. You know everything is in place. I need your brain to finetune.

Lesli: I'm your woman. 😊

Toni: You and Titus broke up? You comin over to taste the rainbow? 😏 💅

Lesli: Cease! 😖

Toni: I don't need to remind you. As long as I gotta face... 😬

Lesli: 😖 I opened myself up for this one. You already know, if I ever go gay, you my first choice!

Toni: And I know this! 😅

Lesli: What time later?

Toni: 7?

Lesli: Cool. Our favorite spot?

Toni: Always.

Lesli put her phone on her work table out of eyesight. She didn't want any more distractions. She kept typing, feeling more energetic and inspired since she would see her friend at Teavolve later, a guaranteed five star experience.

⭐ ⭐ ⭐

Friday 1:00 p.m.

Zing Post – Bree McDee's The Sauce Mobb

Bree McDee (post): Hey, Sauce Lovers, Mobsters, and Queens 😬 👑. This is just a lil' dash of Tabasco, ole skool flava for ya' 🌶. So I hear the natives are restless over at the King of publishers. Folks a lil' unhappy maybe? Who you think might be leaving the castle? Hmmm...We shall see. Tell me what you think. Drip, drip bitches! 🩸🩸🩸

Reactions: 897 Comments: 954 Shares: 445

(Load previous comments)
Ferra Faucet: I have no clue. Just here for the comments.
Lance Fairchild: I bet it's Amber.
Diminka Johns: @Lance Fairchild Amber Alise? I don't think so. She has been so successful at Dominion.
Lance Fairchild: Yeah, but she got other publishers trying to get at her. I know for a fact! 💯
Mia Brown: yall naming a lot of authors. Might be an executive. shit! might be the ceo himself!
Taj Wright: Dang! Not the ceo, yo. smh 😕
Britt Joni: Y'all tripping. Hiram will go down with the ship! 🚢
Bree McDee: Naw. Not Hiram. I would say definitely not.
Sade Nelson: @Bree McDee Yo' ass probably already know 😀
Bree McDee: 😳

Bree lounged on her jumbo multi sectional in the family area of her apartment. Unlike many apartment communities in Seminole City, her apartment building was a rehab of an old plantation manor, so all the rooms were huge and plentiful. Large picture windows allowed lots of daylight to brighten the home she shared with her two children. She continued to scroll through the comments on her tablet, totally entertained by The Sauce Mobb's commentary. Her phone rang.
"What's up, Mace?"
"Ain't nuttin, ma. I'm around the corner."

133

"You pullin' up?"

"As we speak. Got sumpthin' for you."

"Okay. I'm comin' out."

"Aight." He disconnected the bluetooth call. Maceo opened his trunk and pulled out a fully refurbished big wheel, decked out with chrome wheels, chrome pedals, and a black leather seat cushion. Bree's son saw her old big wheel at her mom's house and had been bugging Bree about it ever since. She rarely rode it as a child, but it still needed to be cleaned and repaired. She told Maceo about it and he picked up the toy from her mother and gave it to his mechanic homeboy Rod to get it right. And in true Rod fashion, he tricked it out. He put a horn on it, painted it black and silver, and chromed it clean down! Bree watched Maceo's shiny bald head glisten in the sun as he strode up the two sets of stairs to the front porch of the apartment house. She was so sick of him sometimes but she loved him. He was her friend and her brother.

"Oh my gawwwwd!" She jumped up and down when she saw the big wheel in its full tricked out regalia. "This is so fie!"

"Rod is the man."

"Yes he is." She covered her mouth in amazement. She stretched her arms open. "Thank you, Mace. I love you, bruh."

Maceo put the toy down on the porch and hugged his number one author.

"And I love you, my lil' Bree Wee." He rocked her tenderly. He sat on the banister of the porch, pulled a pack of gum from his pocket, and offered Bree a piece.

"No thanks. I'm cool."

"You burn that evidence?"

"No."

"You need too."

"Why do you care? You won't even let me share the info with you."

"Right. Plausible deniability. I don't want nothin' to do with this bullshit."

"Fine." She sighed heavily shifting her weight to her right hip, her oversized night shirt revealing the cut off sweatpants loosely hanging around her thick cocoa thighs.

"But you need to burn it."

"I'm gonna give it to Hiram."

"When?" He upgraded his attention to their conversation.

"He's gonna come get it."

"When he comin'?"

"I don't know yet. But we agreed to an exchange."

Maceo stood, squared his stance, and crossed his arms over his chest. "What kind of exchange?"

"Twenty G's."

"Whaaaat the fuck?! Breeeee! Yooooooo! Ma!" He craned his neck toward the sun disappointed and disgusted with his bestselling author.

"What? He wants the stuff, so he said he would pay."

"Your idea or his?"

"Well I asked him how much is it worth to him."

"What the hell?!" He rubbed his entire head, running his hands up and down his face and around his shiny clean shaven crown. "Bree. Do not take Hiram's money. I told you about this nigga. Don't take his money. Tell him you can drop off whatever you have and be done with it."

"Whatever. Fuck him."

"You know what. I'm not talkin' about this anymore. You do you." He walked to the edge of the porch preparing to leave, his back to her.

"Good." She stood up straight, readying to return to her tablet. She didn't care to hear Maceo's extended soapbox dissertations today.

"But I cannot see why you have such a glutton for this man's demise? What is it? Seriously."

"He owes me. He promised me an advance. He promised me million dollar sellers. He promised me the world. We had a deal. I signed on the dotted line. He rescinded my book deal after I refused to fuck him."

Maceo absorbed her revelation, contemplating the mixture of her emotions. While he understood her anger, he had more deference for the truth about Hiram and the truth about his own thug nature. In his heart, he was a street warrior, wearing the hat of a CEO. He listened as she vented, recounting the episode.

"He gon' tell me…

"So I got your sample chapters…"

"Yes. What did you think?" I love the whole concept. Just Enough For The City. Your main character is a helluva woman. So spicy." Hiram was referring to Bree's character Beatrice 'Butterbee' Brown a lawyer who goes city to city, solving one mysterious cold case per city. The cases always led back to municipal corruption as the motivation for the murder. "We will do so much with this. I wanted to talk to you personally so that you understand just how big this is gonna be."

"Really? Wow. I can't wait!"

"Yeah. We got your contracts ready. Everything is a go."

"Thank you so much for this opportunity."

"Yeah, yeah. Of course. So yeah. I got the sample chapters. You got any more samples over there?"

"I have two completed manuscripts. One for New Orleans. One for Miami. I can send both of these."

"Mmmm. Yeah." He massaged a picture of Bree sitting on his desk with her file, mesmerized by her smile. *"No, I'm thinking of some other samples. I mean your pen is dripping. Dripping with...hmmm...so much."*

"Wow. Thank you. That means everything coming from the CEO. I do have other stories."

"Yeah. But are they dripping like your city series? And like you? I bet you drip. Drip...slow...and easy."

"Huh?"

"Yeah. I want some more samples. Samples of your drip. Of the ink, from your ink well. I bet it tastes exactly like chocolate syrup." He smacked his lips.

"Uh-huh." Bree's excitement deflated. Her brain swooned; her heart buckled.

"So, can I dip my pen in your inkwell? Drip...drip..."

"Don't you have a wife, Mr. Rivers?"

"Of course I do. She doesn't have anything to do with this. I am asking you about your samples for me."

"Yeah. Okay. And no. I just have sample chapters of my books."

"Alright. You will hear from us soon."

"...And he hung up. I never heard from him or anyone at Dominion again. I called and called. They just put me off over and over again. So, I let it go. And I've done all the letting go I am gonna do. He thinks he can do whatever he wants because he's rich and powerful. Fuck Hiram!"

"Okay. I got it. Now, you. Get over it!"

"Get over it?"

"Yes, sis. Get *the fuck* over it!"

"I am not getting over it. Not right now. I was supposed to be the princess of Dominion! Not Kendali!" she screeched, stiffening her arms by her sides.

"Well, you the Belle of The Butta. That's not good enough for you? You not happy with us?"

"C'mon, Mace. You know I love us. I love the whole GB fam'. I'm just sayin, fuck Hiram!"

"Girl, you betta get over that shit and stop fuckin' around with Hiram."

"Whatever. You done?"

"Oh! You tellin' me to leave?"

"No. Well, maybe yeah. I'm done. Now, *you* let it go." She flip-flopped to the doorway and paused. "Oh! I almost forgot to tell you, since you were so busy lecturing me." She brushed her hair behind her ear. "Your homegirl Monique is ready to leave Dominion. Wants her own house. Needs financing."

Maceo's ears perked up. "You jivin'? For real?"

"Yeah. For real."

"Okay. Thanks, ma."

He was still pissed with her, since she basically said fuck him too. Bree was an information magnet. People just told her stuff. He hated the gossip mill where she always seemed to serve as chief miller, but loved when she had useful tidbits for him. And the Monique thing was definitely something useful. "Aight, I'm in the wind. Got work to do. I don't have the luxury of kickin' back two to three months at a time collecting royalties. And find something else to do with your power, Bree. Like writing you're your next bestseller." He hustled down the steps toward his truck, waving deuces in the air.

"Yeah, yeah, yeah," Bree murmured walking across the threshold of the doorway. She happily returned to her couch and

The Sauce Mobb, unbothered by Maceo's admonishment. She opened a browser window on her tablet and searched for tropical destination packages, anticipating a much needed vacation, courtesy of Mr. Hiram Rivers, CEO & Chief Asshole of Dominion Publishing. "Hmmm. Ghana sounds nice. Maybe I will pop up on my dad in Accra."

�֍ �֍ ✷

Friday 4:00 p.m.

"Yeah, Meena. May not be good for Dominion if Monique leaves." They lay on his office floor staring at the ceiling.
"True enough, but Monique has to do what's best for Monique."
"No doubt about it." This was the first time they had a chance to thoroughly discuss Georgette's revelation about Monique's exit. "It's not good to hold her hostage like that."
"I basically told Georgette that. She needs to examine herself and her motivations about withholding support for Monique's venture. She needs to apply the old adage, *If you love something, let it go*...You know the rest."
"Precisely. But it ain't no love. They fakin' the funk. Buncha fake ass niggas. The whole lot of them. They couldn't publish all that loveless trash if there was love in 'em."
"Now, my dearest, sweetest husband. We know you and I disagree on this point." She touched his fingers. He wrapped his pinky around hers.
"I know, I know. They trying to find their way to love. Right. That's what you say."
"That's really what it is. Just trying to find their way...write their way...back to love."

139

"Meena, they just about money. Period. That is what they love. Money. And I get it. But that ain't cool to me. For our people. Hiram and Georgette squander their power. They are clueless about how strong a force they are. And it angers me."

"I know, Mustafa. Maybe you will help them find their way."

"Yeah. Maybe." He dropped a tender peck on his wife's hand and settled in his office chair.

"Uh-oh. I better go," she said rising up from the plushly carpeted floor.

"No, Meena. Stay. I think you will love this one."

Zing Live - Mustafa

Peace Love and Blessings, Black Family. To my people out there on this bubble in the struggle. I'm gonna be brief because the wife has been monitoring and minimizing my cyber time, but y'all still gon' get this business. Straight to the point...They say the natives are restless over at Dominion. Now if you love something, you let it go, because love is freedom. Freedom is love. Folks gotta feel free, dammit, in order to feel love. So, where is the damned love? Huh? Where is it? Apparently not at Dominion if members of the court want to leave the castle. Y'all ain't surprised, right? Look at what they publish. You read their books. Page after page of lovelessness. Why do we negate the power of our thoughts and might of our pens? Do you know why there is no love? Because that's not what is in their spirits. It's not in their hearts. It doesn't spill from the ink of their pens nor does it claim a rhythm on their computer keyboards. There's only hate and devolution. Misery. Ill-wishing. We seek to depress, oppress, and impress all in the pursuit of success. There's no love. There's abuse. Dishonesty. Ulterior motives. Monopoly. Exploitation.

Literary injustice. Yeah. I said it. Y'all are really trippin' out there with these beefs over books and shit. Holdin' your employees hostage in your corporate HQ. Holdin' your authors hostage in profitless contracts. Holdin' readers hostage, bound and gagged by the loveless stories of these so called writers. Quit it. For real. Because this is not who we are...or are we? Think before we write. Find love from somewhere and write from that place. Because what we are doing now, is not a good look. And it's not love. Let's get to lookin' like love, Black family. And on that note, I'm out. As always, business over bullshit. Peace.

Zing Live End

Reactions: 808 Comments: 324 Shares: 126

(Load previous comments)

Tiffany B: Oh shut up, Mustafa! Go comb your beard. You publish Black Blood Gang! Love you say? whatever 😬

Mike Money: Yeah, sis. But you missing his point. You can still write about gangs, gangsters, but there is a way to write so that a story is more whole. More balanced. A lotta these books are just over the top nonsense. Savage for no reason. Books ain't got no rhythm

Debra Gordon: That's an interesting point when you say it like that

@Mike Money No rhythm and savage for no reason. I get it. Yeah. A lot of these books are just over the top.

Chelsea Williams: I don't see why people come over here and listen to Mustafa knowing he going straight for the jugular. I mean I see some of his points but HE is the one who's over the top! 😬

Liah Harris: Right on, brother #blackpower✊🏿

Akilah Butterfly Jones: I see the point. Delivery is a little strong. Abrasive. But he has a point.

Noah Dandridge: Stop reading the books, ninja. Shit. All that ranting is unnecessary. I love my trap books. My trap music. And my trap authors. 📖💜

Faye Fite: I don't agree. But I don't disagree.

Helena Wright: Get off the fence. Pick a side! Mustafa's right! We get tired of reading that over the top loveless bullshit. Ijs 🙄🙄🙄

Friday 7:00 p.m.

Teavolve buzzed with its customary soulful vibrations, afros and beaded cowrie shelled braids swaying to the rhythms of local jazz fusion sensation, Ghetto Butterflies; aromatic house blended teas bubbling in handmade clay pots; and the best homemade vittles that fresh urban gardens could produce. Toni Griffin sipped her ginger lemonade iced tea waiting for her favorite Butterfly to appear. Her PQ notes lay open on her tablet, color coded and efficiently ordered for seamless execution. She twirled the auburn dyed dreadlocks hanging around her shoulders, her diamond one carat studs peeking through her shiny natural coils. The diamond watch, a gift from her mother, sparkled in the mostly torchlit venue and gave a clear view of her acne prone skin, cured for the day by her Proactiv ritual. She spotted her friend floating through the crowd toward her. Lesli's afro puffs distinguished her from the mass of people networking on the main floor of Teavolve. She donned a green and white Adidas sweatsuit, with green and white shell toes to match. Toni prepared herself for their sneaker show greeting.

"What's up, chica butterfly?!" Toni inched her stout frame out of the booth and wrapped her fluffiness around Lesli. Lesli smiled and buried her head in Toni's shoulder catching the scent of coconut oil wafting from her hair and skin. Lesli stood back.

"Girl. It is so good to see you. Lookin' cute as ever."

"Tryin' to keep up with you." Toni pointed her toe in Lesli's direction, showing off gold and burgundy Saucony Low Pros.

"Aight. Let's see 'em."

Lesli hopped one time toward her friend's pointed toe, like she was splashing into a puddle. Toni admired the classic shell toes.

"Ahhhhhh. My A-didas!" Lesli echoed her delight, pleased with her introduction at their shoe show, imitating Run DMC's hip hop hit.

"I thought I was sneaker obsessive. But, damn Butterfly. You win. You must own every pair of shell toes Adidas ever made."

"Actually I don't. And I don't win, Toni Tone. You are the sultana of sneaks. Worse than any sixteen year old boy."

"Naw, sis. I think you got me beat."

"Impossible!"

Toni chuckled and returned to her seat. Lesli joined her. "I'm starving. Been writing all day, almost non-stop."

"For real?"

"All day long, all day strong."

"Well, let's get some food in you and we will work on PQ along the way."

"Good!"

They ordered a table full of appetizers, a bottle of wine, and a pot of black pekoe tea. As they were finishing their food, Toni opened her notes on her tablet and emailed them to Lesli.

"Girl. Your blog today."

"I know right?"

"Girl. But you see how many people wanna say what you're sayin'?"

"I do."

"I'm surprised they didn't have you delete Ebony's name."

"They wanted to, but I won that argument. Brad lets me have my way."

"That's why they can't stand ya' ass."

"No, they can't stand me because I tell the truth."

"And that! Izzz the truth, sis!" Lesli laughed while Toni savored her last mini spinach quiche.

"Alright. Let's dig into the PQ." Lesli set up her tablet and wiped the screen with a napkin. "I emailed your logistics outline. Same move as last year. I hired the logistics people, but they gotta answer to you."

"Cool."

"Everything is in the package. Review it word for word. Call me with questions."

"Got it."

"You have to meet with the logistics leader and coordinate with her. Fine tune their layout, their plan. They understand conferences; we know books."

"Exactly."

"So, get that meeting done in the next 5 days or so."

"Absolutely."

"That's it."

"So, the big PQ. Is Kendali gonna get it?"

"Yeah. The board decided we can't withdraw the award based on gossip, speculation, conjecture. It's not a good look. We already slated her for it, so we have to follow through. And it's really a people's choice, so…"

"That's true. I just wish…I dunno. I just…"

"I know. It's all so dumb. So idiotic. Just wish these authors would respect the craft. Respect the art."

"Mmmm-hmmm."

"You straight now?" Toni chuckled watching Lesli guzzle her last drop of wine and plunge into a satiated ecstasy.

"Girl. I was so hungry."

"I see. You have said about five words this whole conversation."

"I know. Forgive me. I'm good now." She grinned slowly picking up one more honey buffalo wing. "And I haven't had Teavolve in so long. I think they might have the best wings."

"Naw. Not quite. Not betta than Nina's. Close though."

"I won't argue with that. Nina's is everything."

"Undoubtedly." The two sister friends enjoyed the Friday night festivities, good food, good drinks, and good people. Different folks popped in and out of their area, pulling up a chair to talk or sliding in the booth to share a thought, ask a question, or just show some love. After a few hours, they called it a night and made their way to their cars. It had been raining; puddles rippled throughout the parking lot.

"We have to do this more often, sis." Toni hugged Lesli's neck tightly, feeling a relaxing comfort from Lesli's double D's pushing against her own C cups.

"I know we keep sayin it, but we gotta start doin' it."

"Yeah, we do." An engine revved loudly, disturbing the sisterly vibration. Tires screeched and high beams blinded the pair.

"What the-" Toni murmured. The vehicle intrusion sped by nearly running Lesli over splashing rainwater all over her green and white sweatsuit.

"Drip, Drip, be~atch!!!!! Write a review on that, ya' monkey thot!" A female voice yelled from the terrorist car while other female voices cackled, backing up the malediction with evil laughter.

"Get out the car, you bitches!" Toni yelled running to the car.

"Come back and get some of this, weak ass, punk ass sluts!" Toni ran faster, gaining on the perpetrators. The car increased its speed and raced out of the parking lot. Toni rushed back to aid Lesli. "You alright, sis?"

"Yeah. Damn! I'm so sick of these whores."

"Yeah. Me too."

Lesli looked herself over, observing the splash marks on her clothes and kicks. "Fuck!" She pulled her phone from her bag and dialed Titus.

"What's up, babe?"

"Hey, T. Somebody just tried to run me over."

"Run you over?"

"Yeah, me and Toni are leaving Teavolve. Titus, I don't know what the hell is wrong with these broads."

"You alright?"

"Yeah. More mad than anything." She could hear Titus readying to leave, probably putting his gun on his hip, lacing up his Timbs.

"Yeah, aight. I'm on the way."

"T, you don't have to come."

"The fuck I don't. I told you, I ain't playin' wit' deez bitches. They can catch a bullet just like a nigga can. I do not discriminate. I'm for equal rights for all the Miss Independent Women."

Lesli giggled. "No. Really, baby. I am gonna get in my car-"

"Lesli, sit ya' ass still. I am coming to get you. Y'all go back inside. Don't argue with me, Fly."

"Okay."

He hung up.

"Titus is on the way."

"Datz right. My nigga. Come getcha woman." Toni patted Lesli's afro puffs. "Let's go back inside." Lesli offered a half smile at Toni's comments. While waiting for Titus, she revealed her dead flower incident.

"Yeah. I don't know who sent them."

"Damn, sis. Hmmm."

"I know right. Completely crazy. It's some bullshit. These broads are out of control. Just a waste of energy. Waste of their power."

"No doubt. If they put that much focus on improving their writing, you wouldn't have to spend your time criticizing dey dumb asses."

"Precisely."

"But for me, this tells me that I will have to increase security for the PQ."

"Probably a good idea," Lesli agreed.

Titus arrived about ten minutes later with his cousin Raj. Raj followed them to Lesli's house driving her car, parked it, and ordered an Uber to take him back home.

"I appreciate you, kinfolk," Titus told Raj. He handed Raj a fifty dollar bill.

"Naw, cuz. We cool."

"Come on, man. Get my baby cousins some fries. Money ain't for you."

"Aight, bruh. 'Preciate it." They dapped each other and Raj left in the Uber.

Titus hustled into the house where he found Lesli Lyn spread prostrate on the floor crying. He picked her up with the power and passion of his strong lean body and she rested her head on his big muscular shoulders. He planted a wet kiss on her face.

"Babe, it's gonna be okay."

"I'm so tired, T. I'm so tired of being...of being me."

"I know, love. But it's gonna be okay."

"I just want us to be better. To be all that we can be. To be excellent. That's all. Why are they so mad with me?"

"They are not mad with you, Fly. They mad at the truth, love." He laid her on the bed and she whimpered as he peeled off her clothes. "Everything's gonna be okay. I am going to drive you everywhere you need to go. I am your protector."

"But you have to prepare for school. Your kids...and..." she said referring to Titus' position as an eighth grade math teacher.

"You let me worry about that. I'm taking care of my woman first."

He continued undressing her until she was naked. She lay on the bed while he ran a bubble bath for them. He stripped off his clothes, and returned to his Butterfly. She had drifted off to sleep. He picked her up and put her in the tub and slid in behind her. He washed her body beginning with her neck. She was awake and drowsy, folding into his movements as he cleaned her, purging the day away. He soaped and rinsed himself and carried his fiancee back to the bedroom. His greased her body with coconut oil, massaging every inch of her, lingering around her breasts and squeezing the abundance of flesh as she lay atop the yellow comforter. He sucked on her nipples. They hardened in response. She moaned as he kneaded her pussy lips, and tickled her clit, the oil heightening the sensation for both of them. His fingers slipped in and out of her vagina with erotic ease, stirring her pot until the cream thickened like butter. He plunged into her, kissing her cheeks and licking her lips lovingly with his tongue. Her pussy wrapped around his hot phallus, her butter dripping down the shaft and then running onto her thighs. She caressed his freshly cut head of hair, trimmed to homeboy perfection, murmuring confessions of her love for him. He confessed the same. His slow strokes played an enchanting rhythm inside her soul. He whispered the accompanying lyrics into her ear, "You have nothing to fear. I gotchu." He thrust into her more forcefully, their souls melding together, a sensuous symphony. "And you have to be you, Fly. No matter how hard it is. The world needs the soft, beautiful power of butterflies."

🦋🦋🦋

Chapter Nine
Kendali, The Killer

Monday 10:00 a.m.

"Oooooo, KD lunch boxes." Monique rubbed her hands together hungrily as she entered the conference room.

"Yes, Mo. KD lunch boxes." Hiram smiled. Monique's delight warmed his heart. He loved her for co-building his empire, every step of the way.

Her eyes glistened, taking in the lunchtime setup. Black and gold boxes, lined with gold tissue paper, matching plastic cutlery, and KD's custom logo napkins and cups made for an inviting welcome table. She did a happy dance in her cap sleeved denim skater dress, twirling like an excited three year old in nursery school anticipating peanut butter and jelly snacks.

She opened a lunch box and salivated at its contents, a super-sized fresh lobster roll, two bags of gourmet chips, a generous portion of broccoli walnut salad, Monique's favorite from KD's, and a heaping of KD's blueberry cheesecake explosion. "You must want me to agree to something I ain't gonna agree to, judging from the contents of this box."

Hiram's laughter bounced off of every wall like a pinball machine. "Go 'head, Mo."

"Uh-huh. I know something's up. I told you I let go of the publishing house conversation with you. So it's cool."

"I know," he responded. "Our meeting has nothing to do with that."

"Then what is it?"

"Dang, Mo. You act like I don't treat y'all good or something. I always get KD's for us. Our people. Our authors."

"Yeah, Hiram. But this is a fresh lobster roll. Super-sized. Something is up!"

"Well, something *is* up. But I just want you to listen and be open-minded about what's going on and what needs to happen."

"Hmmm. Yeah, okay." She reluctantly carried her lunch box and a bottle of water to a seat at the humongous all white lacquer conference table. "Where is everyone? And who are we meeting with anyway?"

"Mainly Crispus. He is in the building. On his way to us."

"Oh my God." Deflated by Hiram's reply, she slumped in chair. "Crispus? Lord! What is going on?"

"Just wait. He will give us everything we need. Everything is fine." Hiram picked up a lunch box for himself and placed it in front of a chair across from Monique. He peeped out the door. Crispus and two men were approaching; one was Dominion IT director, Jeff. Hiram did not recognize the other young man.

"Good to see you, Crispus." Hiram embraced his well-paid investigator/everyman/go-to guy.

"You too, brother."

"Y'all come on in," Hiram said ushering Dominion's guests into the meeting room. He shook Jeff's hand.

"What's up, boss?"

"Ain't nuthin, my man," he replied to Jeff.

"Lunch!" Crispus bellowed with twinkling eyes.

"Y'all are the hungriest damn negroes!" Hiram laughed at Crispus' excitement. "Y'all ain't eatin'? Am I paying y'all enough?"

"I'm not gonna answer that." Monique popped a chip in her mouth. Hiram smirked at his right hand.

"Hey, Mo." Crispus walked over to her and hugged her neck.

"Long time, Cris." She patted his forearm resting on her chest.

"Yes. And that is a good thing."

"So true." She giggled. "How do feel being a kinda grim reaper?"

"Somebody's gotta do it, Mo." He moseyed back over to the lunch display. He and his comrades gathered their meals and settled themselves at the table with the two chiefs of Dominion. Crispus bit into his roll and chewed slowly savoring the flavors of the seasoned lobster. "Kaaay-Deee! Hmmmph!" He sighed, took a swig of bottled tea, and opened his manila folders, one at a time. "First, meet Toussaint. Toussaint Sinclair."

"How's everybody?" Toussaint waved his hand at the rest of the attendees and grinned a nerdy grin. He had a coal black medium afro, circle rim spectacles, thick eyebrows, bright eyes, and a thin mustache. He wore multi colored suspenders with a matching bowtie, a plain white shirt, and khakis.

"Good."

"We're good."

"You can call me Tou, you know for short."

Crispus thumbed through his papers while Tou opened his small netbook. "Now Tou is going to conduct a cyber investigation of all Dominion networks, hardware, and software. We have concluded that your systems have been hacked which is how Bree's secret source got the intel on Kendali."

"Hacked? You can't be serious?" Monique dropped her sandwich in the box. "Hacked? Why would anybody wanna hack us?"

"Well, we are pretty sure that Kendali's stalker and the hacker is the same person. This meeting's purpose is simply to update you all on how the cyber investigation works and to introduce you to Toussaint because you will see him moving around your office. We need everyone to give him full cooperation. He will access every single byte of data in the Dominion cyber setup."

"Every byte?" Hiram asked wiping his hands with a napkin.

"Yes, sir," Toussaint assured. "I am very meticulous. Very detailed in my process."

"Yeah, you look like you thorough." Not even Crispus caught the sarcasm in Hiram's tone. He wondered how deep they planned excavate Dominion's inner workings.

"Yes. Tou is the best of the best. Cream of the crop. Even got kicked out of MIT!" Crispus slapped Toussaint on his back with fatherly admiration.

"Kicked out, eh?" Jeffrey quizzed. He had been listening intently and the tidbit incited his curiosity.

"Long story," Toussaint explained. "I can tell you about it later."

"Not a long story. They couldn't handle your big brain. Too smart for them."

"Mr. Adams, you give me way too much credit."

"If you say so. Bottom line, good people, Toussaint is the best. He will uncover the breach. So, meet with your people and be sure everybody gives him a warm Dominion welcome."

"So, you are gonna check emails?" Monique needed to understand.

"Oh definitely. Emails, phone communications, software, hardware, all records, documents, everything that passes through your servers. Your storage. Everything. And I will need your phones. I suggest you get new phones."

"New phones?" Monique was disgusted. Her appetite was fading and she became angry, especially since she didn't get to her cheesecake explosion.

"Yes, ma'am. We are uncertain how much of Dominion's cyber security has been compromised. If this person has hacked your systems, he may have done the same to your phones. So, erring on the side of caution, we must get you all new phones."

"Sweet Jesus. My whole life is on my phone." Monique shook her head lamenting her lunch.

"Well, hopefully we can download what you need from your phones, but only after we do a thorough data analysis of your devices. To make sure they are clean."

"How long will all of this take? And are we talking everyone's phones? There are just a few of us that have Dominion-issued devices." Monique envisioned the mental meltdown of her staff after she instructed them to turn in their phones. She shook off the miserable scene.

"Oh, I would say, we are only talking about people who have frequent contact with Kendali."

"Oh good!" She breathed a sigh of relief. Her cheesecake explosion seemed deliciously inviting again.

Hiram asked, "How long will this take, Toussaint."

"I can't say definitively. There are many variables. But my guess, and this is only a guess. Up to two, maybe three weeks."

Silence prevailed. Jeff, Crispus, Hiram, Monique, and Toussaint quietly chewed their KD vittles, sipped their drinks, and contemplated the possibilities of the data investigation. Jeff hoped he would learn a lot from the young IT wizard. Crispus' military mind looked forward to the quick completion of his mission. Hiram wished there was another, less invasive way to find the culprits; he abhorred the idea of people digging around in his business. The mystery envelope flashed in his mind. Monique anticipated this ordeal as her final lesson from Dominion, a very good teacher preparing her as the leader of her own publishing house, MoJo Publications. Toussaint was just thankful for the opportunity to work with the big dawgs, another job well done to add to his resume. And while they all had their own goals in mind, their common goal voiced by Crispus

154

adjourned the meeting, "No worries, folks. It will all be over soon."

■ ■ ■

Bzzz...

Kendali ignored her phone for the fourth time within the past 5 minutes, and kept applying her makeup. Butterflies in her belly, she was a nervous wreck prepping for her interview with media monster Myesha Morgan. Several interviews with local radio stations and one popular morning show proved alleviating for the scandal. The ghostwriting controversy was subsiding and while some fans discarded her as their favorite author and others were just plain angry, according to Hiram, she gained substantially more readers than she lost. He monitored the Muse downloads closely and his records indicated a quadruple increase in sales and page reads since the madness kicked off. "I told you, I gotchu, Kenni." The memory of his reassuring words floated in her head, meandered into her chest, encircled her heart and slid down inside her pussy sparking her desire for him. Since Bree's cyberattack, the mystery stalker, and the heightened security, she and Hiram had not rendezvoused. The longing for his powerful, passionate, wanton lovemaking was torturous, her body aching for his ravenous affections. Dre had always been a good lover, pure, honest, and meaningful, but Hiram awakened uncharted passion that lay dormant deep inside her bones. He held her, hugged her, cradled her body as he sunk his love steel into her sensual secretions with uncontestable authority. He commanded and demanded her femininity with warrior's might laced with the gentle touch of a brotherly love. Her fingers found their way inside her panties and just when she was about to pluck her fruit, her phone buzzed again.

"Fuck," she murmured. She stomped to her night table to check the ID of the interrupter. "Tea?" Latoya "Tea" Mitchell wasn't just the administrator of Tea Thyme Zing group. She had been Kendali's loyal and trusted confidante dating back to her video days. Tea used to do photography and promo for some of the record companies. They met on a video set. Tea snapped photos of her on the set of Cash Cole's famous video *Don't Judge Me* in which Kendali was the star vixen. They struck up a conversation after the shoot, went to dinner, and slowly became friends over the next year, bumping into each other at shoots, parties, and industry events. Kendali read the messages.

 Text Message

Tea: Kay Kay

Tea: GM, Kay Kay

Tea: You there? Talk to me, ma. I'm sorry. You should know I didn't mean any harm. You KNOW this! I'm your biggest fan

Tea: Okay. You're not talking to me. But I know you have Myesha Morgan today. I am going to be there to support you. Love you

Kendali: Thanks, Tea. I love you too

Tea: You betta love me, girl.

Kendali cried tears of sadness and joy. She gladdened that somebody out there realized she needed more support and more love and that loneliness had been eroding her heart for the past several weeks.

They had not spoken or had a text exchange since the ghostwriting fiasco. Tea had texted her a few times, but Kendali just ignored her even though Tea continued promoting, sharing, and liking Kendali's Zing posts. Tea never wavered, supporting her author friend, regardless of their disagreement and Kendali appreciated Tea's dedication to their friendship.

She skipped into the bathroom and applied the finishing touches to her makeup. A heavy handed smearing of MAC foundation made her television ready; their cosmetics earned a special place in her heart fulfilling all her celebrity requirements since her hip hop days. She wore her natural light brown curls and selected a simple short sleeve black dress with lush silver, white and red gardenia flowers cascading down one side of the garment, from the waist to the hem. A patent leather peep toe pump, with a white flower on the heel and matching purse added flair to her ensemble. Her sparkling diamond jewelry rounded out her look: simple stud earrings, a teardrop pendant on a silver filigree chain, and an encrusted bangle set in platinum, a present from "Dominion" for being their pen princess. The bangle was really Hiram's love token, his slick way of masking a very expensive gift.

She dashed out the door where Black was waiting, truck door wide open for her entry into the soft leather backseat. They made a quick stop to pick up AJ, who reluctantly agreed to attend the show with her, and arrived at the Myesha Morgan studio with ten minutes to spare. They pulled up to the guest entrance on the side of the building. Attendees were hanging out in front, meandering into the studio slowly, but surely. As Kendali exited her security truck, she noticed a familiar face in the distance.

"Black, I gotta go say hi." She hurried along the black tar ground.

"Kendali! Wait!" He ran up behind her. AJ stood by the entrance door, casually observing their surroundings.

Kendali approached the handsome geek wearing a low fro, glasses, green polo, khakis, and two tone Docksiders.

"Max? I thought that was you."

"Yeah, it's me. And I know that's you." He smiled at her and she hugged him in return. They inhaled each other's fragrances conjuring memories of their too brief affair.

"What are you doing here?"

"The show is one of my clients. I check it out from time to time. I heard you were gonna be on, so...all the more reason to come today."

"Awwww, that's so sweet, Max. I'm so glad to see you."

Max was an IT guy, an all-around tech geek that worked in Dominion's IT department. He had released a few unsuccessful novels on Dominion. He and Hiram had a volcanic disagreement about creative visions and Max accused Hiram of skimming royalties. Max made a dramatic exit replete with police involvement and lawsuits that were later settled out of court.

"It's good to see you too, Grace."

"Yeah," she lingered inside his soft, sweet countenance, reminiscing.

"Well, let me get inside and get a good seat."

"Yes. Yes. Thanks for coming, babe." She squeezed his hands with passionate gratitude.

"Yes, Grace. Always. Have a good show."

"Bye, Max." She kissed his cheek and sauntered away. He watched the lusciousness of her Amazon hips and the jiggle of her booty making erotic promises beneath her perfect fit dress.

He could smell the lavender and vanilla sweetness of her skin conjuring memories of their tryst. The supple softness of her breasts, his sucking of her nipples, as she bounced her booty up and down on his ten inch steel created a heat in his groin. He remembered how her flesh slapping his thighs brought tears to his eyes, a new juicy pleasure experience for him. They would meet up, have dinner and drinks, and discuss how to be better storytellers. Their rendezvous ended at his house or a hotel suite where they would make love and fuck for hours on end. He shared his rare book collection with her, including a tattered raggedy book from the early 1900's called *The Mondawmin Indians*. "This is about a fierce warrior battle on American soil. Ancient American nation, literally fought the colonists to the death. These are our ancestors, yours and mine. My grandfather told me that we are direct descendants. Very few of the bloodline remain. It was the bloodiest documented battle ever on American land. That's why the elders taught, 'The only thing left are cowards and fools.'" She was intrigued by his intelligence and his sense of pride. Their reading tastes were similar; they both loved Richard Wright, Langston Hughes, Gwendolyn Brooks, and Gloria Naylor. They loved biographies, cookbooks, and books about travel and spiritual development. She was shocked that her *Vixen Notebook* series was on his shelf.

"You read my books, Max?"

"Of course. Why wouldn't I?"

"Seems beneath you."

"This is what you write today. Tomorrow is a new day. I have faith in your evolution. Your soul is pure, Kendali. The world turns us into these other things. But love, love brings us back to our purity. Back to our souls."

The deepness of his kiss in that moment took them into an abyss they had never known before, filled with confessions: she told him he was the best lover she had ever had, sweet, long lasting, kind, gentle, strong, patient, and powerful. She said he was the perfect prince and a perfect fool for falling for her.

"But aren't you falling for me too, Grace?" he had said.

She gazed past his sorrowful eyes, no answer for his question. "Well aren't you? I can feel it. I feel the rhythms of your soul speaking to me. You love me, Grace."

"Max, we can't."

She broke him, the marrow in his bones dried up with her statement. His heart froze, an icy organ, cracking then melting into sadness. They made love in spite of the despair, he beseeched answers from her as he plunged in and out of her wet canal all night long. *How can you turn away from love, love? You know you wanna be with me? Why won't you just fall into this? Why don't you get what you need most? Promise, you will think about it. Promise, you will stay open to me.*

I promise. But she lied. And he died that day. A different man walked into Myesha Morgan's studio, found a comfortable seat in the back, and waited for the show to start.

Monday 12 noon

The audience was loud, live, and laughing as Kendali, AJ, and Black were ushered to the dressing room for makeup and preparation. Myesha peeped in while the makeup artist added a light dusting to Kendali's face. She had left little for him to do since she MAC'd herself up before she arrived.

"Knock, knock, lovelies." Myesha was cute in a bright red dress and heels, and bloody red lipstick. She wore chunky gold accessories adding an ethnic sparkle to her outfit. Kendali looked in her direction, less nervous than she imagined she would be. She trusted Hiram's words of comfort about Myesha tempering her monster demeanor for the show. AJ, who had a certain guard dog energy with Kendali, was present. AJ detested the gossip gorilla Myesha types and their shows even more than she hated Kendali's success and the state of urban fiction books, so she was ready to pounce if necessary. Essentially, Kendali Grace had *two* bodyguards since Black was right at her side walking in sync with her.

"Y'all doin' okay?" Myesha asked.

"Yeah, we're okay," Kendali replied.

"Don't be nervous. Just think of this as a girl chat. Me and you just talkin'. The audience is just listening in because we are soooo mah-vuh-lus."

Kendali chuckled. AJ rolled her eyes. Black remained stoic.

"Thanks, Myesha. So much. For the opportunity to be here."

"Of course, my darling. We love Dominion. And we love your books around here."

Kendali grinned a wide smile while the makeup guy fluffed her hair. She winked at Myesha. "Awwww, Myesha. Thank you so much."

"I'll see you in a few."

"Okay," Kendali said.

Myesha blew her a kiss. The makeup artist finished giving Kendali a television face polishing. She and AJ left the room and found a quiet corner backstage to wait for Kendali's queue.

"AJ, I know you didn't want to come, but I'm glad you did."

"It's okay. I'm here to help." She almost felt sorry for Kendali, a prisoner inside her success and her experiences.

161

"Thanks." Kendali liked AJ. She was smart, pretty, nerdy, and no-nonsense. Her dedication to her craft was creatively inspiring. Kendali peeked out into the audience and spotted Tea on the second row, center. She sent her a text.

📱 Text Message 📱

Kendali: Eye see you👀

Tea: Hey girl. 😊 You nervous?

Kendali: Surprisingly-no 😊 I have 1.5 bodyguards.

Tea: 1.5? 🤔

Kendali: Hiram hired one. dude named Black. He kinda sexy too. You might like him. 😊 And AJ is here. She gotta lil' Rottweiler in her. 😬

Tea: 😁 AJ is cool

Kendali: She hates these gossip shows. reality tv. all that stuff. So she is ready to pounce on Myesha-one false move and Myesha is dinner! #woofwoof 🐶

Tea: 😁 Well, I'm glad you're not nervous.

Kendali: And I'm glad you're here 😊

Tea: You know I love yo' ass 💚

Kendali: 🐾

The audience was rambunctiously chanting, clapping, and stomping, excited about the departing guest Nina Black, the hottest hip hop diva on the scene with two number one singles on the charts. As the crowd simmered down, Myesha began to speak.

"Ooooo, yes! Nina Black. She is so everything." Myesha cooled herself with her signature Chinese style hand fan. "Okay, love children. Our next guest you are gonna absolutely adore. She rarely does interviews, and I guess not because her work speaks for itself. She is bestselling author of the ten part series *The Vixen Notebook*. Please welcome the deliciously gorgeous Kendali Graaaaaaaay~ssssssss!!!" The audience cheered loudly, waving their arms and leaping to their feet. Kendali walked across the stage, waving, smiling, and blowing kisses. She stopped right before the raised platform where Myesha was standing and took a deep curtsy. She held the curtsy for about ten seconds, the crowd screaming louder, the longer she held the humble posture. She hugged Myesha and sat on the sofa. Her eyes zoomed in on Tea, who was bursting with pride.

Tea winked. Kendali smiled and exhaled any residue of fear lurking in her mind and heart.

"Okay, so. You look gorgeous."

"Why thank you, Myesha."

"Shame you don't do more interviews. I mean you are stunning. Isn't she stunning?!" The audience erupted with clapping and shouting.

"Awwww, thanks so much," she responded coyly, bowing her head to the audience.

"You are very private."

"Somewhat. I am public private. I mean I share a lot on social media. But I spent so much time on camera...in the videos...at the center of so much drama. I have learned to kickback, lay low, and I love it." The audience applauded her testament of growth.

"Yeah, yeah," Myesha acknowledged. "Okay, guys. Give us the jewelry cam. You know I love jewelry." The camera zoomed in on Kendali's sparkling baubles. Myesha stretched Kendali's arm outward so her bangle would be in full view. "Now, I ain't no thief, but ummm-" She smirked and looked into the main camera at the audience. Kendali and the audience laughed. "Girl, this bangle though. You sellin' a whole lotta books, huh?"

"I've sold a few."

"Tony give us a supersized close up on this gorgeous piece of art." Tony, the number two camera man zoomed in on the bangle. "Y'all see that?" The audience oohed and awed as the camera slowly creeped in on the bracelet. Myesha twisted Kendali's arm to get various shots. "I don't even want to touch it. I think I'm in the wrong business," Myesha scoffed.

"Myesha, stop." Kendali shrugged, her smile lighting up her round face.

"No, I am serious. Tell us about the bracelet. Precious or costume?"

"It's all real. Crushed diamonds, set in platinum."

Myesha released her arm and they settled into their seats. "You gon' help me write a book, girl?" Myesha asked playfully.

"Definitely. I would love to collab with you." The audience whooped at Kendali's comment, excited about the possibility of a collaboration with the two tell-all divas. "But the bangle is a gift from my publisher. Shout out to Dominion Publishing!" The audience clapped.

"They givin' it up like that?"

"Always. They have been awesome. So loving and generous to me."

"Good. So good to know that we have Black business doing good business. Taking care of us. Taking care of each other."

"Yes, we do. Definitely."

164

"Now, speaking of collabos, you know we gotta talk about the scandal."

"I know." Kendali turned her head to the side, feigning little girl shyness.

"You want me to start, or you start?"

"You go ahead."

"Ghostwriter or not?"

"I have a team of people that help me, writers and editors."

"Now, you know I can't let you get away with that answer, girl. This is the Myesha Morgan show."

"Okay. Let's just say this. Do I write every single word- no. There are editors and writing coaches on Dominion's staff that assist authors with polishing the final product. Do I write the story- yes. It depends on how you see ghostwriting, you see?" She moved closer to Myesha. "Listen, there are authors out here not writing at all, not one single word."

"Mmmm-hmmm. Really? Not one?"

"Not one word. They are putting their names on the books and selling the work as their own. They may not even read the book or know what the book is about."

"Whaaat?"

"Yes. And some very popular authors you all know and love are doing this."

"Really?"

"Yez, girl. Yezzzzzz."

"Wow. Okay. So, no ghostwriter for you."

"I don't do that."

"Okay, okay. We hear ya'. Well, we love your work. And so do a lotta other folks including our people at The Platinum Quill. You are receiving their top award, Author Of The Year, true?"

"That's what they tell me." Kendali's eyes glowed with happiness and humility. "It is such a great honor. Truly incredible. I am thankful to Toni and all of The Platinum Quill board and staff. They are truly beautiful people."

"They are. Congrats on that, sis." Myesha clapped and the audience followed suit. Kendali bowed her head to the audience. "Now, with *The Vixen Notebook*. I love figuring out who you're talking about because you never name names."

"And I won't."

"Yeah, but anybody with half a brain can figure out all the characters."

"Well, I leave that to the readers."

"You know I know all these kneegrows, so anybody reading Kendali's books and want some help unveiling the characters, y'all hit me up," Myesha shouted waving her arms over the audience. They responded with whooping laughter. "Now your upcoming release is the final installment in the series?"

"It is. Book 10! Issa wrap!"

"Wow. A ten book series? That is so awesome. Congratulations on that, love."

"Thank you. Thank you so much."

"Now that's unusual, a ten book series for the genre of urban fiction."

"It is probably the longest series in the genre, right now. Maybe ever."

"That is such an awesome achievement. Why do you think folks keep wanting your books?"

"Good stories. Good writing. Good promo. No secret formula. That's it."

"And that's a plenty!"

"Yes."

"So, you're goin' out with a bang?"

"I think so."

"Give us a lil' morsel. Wet our appetites, sis."

"Well, the finale is going to show you the under underbelly of the music industry. The stuff nobody wants to talk about. A really ugly, evil side."

"Really? Wow. Okay. Like what?"

"The criminal nature of the business."

"Ohhhh-kay…" Myesha wanted more.

"Just know this: people don't realize how much hip hop is supported by illegal drugs, the porn industry, and sex trafficking. I mean for real. You have no idea."

"No, folks don't have any idea. They really don't."

"And politics. You see hip hoppers posted up with governors, mayors, presidents, etc. This is not new and the relationships run deep. Real deep. Deeper than you think. Deeper than they have shown you in any book or any movie."

"Girrrrrrrrl, you know I know. You fiddnah tell on these fools?"

"Well, I am gonna tell the tale. The readers will see and get what they need to get. Really- if you payin' attention, most of this is happening right in front of your face."

"So true. But most of us ain't lookin'. We listenin' to the beat."

"Exactly."

"I love it! I am glad you are writing it. I want you back on the show when you release the final piece. Release date yet?"

"Not yet. But really soon. Probably before the year ends."

"I can't wait!" She turned to the audience. "Listen, y'all. If you haven't read her series *The Vixen Notebook*, get started now, so you can be ready for the finale when it drops. Tell us the title of the finale."

"*The Vixen Notebook: Age Is More Than A Number.*"

"Oooooooo, girl. Yes! Listen. Y'all get started! Follow Kendali Grace on Zing, Sensa, and Wired. All her info you should see on the screen. Get on over to Muse and download her books. If you missed anything, you know you can always visit Myesha Morgan dot com and search Kendali Grace or *The Vixen Notebook* to get links, snippets, and updates on Kendali and the happenings with the Myesha Morgan show." The two women rose from the cushy sofas and embraced each other lovingly. "I am so glad you spent time with us today. You gotta come back and see us."

"I will. Thank you so much, Myesha."

"Thank you, sis." Myesha grabbed Kendali's hand and held it straight up toward the ceiling, a triumphant stance. "Kendali Grace, y'all." She received a standing ovation. She offered another humble curtsy, kissed Myesha on the cheek, and waved to the crowd as she exited. AJ was backstage, excited to receive her.

"How'd I do?"

"You were ravishing. They love you. Outstanding job, Kendali." She fell onto AJ, resting her head on her petite shoulder and cried a single tear. "I needed you to say that."

AJ patted her on her back, feeling awkward in the moment. "You did good." Kendali stood up and AJ handed her, her purse. "Your phone has been buzzing like a beehive, making honey."

"Really?"

"Yeah."

"Okay, ladies. Let's exit."

"Black, I wanna go to lunch with Tea. She's in the audience."

"Are you meeting her? Or is she coming with us?" Black asked.

"AJ, you comin'?"

"No, I need to go back. People are excited about your book. I gotta make sure it lives up to the excitement."

"Aaargh, come out with us."

"No, y'all go on. Drop me at Dominion and y'all go ahead. Besides, I have my lunch in my fridge at my desk. I'm okay."

"Well, okay," Kendali expressed with disappointment. She was so excited about making a connection with AJ and hoped to share more with her, but the forces didn't feel it was time.

"Ladies, I want us to get goin'." Black was growing impatient. The mission was complete and his training taught him to move, mission to mission, period.

"Okay, I will text Tea and tell her to meet us at KD's. And we can drop AJ off at the office."

"Good. Let's go." Black led them to the bulletproof Suburban and they drove away.

Monday 7:00 p.m.

Tatanka Villa Resort offered a quiet, relaxing getaway for Seminole City residents and surrounding areas, approximately a three hour drive away. Kendali was so grateful for the welcoming staff, the gorgeous gardens, the premium delivery services, and its full spa. She wasn't so grateful for her twenty four hour tag along, but Hiram and Crispus insisted. She realized just how serious the situation was when Black gave her a new phone and took her old one without allowing her to clone it. No one was allowed to transfer anything from the old phones. Crispus and his cyber security specialist, Toussaint, were issuing complete data scans of all mobile devices and computer equipment checking for spyware and hacking codes. Meanwhile she indulged in a retreat at Tatanka. Black secured the rear entrance of her villa with an infrared alarm switch that would alert him if anyone crossed the threshold of the villa's terrace door while he guarded the villa's front entrance,. After Black performed his security check, Kendali unpacked, took a long, piping hot bath, and buttered herself up with lavender vanilla body cream mixed with coconut oil. Incense and candles set the mood.

Hiram tapped on the adjoining suite door. He arrived secretly, renting the villa next door to his long lost Kenni. She greeted him, glistening, butterball naked, and ready. Upon seeing her, his erection grew another inch of soldier salute steel. Mesmerized by his lean stature and piercing eyes, she opened her arms to receive him. His touch chastised her for being away from him, even though he designed their separation, standing as her fierce protector. Her breasts accepted his punishment with every forceful squeeze. His tongue lashed in her mouth with anger created from his yearning and sadness from his waiting. But his relief was in the tasting and enjoying her tongue's eternal sweetness. Her mouth acquiesced to his admonishments, a delicious surrender to her loving savage, a beautiful beast he was. He pushed and pulled her body simultaneously a sensuous confusion that their longing created. She melted into his touches torturing her skin and his grabs crashing upon her flesh; her hips and ass endured most of his love whipping. Blasts of perspiration showered her face and neck from his pores. She apologized with her reception of his sweat laden lust, baptized in his juices. Her own nectar stirring in her vagina, she readied for his dagger to dig its way deep into her center cutting out the ache she had been feeling in her belly.

They made it to the bed after the initial feral greeting. He sucked and bit her neck with a ravenous voracity and held her hands to comfort her in the painful pleasure. She whimpered. He ate her like a king's buffet; her body boasted a variety of delicious delectables that the most-high chef prepared for the palette of a sire. He ruled her. And she ruled him with her strong Amazonian, yet delicate femininity. She climaxed repeatedly until her senses dulled and her pain of longing dissipated.

"I missed you, Kenni. I missed you so much," he confessed between slurps and sucks of her vulvanic bowl that poured forth erotic promises of bliss. He continued to feast as long as she continued to feed.

"I missed you too, baby."

She showed him her yearning, devouring his erection until she felt the force of his seed rumble to the tip. She stopped. He cried out, his man jewels throbbing. Her tongue twirled about on the tip as she squeezed his buttocks. The cradle effect of her large and powerful hands turned him into a baby. He sucked his thumb unknowingly. She swallowed his shaft again after his semen retreated, intensifying his desire for orgasmic satisfaction. He pulled her onto him and she assumed the cowgirl position in one smooth move. She rode and they enjoyed the ride. He forced her under him and he stroked her until she squirted, his steely passion finding its way into the darkest moistest places inside her. It was good. And he came, finally, after her final squirt. He screamed without care or concern. She muffled his expression with a long passionate kiss and he heaved life in and out of his lungs uncertain if he was crossing over to heaven. He didn't care if he was standing at the pearly gates; this was the way to die.

They lay stretched out on the California king size bed, taking turns on a blunt and drinking wine.

"Your interview was awesome. I mean the camera loves you. You execute so well."

"Awwwe, thanks babes." She lay her head on his shoulder.

"You do. So well, you got these niggas shook about this finale."

"Yeah. I know. I got a few phone calls and texts. I ignored them." She sucked in the premium herb and exhaled slowly feeling her intoxication intensify.

"Well, Dominion's lines were blowin' up after the show. I ain't talkin'. I'm lettin' Mo go for what she know wit' this one. She wanna be a CEO so bad, then boss up. Shiiid."

"CEO?"

"Yeah. Wants us to help her finance her own publishing house. I'm not opposed. Just not sure she's ready."

"Are you kidding? Mo built Dominion."

"Yeah, but being the chief overseer of a company isn't the same as CAO."

"Hiram. Baby. Stop." She rolled over on her back and turned her face to him. He stayed in position on his stomach dropping ashes into the ashtray on the floor.

"What?"

"You need to help her."

"Well, let's see what happens with all the drama you are stirring. What the hell you got on these niggas?"

"Way too much." She stroked her hair thoughtfully. "I guess this thing is really serious. Huh?" She rolled over closer to him, her breasts pressing into the love soaked sheets reeking of lavender and Hiram's Aramis fragrance. He passed her the reefer again.

"Yeah, it is. You thought I was crazy for hiring security after the flowers. Now, this book controversy."

"Well, I didn't think you were completely crazy. I told you about the mysterious car."

"Yeah. And you should have told me when you first saw that, but no need to have that argument again." He kissed her lips and she blew smoke all over his mouth and face. He received her herb laced gesture, closing his eyes.

"I mean taking our phones. Security professionals. How long will this go on?"

"I don't know. Hopefully not much longer. I cannot keep missing you like this." She blushed. "I can't."

"I know. Me either."

"I got an envelope too. Just like Bree. She got an envelope with the emails, text messages, details about the ghostwriting. That's why Crispus is sure the hacker and the stalker are the same. Fuckin' with all of us."

"What's in your envelope?"

"Too much."

"What is it, Hiram?"

"You already know. Like you said, 'way too much'."

Chapter Ten
Legends, Launches, & Lionesses

Wednesday, 10:00 a.m.

"I don't care, Love. I am your protector. You are my responsibility. I am picking you up, taking you everywhere you need to go, Fly. Period. It's not up for discussion." Titus put his Toyota Sequoia in park.

"T, I'm just sayin'. It seems so inconvenient." Lesli rolled her head side to side on the headrest.

"How are you inconvenient? You my woman. And until we get to the bottom of this bullshit, if there is a bottom, you stuck wit' me, ma. Besides, you're such a beautiful inconvenience."

She stroked his thigh, gazing into his serious, sincere eyes, thankful for him. "I love you, Titus Dixon."

He leaned over and planted a juicy lip smack in her mouth. "And I love you." He kissed her cheek, then her chin. "And I'm gon' marry you."

"Yes."

He kissed her other cheek. "And we gon' keep loving each other."

"Yes."

He pecked her nose. "And we gon' buy a big house."

"Yes," she moaned, her spirit absorbing his romantic playfulness.

"And we gon' make babies."

"Yes."

He nibbled her ear and whispered, " Four or five babies."

"Whoaaa...whoa, homeboy! Pump ya' brakes. You had me, but-"

"What, Fly? All dem titties you got? We gotta have at least four babies."

"Maaaaan. I'm goin' to work." She pushed him away from her. He persisted, pushing weight on her bubbly breasts, burying his head in her double D's. "Titus!" She laughed out loud trying to wriggle herself free from his indulgence.

"Mwahhhhh!" he said loudly kissing her in the center of her chest. He relented falling back into the driver's seat. "I love you, Fly."

"I love you too." She kissed her hero goodbye and exited the vehicle. He watched her walk into the Meade Comm building, her africoid antennas moving with the morning breeze.

"Hey, Sam!"
"Hey, Lesli Lyn. Good morning."

"Good morning, love."

"Bradford wants to see you right away. He has been asking me all morning about your arrival. You not answering your phone?"

"Shit! I ain't looked at my phone since last night. Been in a lil' funk."

"I know. I get it. Don't worry about deez hoes, girl. They just trynah bring you down. Fuck 'em. You Butterfly Brooks! They can't catch you, girl with them fluffy wings you got." Samara winked.

"You always know how to make me smile," Lesli responded

pulling her phone from her bag. There were eleven missed calls from Brad. "Okay, lemme see what our boss wants."

"Yes. Let's see. And let me know."

"Girl, you a mess." Lesli trudged toward the elevator. She hoped that Bradford had some good news, something wonderful to rejuvenate her. The current state of funk was exhausting for her and her caped crusader. She said a silent prayer thanking God for Titus. Her office welcomed her with the scent of sandalwood and pineapple, an aroma still lingering from the candle she burned late last night as she sat typing on her computer. Titus had camped out with her on the supersized comfy sofa until she finished her writing goals for the day. She put her bag down and sent Bradford a text telling him she was in her office. She started her computer, checked her calendar, and began her daily tasks.

"Les!" Bradford floated into her office beaming, his caramel eyes creamier than usual.

"What's goin' on, brother?"

He stood in front of her desk in his seersucker suit and yellow tie ensemble. "I know you been down because of your hate mail, the drive-by...Thank God for Titus and you know I'm here for you because I won't kick a bitch ass, but you know I'll get a bitch's ass kicked."
Lesli offered a half chuckle. "Bradford."
"Right. Right. Back to the point. And I mean, we know your heart don't pump kool-aid. Deez broads really do not understand you." She switched her weight to the other side of her chair

impatiently. "Right. Why I have been blowin' up your phone. The Times. They did an interview with Maya Walker Bambara."

"Okay."

"She quoted you!"

"Quoted *me*?"

"Yes. She quoted your blog piece from about a month back. The one on editing errors. I've already got Tomeika writing a piece on you about the quote with a reprint of your original blog."

"Wow. I can't believe it." She gazed across the room in amazement, past Bradford, past her work table, fixing her eyes on the black butterfly painting on the wall. Just when she was ready to give up, throw in the towel, and be somebody else, because being herself seemed too hard, Maya Walker Bambara reminded her that Titus was right: 'The world needs the soft, beautiful power of butterflies.'

"I don't know why you can't believe it. Believe it! You Butterfly Brooks."

"I know. But *Maya Walker Bambara*?"

"Yes, *thee* Maya Walker Bambara. Now, some of this madness with these crazy ass broads attacking you will probably die down."

"Hmmm. You think so? I don't know."

"Oh yeah. You have been courageous enough to speak the truth. They gonna quiet down. Now you have a legend backing you up."

Lesli shrugged and smiled proudly. "I gotta see this." She turned to her computer screen and clicked *The Times* icon on her home screen.

"The headline story of the arts and culture section," Brad instructed.

"Wow. The lead story?"

"Yeah. It's a big deal. She hasn't given an interview in years. She has a book coming out, so she is doing interviews and a short tour."

"Oh, wow." Lesli moved closer to her screen browsing *The Times*. She clicked the Arts and Culture tab and there she was in all her artistic regality, a gorgeous picture of the literary goddess draped in a beautiful white caftan. A few of her soft locks, wrapped in a white and gold scarf, dangled righteously around her ears onto her chest. The photo was a natural shot, her in a relaxed mode, clearly dropping pearls of passionate wisdom from her lips. Lesli skimmed the article intending to reread every word later on, but in the moment she wanted to see the quote.

MWB: Well, there is a young woman at one of the Meade companies. You may not know Meade, but your bosses do.
RB: I'm familiar.
MWB: Well they have a young sista. A writer. She blogs. I read her blog often. But she talks about the state of African American fiction. Literature. And there was one blog article I was reading.
RB: What's her name? Which blog?
MWB: She calls herself Butterfly Brooks. The blog is The Kaleidoscope. You know what a kaleidoscope is, Rob?
RB: A colorscape. Something of many colors and shapes coming together.
MWB: Yes. But also, it is the term for a group of butterflies. Like a school of fish. A herd of sheep. A murder of crows. A kaleidoscope of butterflies.
RB: Oh, I see. I didn't know that.
MWB: I didn't either. Butterfly Brooks taught me that. (smiling) Well anyway. I am paraphrasing but in one of her blogs, she

talks about the poor editing and rampant errors in many of the books labeled African American fiction. She goes on to talk about the need to still maintain a standard even if you write about guns, drugs, you know. The ugly side of us. At least write it well. As error free as possible. And make it good writing for good reading. She says there is no excuse for mediocrity amongst our people. She says mediocrity is murdering us, as a people. Even in our books. And we must arrest Mr. Mediocrity without trial, he is guilty and he must be burned at the stake. Something like this she says. And she is one hundred percent correct.
RB: I will have to read her blog.
MWB: Yes. You have to.

"Oh my goddess." She sat back in her chair, her mouth agape. Brad walked around to her, hugged her around her shoulders, and kissed her on the forehead. "You are soaring, Les. You are the best!" He kissed her again and shuffled happily to the door. "Now! Get to work! I will see you after I get back from my meetings."

"Yessir!" she shouted, flapping her arms imitating the fluttering wings of a butterfly. She texted Titus the good news and thanked him for taking care of her through her funk. Then she reread the article word for word. She clicked the link to her Kaleidoscope blog entry that Maya Walker Bambara quoted included in the piece and read it:

My oh so precious butterflies. I descend upon you with soft, silky wings, bestowing messages from the garden.

I am getting straight to the point because I have to get back to this bottle of unfinished wine from Nappy Vines. For those who didn't know, were grossly misinformed, confused or just don't give a damn, this is for you. Trust: Writing is an effective form of communication. It is most effective when well written and easily comprehended. If you want what your writing to be universally understood and lovingly received, then there is some due diligence that must be applied. Thorough editing is required. Poor slipshod editing is a clear indication that you and your publisher don't give a damn the craft. Misspelled words. Subject/verb disagreement. Lack of punctuation. Incorrect word usage. Sloppy sentence structure. Word repetition. Kindergarten styling. The overabundance of errors in your work deplete your catalogue's value.

Once your manuscript is in your publisher's hands, your credibility is on the line. Your masterpiece, that took you forever to write, is supposed to be polished and refined. Unpolished, error-ridden books will not get a read from me or a huge number of readers who seek the comforting escapism and enjoyment of a good novel.

Great stories are killed by poor editing. Start checking these editors and publishers because they are misrepresenting you, themselves, and the literary arts. Writing isn't for everyone. It's not everyone's calling and if it's not calling you, please don't answer. You all have your inspirations and motivations in a tight spot. Read. Study. Hone. Practice. Be better. Write better. No edit, no credit. Period. Now, I have a bottle of Nappy Vines to attend to.

This is L~Double. Silky, Soft...and Signing off...Float on 🦋
She confessed, "It *is* a soft beautiful power."
🦋🦋🦋

"Look here, bruh. Before we go inside," Thaddeus began as he and Mustafa arrived at Nina's. They were there for BlackOut's meeting about Isis, Mustafa's brainchild.
Mustafa put his car in park, "What's up, my man?"
Thad leaned closer to the dashboard looking around the parking lot. "I am wondering why it seems like I get a lot more money from BlackOut than Dominion."
"You know Hiram ain't the straightest arrow in the bunch. Tell me what's goin' on."
"I started comparing BlackOut's royalty reports to Dominion's. Now, I expect a decrease in those older royalties, but...just seems off. Too dramatic a difference."
"Do you have your Muse reports? You see we always attach your Muse report to your royalty statement."
"Yeah, y'all do. A Muse report from Dominion? No. Ain't never had one."
"Well, you have a right to see all documents pertaining to your money. It's in your contract. So, ask for the Muse reports."
"Yeah. I think I got something like three g's on Black Blood Gang this past quarter."
"Whoa! Wait. What? Three g's?!"
"Yeah, man."
"Oh, no way. You should have waaaay more than that."

"I know. I mean, y'all just gave me a royalty of 5 g's for the Black Blood TV series. I know folks gotta be buying the book more. You see?"

"Uh-huh. Hmmm. Yeah. Definitely." Mustafa scratched his head. "You betta get those reports. But you gon' know what's up when you ask for them. The response will tell you if something is afoot."

"Yeah, ahk. I'm on it. I appreciate you, man. Best decision I ever made, leaving Dominion and coming to BlackOut."

"Yeah. Hiram is our brother but he is flawed. Corrupt. I really think that behind the scenes, he talked BlackTV out of renewing your show."

"I wouldn't doubt it. That's why he still clinging tight to Black Blood Gang. I am glad I retained screen rights. Hiram crazy."

"Yeah. He cut off his nose to spite his face. The show was helping to sell more of your books in Dominion's catalogue. More green for all of us. But hey...fuck 'em. We onto bigger and better, my brother."

"All day."

Thaddeus gave Mustafa a pound. Mustafa held onto Thad's fist for a spell saying, "But getcha dough, yo." They laughed and headed into Nina's.

▲▲▲

"Maaaan, I am telling y'all. This is the motherlode. It is the ultimate Black media EVERYTHING," Mustafa said ending his slide presentation. He guzzled his tea, relaxed and excited to share with some real power brethren in Black media. He had reserved the banquet room at Nina's for their meeting- him, Brad, Malachi Green, former CEO of Unique Magazine, and Thad. The rest of the power crew flipped through the accompanying 200-page, first stage proposal of Mustafa's brainchild, Isis dot com, a full service multimedia platform offering all things Black media. Isis was essentially the all Black version of Muse dot com with books, movies, streaming services, magazines, dailies, blogs, Black studies educational lecture archives, and rare book reprints.

After about fifteen minutes of silence, Malachi spoke first. "You definitely in godfather mode; this is an offer we can't refuse."

"No doubt," Bradford concurred.

"Yes! That's what I want to hear, brethren."

"My only thing is," Malachi stated. "The buy-in. Your marketing strategy is tight. And I know Rondell over at Paradox. I would like to see that plan executed first. Get people signed up for the beta test now, and then see if it makes sense."

"I'm ahead of you, bruh. See page 108. Outlines the beta test launch, pre-launch, and launch phases. And I will need your funds for all phases, brother. I have exhausted all my capital thus far."

"Good. Now *that's* what *I* wanna hear, a brother investing his all in his *own*. I gotchu. I got the dough. I will have my people setup a wire in the morning."

"My brother!" Mustafa gave Malachi a fist bump.

Bradford asked, "Now what do you need from me?"

"Well, any funds you have available, we want you to invest. And we want real content for the beta test. As you saw in the presentation, our current beta model includes mock data. We want to include real content for the beta launch."

"Okay. So, I will link you with our catalogue and archive directors and our legal team so you can sort it out."

"My man," Mustafa acknowledged Brad's input with a wink and a point of his finger. "Brother Thad! Anything to add?"

Thaddeus, who was there for moral support mostly, looked up from his plate of Nina's herbed cabbage and potatoes. "Just looking forward to the project's completion. And thankful to be in the number. I do have to ask, whatchall gon' do about security?"

"Security?" Malachi asked.

"Yeah, security. Cyber and otherwise because you know them others gon' come for y'all." The three men absorbed the weight of his statement, knowing his point bore a validity they did not want to accept. "You know when the negroes get together, the others get worried. Say whatcha want. It may be a new millennium, but it's filled with old ideals. And whitey gon' be on our asses." A hush fell over the room.

Wednesday, 2:00 p.m.

Because Crispus had seen his share of rolling hill estates, mansions big and small, he wasn't impressed with Tasir Samaan's twenty-six room Mediterranean style manor. Yet, he was moved by the dark energy surrounding the modern day palace. Even its bright peach colored exterior and the midday sun could not hide its sinister vibration. He checked in at the security gate, drove slowly uphill, and pulled into the cul de sac, parking behind a vintage Bentley. *Vintage Bentley is a sure sign of a nut case*, he thought. He sat for a few minutes reviewing the contents of a manila folder filled with pictures, profiles, news articles, his scribbled notes, and reminders. Tasir Samaan, a swarthy Arabian prince with silver spooned mouth, came to the United States with his younger brother and sister when he was a very young boy. His father and his siblings inherited an oil empire from their forebears. They were members of the royal bloodline as the wealthy cousins of the Royal House of Rasaan in the Middle East. His father studied medicine and became a surgeon while his mother was a classically trained harpist. Tasir studied music like his mother, and was especially gifted on the eighty-eights, but he also mastered guitar and violin. He played professionally for a short time, then decided to start his company, Palace Records. He was a legend in the music business having signed so many pop, blues, and soul legends to Palace. With the financial strength of a blockbuster catalogue, he bought several other small, fledgling, innovative, independent labels along the way which helped Palace remain relevant in the music industry. There were rampant rumors about his sadistic predatory and savage nature. Stories abounded about his use of sadomasochistic tactics, violence, rape, bestiality, and even pedophilia. A real low life terrorist.

When Crispus approached the front door, a butler was standing, waiting with his hand on the ornate handle. His attire was simple, white slacks, black long sleeve shirt, white bow tie, and black and white bucks on his feet.

"Lord Samaan is waiting for you in the salon."

Lord? Salon? Yeah, this sand nigga crazy, Crispus noted mentally.

"Okay. Thank you," Crispus replied stepping inside. He surveyed the high ceiling foyer decorated with an oil portrait of the Samaan clan, Tasir's nuclear family, his parents, and the families of his siblings. While Tasir appeared as the darkest figure in the group, no one seemed to possess much light, their eyes telling the stories of the unchecked appetites that infinite

185

fortune brings. Intermittent notes from a piano played in a low hum serenading the empty hall.

"Follow me, sir. Welcome to The Oasis."

"Yes." Crispus observed the mosaic tiled floors as they passed the semi-circular staircase. The library on the left had heavy wooden doors and ornate handles almost identical to the front door with hand carved bookshelves lined with strange, obscure titles.

As they arrived at the salon doorway, the butler asked, "Would you like a nice cold tasty beverage or a delectable hor d'oeuvre?"

"I am fine thank you."

"He is expecting you, so make yourself comfortable on the flower printed chaise. Please do not sit on the bright green solid colored sofa."

"Okay." Crispus stepped toward the entryway.

"And please do not interrupt him at the piano. He knows you are here. Just let him finish and then he will speak to you."

"Hmmm. Yeah, alright," Crispus answered half-heartedly. The odd fellow continued to the back of the house toward the kitchen while Crispus found a comfortable spot on the flower printed sofa as he was instructed. He decided to wait a few minutes for his lordship to complete his concerto, setting a five minute wait time in his mind. He would not kowtow to the rich psychopath.

Tasir sat hunkered down on the piano seat, plunking the keys and then pausing to write notes on his sheet music. His hair, usually pulled back and braided neatly in a ponytail, was wild and untamed, the salt and pepper strands bouncing about his shoulders and dropping around his deep olive tone face. He moved back and forth between the keys and his paper and pen with great vexation. Simple furnishings and a plethora of fresh flowers adorned the room. The chaise where Crispus sat, the green sofa, two oriental styled wooden chairs with bright green cushions and one gargantuan painting of a 1960's nightclub scene, depicting many Black music legends, made up the madman's personal concert hall. Around the two and a half minute marker he spoke.

"It is, what I imagine, if all the greats got together on a stormy night just hanging out. No pay for play. Just making music."

"Yes. It is a remarkable piece."

"It is. Sarai is an extraordinary talent. A lousy lay though." He grimaced remembering his brief encounter with the painter of the musical homage masterpiece.

"Mmmm." Crispus wiped his brow with his handkerchief feeling sweat building under his Hawaiian printed shirt.

"I generally have the air conditioning very low in this room so that it holds some heat." His mild Middle Eastern accent lingered inside some of his language. "It is the heat, Meester Adams, that makes the music come alive. Music is a heat. An energy. A power. Why do you think it is so tightly controlled, eh?"

"I don't know. I never thought about it."

"Because. It is not the money. Men in music can make money anywhere. Most of them have other fortunes. Other interests. It is the power. You know the story of the pied piper?"

"I do."

"So I do not need to say more, ah?" He leapt from his seat and seemed to fly directly in front of the investigator. Crispus leaned back slow and easy hoping he would not have to crack his skull or snap his neck. He quickly assessed that a neck snap would be easiest for he was very slight in build and short in stature. *Crazy ass sand nigga acting like he might carry around a pocketful of human liver or a lunchbox full of dead muthafucka.*

"No. I understand."

He moved in a womanly fashion to the double doors leading to a beautiful terrace garden filled with a variety of orchids. Crispus footnoted the orchids, same flowers that were sent to Kendali. He remembered that the florist said an older lady ordered the flowers. Tasir's mother? Another female relative? How truthful was the florist? Tasir had more than enough means and power to pay or to convince anybody to say anything.

"So, what did you want to ask me, Meester Adams?" He turned his head to Crispus in a seductive fashion.

"I want to talk to you about your relationship with Kendali. Kendali Grace."

His eyes bubbled from the sockets like hot lava pouring from a volcano. The olive tones in his skin turned to pea soup, bland and flavorless. "Kendali? What about her?" he purred sounding like an Earth Kitt drag queen.

"Just what your relationship was like."

"Has something happened to her?" he asked with a sense of excitement.

"No. She's okay. We are doing a background check on her. She is considering a contract with a large corporation that requires certain kinds of clearances. My firm has been hired to check her out. Her fame and background make her a risk automatically, but the company wants her for some other non-sensitive tasks. Even so, they want to do the standard procedure."

"I see." He admired his orchid plantation, rubbing his chin and twirling his hair on the ends. "Well, what do you want to know?" He clapped his hands loudly, five times in rapid succession. "I am just getting the note in my head. The note that I needed!" He raced back to his seat in front of the baby grand piano and hammered the note he wanted, creating a din that startled the former special ops soldier. Crispus jumped back still sitting on the sofa. Tasir jotted notes on his sheet music, then looked at Crispus whose facial expression made the madman chuckle.

"You see, Meester Adams. I love music. I mean adore music. I am in love with music. I have been in love with her my whole life from the first time I heard mother play her harp. Lulling me to sleep as a baby."

"You remember that?"

"Of course I do. Who can forget such beautiful sounds." He shook his head passionately. "Now what is it? About Kendali, yeah? She is a video whore. That is all I know."

"Did you all have a relationship? She said you beat her up and had her followed for a while. Is that true?"

"That would make me some kind of monster, yes?" His thick uni-brow sank onto his eyelids in disgust. His lips crept to the right side of his head in an upward half grin.

"Is it true, Mr. Samaan?"

"You can call me *Lord*. And no!" He flipped back to his piano and banged chords loudly, so loudly that the butler rushed into the salon.

"Lord Samaan, is everything alright."

"Of course, Ramon. Of course. Meester Adams was just asking me about Kendali. You remember her, yes? The video whore?" Ramon moved backward, exiting the salon. "Yes, Lord. I remember." He stood still waiting for Tasir to dismiss him.

"I am fine, Ramon. Carry on!"

"Yes, Lord." He left.

"Kendali is not my type. Video vixen they call themselves. Those types. We went out to de' club. Sometimes. From time to time. That was it. She just pretty face. That's all. Big hips. Not my type."

"You have a type? They say you have all kinds of types."

"Do not believe they, Meester Adams."

Crispus rose from the chaise. "Did you know she loves orchids?"

"She does?" he stated, feigning a question tone.

Crispus caught his pretense. "Yes, she does."

"Is there any other question? I have to get back to my music."

"No. That's all. Nothing else." Crispus strode to the door. "I thank you for your time."

"Ramon!" he yelled for his servant. "See, Meester Adams out."

"I'm okay. I will find my way out."

The psycho musician returned to his composition knowing that the investigator had lied to him about his reasoning for the Kendali questions. And Crispus found his way to the door, a slightly bruised eye peeping at him from the library. Crispus was unable to determine if the eye belonged to a man or a woman, but whoever it was offered a partial grin as he left the mansion of horrors. He and Tasir knew the other was being untruthful in their communication. Bottomline, he proved a strong suspect in the stalking of Kendali.

Wednesday, 3:00 p.m.

Crispus eased his car into the parking lot of McCallahan Shipping. There were workers standing around the front entrance talking and laughing, some leaving for lunch, some returning from their midday meals. He found a parking spot that gave full view of all entrances to the parking lot and the doors along the warehouse. He looked in his file folder labeled "Emory" to refresh his memory of Emory Parker's face. He had been harassing Kendali and eventually Hiram fired him for the harassment. Emory threatened to sue Dominion for wrongful termination, but never initiated a lawsuit. He seemed to move on with his life after landing a job with McCallahan as a shipping manager. Emory didn't possess the knowledge or power for hacking Dominion's servers, therefore Crispus categorized him as a least likely suspect. Drinking the last drop of his sweet tea, he tossed the folder onto the passenger seat and examined the chummy, work-focused employees coming and going. He saw Emory strolling to the front door of McCallahan, his thick muscular body moving swiftly through the breezy air and his dark skin absorbing the sun's vitamin D. Crispus exited his car and approached him.

"Mr. Parker?"
Emory flashed a bewildered glance. "Who wants to know?"
"I am Investigator Crispus Adams. Do you mind stepping over here with me to talk privately? There is nothing for you to be concerned about. I just want to ask you a few questions about Kendali Grace."
His shoulders dropped and his facial expression displayed frustration. "You must work for Hiram's bitch ass?"
"I do work with Mr. Rivers. Do you mind talking to me for a few minutes?"
"Not without a lawyer present. I don't trust none of y'all motherfuckers."
"You don't need a lawyer. I am just an investigator. I have no police authority. We are simply attempting to clear up some personal matters for Ms. Grace."
He paused and scanned Crispus from head to toe. He had an imposing demeanor, but overall appeared harmless. Emory

decided to talk, but very little. "Aight. We can talk over here." Emory motioned toward some picnic tables in the near distance on the side of the warehouse. They walked over to the table area. "What was your relationship with Kendali?"

"There was no relationship. There was only miscommunication. I misread some signals. She misread some signals. That was it."

"Signals?"

Emory stepped closer to Crispus holding out his arms with his palms facing upward, using his hands to communicate his point sincerely. "Look here, man. I was diggin' Kendali. I thought she was diggin'me. She used to flirt with me as much as I flirted with her. All the women at Dominion flirted with me. And I fucked a few. I thought she was tryin' to see what all the fuss was about. You know, about me, you see? Bitches talk."

"Uh-huh."

"Yeah. So really I think Hiram got in his feelings because she began to respond to me more positively. He thought I was gonna get dem' drawers. But we all know dem' drawers belong to him."

"To Hiram?"

"Yeah. They real slick with it and most folks don't think they got a thing. But I know better."

"Better than what?"

"He fuckin' her. That's his meat. That's why he fired me. They trumped up some sexual harassment bullshit. But how you gon' sexually harass a video hoe? I mean come the fuck on."

"Is that so?" Crispus looked at him with disgust and disapproval. Emory noticed his reaction. "Look here. I ain't no harasser, man," he explained apologetically. "I am just sayin'. Kendali got some shit with her."

"You were gonna sue Dominion, right?"

192

"Yeah. But I left it all alone. Moved on. Bigger and better now. I'm doin' much better now than I ever thought. Getting' ready to get my CDL. I'm a manager here now. I got plans. It's cool. I'm done with that."

"I see."

"Yeah. And I need to get back to work. My people can't see the supervisor gettin' back late from lunch. Gotta set a good example." He smiled proudly.

"Yes. Of course. Back to work. I hear you, my man. That's all."

"Alright. Have a good one."

"You too."

Crispus returned to his car. He wanted to rule Emory out, but you can never tell with these situations. People are such good liars. Even so, he labeled his folder in red ink, "WEAK SUSPECT". He started his car and headed to the next interrogee.

✔✔✔

Wednesday 4:30 p.m.

Dre walked into the Seminole City Diner in his green work uniform, thin army green khakis and matching thin army green shirt with a right pocket patch that read, "Walker Green Services". He wiped the sweat from his forehead with a thick white paper towel as he approached the table. Crispus stood to greet him.

"Thank you for meeting with me, Mr. Walker," he said shaking his hand.

"No problem," Dre replied. They sat in the booth at the window overlooking Lake Apache.

Crispus swallowed his coffee, the warm liquid giving him a second wind. He hated interrogations. "How long have you and Kendali been together?"

"Before we split last week, about four years. We got together right around the time she was leaving the music business to started writing books."

"Split, you say?"

"Yeah. We had it out. She thinks I don't know she fucks around. Or she tries to pretend that she doesn't." He glanced out the window at the rippling lake. "Just got tired of being lied to."

"So, you think Kendali is seeing someone?"

"I know she is."

"Who do you think she is seeing?"

"Probably multiple guys." He straightened his torso pressing himself into the edge of the table and opined further. "Let me tell you something about Kendali. She is a video vixen in her core. The wild parties. Wild sex. Orgies. Drinkin'. Druggin'. All of that lifestyle affected and infected her. She may have simmered down, but there is still some of that shit inside her. Some of that life is just who she is."

"Okay. Is it true that you slapped her and threatened her on several occasions in public?"

"She told you that?"

"She did not."

"How do you know?"

"I am investigator, Mr. Walker. I get paid to find out things. To infer, perceive, draw conclusions and gather evidence to prove my conclusions."

"Yeah. Sure." Dre sucked in a deep breath. "That happened one time. Just once. She was actin' like a hoe. We were in the club together and she disrespected me. Letting this guy run his hand

194

up and down her hips and thighs while they were dancing. And then talked shit to me when I checked her on it. It was just a knee jerk response. She cussed at me. She was drunk. I was probably high. Before I even realized I had smacked her, her friend Tea was picking her up from the floor."

"I see." Crispus rested his back on the seat in the booth. "Did she make you angry often? And you had a knee jerk response?"

"I just told you that happened one time."

"Who is she seeing?"

"I don't know. Not for sure. But my best guess is Hiram. But there could be others."

"How long have you known about her infidelity?"

"Like I said, I don't know but I am pretty sure. And probably not too long after we started dating again."

"Again?"

"Well, we used to kick it way back when. As young kids. She went off to pursue her alleged acting career and I went to school for business."

"Okay. Cool."

"So we good? I gotta get back to work."

"Yeah, yeah. Everything is everything."

The two men slid out of the booth and shook hands goodbye. Dre left the diner and Crispus returned to his seat and made a note in his crumpled notepad with his favorite red pen, *"Dre medium-strong suspect"*. While Dre was cool, calm, collected, and seemingly honest, the boyfriend always had to be a suspect in any case like this one. And Crispus detected a temper in Dre that he obviously learned to control. Even so, he had the potential to be a stalker.

Wednesday 6:00 p.m.

195

After taking a long break running errands, checking in with Toussaint, having his car detailed, and enjoying a leisurely lunch, Crispus arrived at the home of Nikki Pennington. Isaac agreed to talk with him not knowing the discussion topic. Crispus simply told him he wanted to talk about industry happenings. Nikki's home was a standard two-story, colonial in Apache Meadows, a cookie cutter subdivision on the outskirts of the city. Nikki greeted him with her mocha fluffy cuteness dressed in a long, strapless, orange and white floral print sundress. Crispus was surprised by her attractiveness. He didn't expect her to be so pretty.

"Welcome to the Pennington Palace," she said as she stepped back to allow him to enter.

"Why thank you," he responded, trying to stop blushing at her beauty.

"We are in the study, working as always." She pointed to the door behind him, he turned, and crossed the threshold to see Isaac tapping on his computer. Nikki followed behind him and found her comfortable spot on the floor sorting books for shipment to several prisons and non-profit reading organizations.

"Hey, brother," Isaac said as he stood and gave Crispus a pound. "Make yourself at home." He gestured for Crispus to sit on the black leather sofa facing his work station.

"Thank you much." Crispus settled on the sofa and started his process. "So, how do you know Kendali Grace?"

"Is that what this is about?" He pushed away from his computer, positioning himself more directly in front of the investigator. "I thought you were some kind of reporter doing a story on urban fiction. Why are you asking me about Kendali?" Nikki's ears perked up as she continued her book packaging task.

"Well, I work for Dominion, and-"

"Aaah...ohhhhh...shiiid. Maaaan. You from the enemy camp."

Isaac put his hand over his face, mentally kicking himself for not paying more attention to Investigator Adam's' phone call. When he rang him, he was between errands, going into a meeting for Black Pearl, fielding texts from Nikki and his baby mama. He wanted to throw Crispus out, but he didn't want to create any suspicions in Nikki. "Okay. Go ahead. What do you want to know? And why are you asking me this?"

"Well, we are trying to clear up some things at Dominion. With the ghostwriting scandal. Rumors about Kendali. Hate mail."

"Oh really? Because we heard she might have a stalker."

"Maybe," Crispus offered with a stoic face. "So, about you and her..."

"I mean we dated a lil' bit. Went out a few times. Nothing serious."

"Nothing serious? You sure about that?"

"Yeah."

"My understanding is you were heavily involved and you didn't take it well when she broke it off."

"Didn't take it well? I mean she went her way, I went mine."

"Yeah, but not before you harassed her with threatening text messages and phone calls. Showing up unannounced at her shoots. True?"

"Well, that's a lil' exaggerated."

Nikki jumped up from the floor. "Nawl! It ain't exaggerated, nigga. Now it makes sense. Why you can't stay off her page! Why you always trolling her. Now I see. You ain't shit, Isaac Cole!" She flung her arms around like a maestro conducting a ghetto girl symphony, while popping her neck in a furious rhythm.

197

"I take it you didn't know your husband had been involved with Kendali?"

"Fuck no I ain't know! And this is not my husband. I'm married to Maceo Grant!" She glared at Isaac. "He always said you were a lame."

"Whoa, whoa, whoa. I'ma need you to calm down."

"You calm down! Fuck you, Isaac!

"Watch your mouth Nikki Pearl." He rose slowly from his chair.

"No. You watch it! How you ain't never, not one time say you were seein' this video hoe? Huh? AND, you were lightweight stalking her?" There was silence. Nikki crossed her arms, rolled her eyes, and leaned her weight on her right hip. Isaac remained still in his office chair. Crispus broke the silence.

"Well, I think I have everything I need. Thank you."

"Yeah, bruh." Isaac shot Crispus a mean stare. Crispus maintained an unemotional countenance as he left the residence. He sat in his car updating his notes, labeling Isaac's folder, with his red ink pen, *Medium-strong suspect*. He started his vehicle and headed home.

Wednesday, 6:30 p.m.

"I don't give a fuck! There must have been a reason for you keeping the relationship from me." Nikki was storming the closets, room by room, throwing Isaac's stuff into an oversize duffel bag she had slung over her shoulder. Isaac followed, on her heels as she cursed him and shouted her displeasure, disappointment, and betrayal. "You must still be fuckin' this bitch!"

"Nikki. I ain't fuckin' nobody but you. You know that, ma."

"I don't know shit!" she shouted tossing Air Jordan sneakers haphazardly into the bag. "A muthafuckin' stalker! This is some bullshit! I shoulda listened to my fuckin' huzzbin!" she roared in his direction. He leaned away in shock; she seemed to morph into a savage sphinx, the most beautiful monster he could have imagined, bulging eyes, wild mane, fangs, claws, and all.

"Nik! Stop!" He grabbed her slinging arm.

"Git da fuck offa meeeeeeeee!" The flames of her hot breath and angry words burned his skin, singed his soul. He retreated and accepted that he could not talk her down from the heights of her inferno.

"Nik, fuck it. I'm gone." He shuffled down the stairs.

"Yes! Get da fuck out!" Her throat burned as she hurled the duffle bag down the stairs behind him. It grazed him on his shoulder and tumbled toward the first floor, landing in the foyer before he did. He picked up the bag and left.

"Muthafuckaaaaaaaa!" she screeched, standing at the top of the stairwell. She heaved deep, long, slow breaths in and out of her lungs, pressing her back against the wall, head to the sky, and prayed for the serenity of the ancient Serengeti.

Chapter Eleven
Between Bree & Thee

Wednesday 8:30 p.m.

Nikki lingered in her Jacuzzi tub, Jill Scott playing low, a half empty glass of sangria marinating, and her phone abuzz with messages from Isaac. She snatched up her cellular device, ready to throw it across the bathroom, but she decided to silence the ringer instead. As she switched over to silent mode, she saw a text from Maceo blinking in the status bar.

📱 Text Messages 📱
Mace: Where you at?
Nikki: Home. Mad. What's up?
Mace: Mad? Why? What's goin' on?
Nikki: Isaac was questioned by Hiram's hired help. Dude named Cris. Older guy. Come to find out he and Kendali used to fuck.
Mace: Not surprising. She was a video hoe
Nikki: Yeah. But it seems like he was caught up. All in his feelings when she broke it off with him. The detective dude implied Ike had been stalking her.
Mace: 😂 😂
Nikki: I cannot believe you are laughing. I'm so pissed off. Now I see why he was so interested in keeping up with her on Zing.
Mace: 😂
Nikki: Fuck you Mace 😝
Mace: Look I know you're upset. But I been telling you the dude is a sucka ass nigga Those are sucka moves. Caught up by the video hoe 😂

Nikki: whatever. What do you want?

Mace: You ate already?

Nikki: Naw. Boys are at my mom's. Ike is with his people. He staying at his house. I threw him out with his duffle bag of nothing.

Mace: You hungry?

Nikki: Not really.

Mace: Not even for Deucey's?

Nikki: 😁 Maybe 😊

Mace: Come out with me for a lil' while. Pack a bag.

Nikki's clit throbbed, her belly quivered, and her grin wrapped around her head like the rings of Saturn.

Nikki: Okay.

Mace: I'll scoop you in about ten minutes.

Nikki: One 💜

She leapt from the tub, dried her body quickly, and twirled around on her tiptoes, pirouetting around the bathroom, happier than any prima ballerina popping up from a young girl's jewelry box. Her excitement and love for her husband filled her soul with an indescribable bliss. She oiled her skin with ginger body butter, applied some simple makeup-loose powder, eyeliner, lip liner, lip gloss, and slipped on a yellow tube top sundress. She pulled her weave up in a ponytail, brushed her bangs to the side, and cold curled one long tendril to dangle down her back. She grabbed her pre- packed overnight bag, locked up the house, and lounged on the porch until her husband arrived.

Maceo pulled into the cul-de-sac and watched his wife sashay down her flower laden walkway. She looked like living, breathing brown sugar. The long tube top dress flowed lusciously over her wide hips. Her lip gloss was poppin', her weave tight and toes right. Her beauty inspired him to feel like beating his chest and howling at the moon in his warrior call proclaiming that he had won the war of the worlds. *My pearl*, he thought. His nature rose, but he played it cool, for he had perfected his icy manner with her, focusing on their friend zone. He didn't want to fall into Nikki again. Not his pride, but his principle motivated him to create their very own 'globally warm' Antarctica. She crossed him, and for that, he could forgive but never forget.

"Hey, Mace." She slid into the passenger seat and hugged her husband. He always smelled so manly and intoxicating even after a long day. She secretly caught her breath and clutched her heart. "Hey Nik," He hugged her back, since warm friendly hugs were allowed in their Antarctica. He put her bag on the back seat. "You look nice."

"Thanks, Mace." Mild surprise washed over her spirit. He hadn't given her a compliment in years. Her Spidey senses activated; something must be going on with him. She wondered if he was going to ask for a divorce because he had found someone. Her belly felt nauseous. She abandoned the desire to divorce Maceo a long time ago and designed a comfortable space inside their married, but separated relationship. They started their journey toward the best chopped fish subs in the city. Smooth roads, the city's night lights, and Robert Glasper playing on Sirius made for an enchanting commencement of their night. "So, what's goin' on?"

"Same ole same ole. Bree is drivin' me fuckin' bananas. She makin' me hate her. I feel like I wanna kill her ass."

"Mace, don't even talk like that."

"Why not? Shit. Somebody gon' probably off her ass. Might as well be me."

"Nigga, you crazy."

"I'm for real. Like a mercy killing. We would sell a helluva lot of books. Fuh' sho'."

Her sweet chuckle swirled around the air conditioned truck.

"Mace, stop. You kill her, then you would have to kill yourself. You love Bree's ass. You'd be sick." Maceo flashed his light-up-the-night grin. "What she do now?"

"Her and that group. You know about the ghostwritin' shit?"

"Yeah."

"Yeah. Well, she is sellin' Hiram her intel."

"Dear Jesus."

"Yeah, exactly."

"Who's the source?"

"Shiiiiid. I don't know! And I don't wanna know. I told her, don't tell me shit. I ain't goin' back to jail for nobody and nothing."

"I know that's right."

"But she did tell me why she hates Hiram so much. She ain't never told nobody. So between me and you."

"Oh, always." Nikki's ability to squeeze a secret into non-existence was one of the main reasons Maceo loved her so much. She sucked secrets up into her succulent tight pussy, purged them out her fat juicy ass, and flushed them, gone forever.

"Dominion had a deal set up for her. All the trimmings. Advances. Everything. She refused to give Hiram some pussy. And she never heard a word from them again."

"Wow. So typical. Never again? No word? No letter of thanks, but no thanks?"

"Never. Nothing."

"Well, few people know Hiram like we do. He is a magician.

Con artist."

"Exactly. An illusionist. David Copperfield's Black bastard brother. The outside child."

Their laughter warmed their spirits as they drove into Deucey's packed parking lot.

Neither of them had been to Deucey's in a long time, so they were anticipating their delicious favorites with romantic nostalgia, the foods that fed their courtship over fifteen years ago. Maceo greeted the hostess and she put his name on the list. They turned to find a place to stand in the SRO waiting area. Deucey entered the restaurant.

"Maceo! Maceo wontcha blow!"

"Deucey!" Maceo and Deucey hugged, rocking each other side to side.

"How you doin', youngblood?" Deucey stepped back and looked at the son of his very good friend, Maceo's father.

"I'm doin' alright."

"Let me look at you. Aww, man." He grabbed Maceo for another hug. He released him again, feeling the spirit of his long gone friend. "It is good to see you, man. You gotta come around more. Ain't seen you in a long time."

"I know, Deuce. So busy, man. So busy."

"Yeah, I know. Me too. You still sellin' dem books, right?"

"Yeah. We still sellin' books."

Deucey noticed Nikki. "This ain't Nikki?"

"Yeah, it's me."

"Come here, girl." She stepped forward for her hearty hug from the neighborhood legend. He hugged her, almost sweeping her off of her feet. "You done filled all the way out, girl."

"Just a lil bit." She smiled.

"And still pretty as you can be."

"Awww, thanks, Mr. Deucey. It's good to see you."

"Y'all eatin' tonight?"

"Definitely. We waitin' to be seated."

"Waitin'? The hell you are. No sir. Y'all follow me. I still got the VIP section."

"For real? I always get takeout. I hadn't paid attention," Maceo remarked.

"Of course I do. And it's real nice now. Much nicer than when y'all was just goin together."

"You remember that, Deuce?"

He halted their VIP sojourn abruptly. "What? You damn right I do. You know I loved your father, Maceo. He was my brother."

Maceo never knew much about his father's death, just that it was a freak accident at the steel mill. His mother got a big settlement including college trusts funds for all five children. And she received a monthly allotment from his retirement in perpetuity.

"I know, Deucey. Brother from another mother."

"That's right," he replied, ushering them onto the refurbished deck facing the city's distant skyline. When Maceo and Nikki were going together it was a rickety porch. "How are the boys?"

"Awww, man. They good. So good."

"Yeah, good and crazy and gettin' on my nerves," Nikki chimed in.

Deucey laughed. "Now y'all order whatchu want. On the house. Your money ain't no good here."

"Now, Unc. I gotta spend some of this book money."

"Not here you won't." He playfully punched Maceo's shoulder with a one-two boxing move. "I love y'all. Enjoy your dinner."

"We love you too, Deuce," they replied in unison.

The icy lovers ate, talked, laughed, and enjoyed their chopped fish subs with everything-lettuce, tomatoes, cheese, fried onions, and hots. A big basket of hand cut Cajun fries served as the perfect complement, with fresh squeezed strawberry lemonade to wash down the hometown goodness and a whole coconut cake to go.

They arrived in Midtown at Maceo's condo located inside an old remodeled warehouse consisting of six gargantuan high-ceiling apartments. Maceo had an eye-catching mural of an urban street scene reminiscent of Ernie Barnes painted on the entire wall opposite the entrance. To the left, a full bathroom ran the width of the apartment. Right up above the bathroom was an open air loft style bedroom for the boys. To the right, the identical bedroom/bathroom layout was for Maceo. To the left of the entrance, there was a huge stainless steel kitchen. In the center of the apartment were two living spaces, arranged with bright colored orange, green, purple, and blue sofas, tables, and chairs. One had video gaming equipment, Lego sets, puzzles and overstuffed book shelves for Maceo and the boys. The other space had a TV, a pool table, an old arcade style Pac-Man machine, and a desk for Maceo's Gutta Butta home office. Nikki looked around for signs of a woman. There was nothing. He took her bag upstairs to the bedroom and came back down, full commando. "I'm gonna shower. You wanna come with me?" Nikki dropped her dress, naked under her clothes. Maceo was excited at the sight of her thickness. She followed him into the shower. They washed each other with careful caresses, three jet streams bubbling the soap on their bodies. Gently cupping her head, he pulled her face to his, and kissed her deeply, looping his tongue around hers. He pressed her body against the shower wall, raised her leg, and entered her center with mild force. She melted under the warm water, the orange ginger bath gel aroma igniting her libido. His steady strokes brought her close to orgasm; he stopped before she climaxed, turned off the water, stepped from the shower, and toweled off while she watched. After drying her body, he picked her up and laid her over his shoulder. She gasped at his strength. He fingered her pussy with his free hand while he carried her up the stairs rubbing her clit until a head-bobbing orgasm racked her spirit. The throbbing wetness delighted his fingers as he pushed deeper inside her pussy. He laid her limp, pleasure-filled body on the bed and sailed deep inside her ocean, his dick growing wider inside her as he increased his speed.

"Mace, I'm not taking anything. You gotta pull out, babe," she whispered.

"Yeah, yeah okay." He kept sailing, full force.

"Ooh, baby. But I'm not taking anything, Mace," she murmured.

"So what? You my wife." He mastered the navigation of her sweetness, riding all her waves as a skilled commodore. "Damn! I still fuckin' love yo' ass!" He swirled around her rushing waters, high tide approaching and she responded arching her back to his erotic command.

"I love you, Mace. And I'm so sorry. For everything." She held tightly onto his shoulders as he rocked her into another climax.

"I know you are." He palmed her ass pulling her harder onto his dick as he smashed his body into her fluffiness.

"Yes, but you gon' pull out, honey?"

"Stop, Nik. I ain't concerned," he panted, lost in the enjoyment of her feminine wiles.

"But we have two boys. Mace, please," she pleaded in his ear. Hanging onto him and holding his neck, weak with multiple orgasms, her pussy tightened, locked up around his dick involuntarily. He growled and moaned.

"Nik! Oooo... Don't worry me 'bout that now. Might be that girl comin'. Yeah! Ummm…Ya' pussy, Nik! Why?! Why can't I get this feeling anywhere else? Huh, guhl?" he whimpered.

"I don't know, Mr. Grant."

And there it was. He exploded inside her, pulled out, then man-squirted all over her, making a sloppy mess.

"Aaaaaaaaahhhhhhhhhhhhhh, baaaaybee. I love you, Mrs. Grant." He plopped onto her voluptuous bosom face-first and sunk his muscular physique into her pillow soft comfort.

"I love you too."

She lay under him in cosmic contentment, as they floated on the ecstasy of their passion. *Well, I guess he doesn't want a divorce.*
♥♥♥

Wednesday, 9:30 p.m.

Bree skipped to her car, leaving Featherstone Town Center after an evening of shopping with her Dominion "settlement". *Ten G's? Ha! That's the least the nigga owes me. I didn't even add pain and suffering. Sorry muthafucka.* She shook off her thoughts of Hiram and turned her attentions to the goodies in her bags. She bought sundresses, sandals, and sunglasses, all the things a girl needs to enjoy an exotic beach. As she approached her car, she saw a small gift bag sitting on the trunk. She stopped and scanned the parking lot and surrounding area, slowly looking up, down, under cars, around poles, at the mall entrances, and the traffic lights in the distance. There were no people in close proximity, but there were a few restaurant goers at the Seminole Grill about eight hundred feet away. She decided it was safe to investigate the little gift bag. Just as she started peeping inside, a white van pulled up behind her. A man in all black, wearing dark shades, jumped from the van, lightning speed, pushed her face down on her car and held her down with a .45 at the base of her spine. She screamed for help and he pushed the barrel deeper into her flesh rendering her silent. She choked on her hollow screams, coughing up tears. The assailant kept the gun steady on her spine and snatched her purse from her shoulder and several of her shopping bags from her wrist. He tossed the stolen goods in his van, knocked her to the ground, and sped away. A few of the restaurant goers made their way to her side.

"Are you okay?" Bree lay unresponsive, but totally conscious; eyes wide open purging raindrop size tears, and mouthing words without voice. "My boyfriend is calling 911, okay?" the comforter said holding Bree's hand. She rose up from the concrete slightly, gave everyone around her a once over, and fainted. An hour later, she regained her senses, awakened by the voice of an attending nurse at Seminole City General.

"Welcome back, Ms. McDaniels. Everything is okay. You are in a safe place." The nurse smiled down at her as she lay on the hospital bed. She tried to push herself up, but her arms were hurting.

"Where's my purse? I need to call my brother."

"You don't have a purse, Ms. McDaniels. We actually got your name from the police. They ran your vehicle tag number. They want to talk to you." The nurse spoke to her in the standard sing-song voice that they are trained to use for bedside manners. "Just relax for now," she patted Bree's shoulder, motioning her to lean back. Bree resisted.

"No! I need to call my brother. That muthafucka took my purse, didn't he? Shiiiit!"

"Ms. McDaniels, please calm down."

"I will not! I gotta call my brother."

"Okay. Okay." She nervously hustled to the other side of the bed, placed the phone on the overbed table, and positioned it close to Bree so she could call Maceo.

"Thanks." She dialed him. He didn't answer. She dialed again. He picked up.

"This better be good."

"Maaaaaaaaay~ceeee~ohhhhhh," she wailed.

"Bree? What?! What is it?" He untangled himself from the good lovin' aftermath snuggle of Nikki Pearl and sat up on the bed."

"I'm in the hospital," she sobbed.

"What hospital, Bree? What happened?" He swerved his body around and put his feet in his slippers.

She choked on her words, snot and spittle running down her mouth and chin. "Seminole General. Emergency room." She coughed. "I don't know what happened. Come get me, Mace. Just come get me."

"Aight. I'm on my way."

Maceo dressed quickly in shorts, a t~shirt, and sneakers. He pulled his .45 from the closet as Nikki watched him. "Not the heat, Mace? You not even supposed to have that, babe."

"Tell that to the streets."

"Sweet Jeeeezzzuz! Maceo!"

"Nikki. I don't know what's goin' on, so I gotta prepare for the worst."

"I'm goin' with you," she insisted climbing from the bed sheets.

"No. I think you should stay here. Just chill. I'll be back."

"No. I'm comin'. Y'all might need some help." She eased into her sundress and sandals.

"Nik. C'mon…"

"Maceo, I don't care what you say. I'm comin' with you. Now, we wastin' time arguing."

"Fine. Fuck it." He went back to the closet and retrieved a .38 for her. "For you, my pearl." He gave her the gun. She gave him an Eskimo kiss and dropped the weapon in her purse.

"Datz my Mr. Grant, Cavalry Commander In Chief. When the streets call..."

"Regretfully, I'm still answering."

🔫🔫🔫

"I'm not talkin' to no po-po!" Bree screeched at the three nurses attending to her. She had been screaming, yelling, and shouting about her ordeal since she regained consciousness.

"Ms. McDaniels," one of the nurses began. "I am reminding you, you need to calm down or we will have to remove you from the hospital or sedate you and take you to the sixth floor."

Bree lowered her voice into an angry hum speaking through pursed lips and gritting teeth. "I don't care about the sixth floor and no removal and no police. You sedate me if you want, I will sue this hospital into the ground."

"Ms. McDaniels," another nurse chimed in. "You have suffered some trauma. You are in shock...and pain. Let me give you a shot for the pain. Just to relax you while you wait for your brother."

"I don't want it! I told you already!" Bree continued to throw her tantrum, refusing their advice.

Ten minutes later, Maceo and Nikki hurried into the hospital and asked the triage receptionist about Bree. "Aubrey McDaniels, please," Maceo said.

"I don't want it!" Bree shouted again.

The receptionist's eyes filled with embarrassment. "That's okay. I hear her." Maceo walked away from the reception desk toward Bree's cries. Nikki followed close behind.

"Sir!" the coordinator beckoned. "You have to sign in. I need your ID."

"Nikki, handle that, babe," he ordered, giving her his wallet.

"I got it." Nikki walked back to the coordinator to fulfill the visitor registration process. Maceo found Bree cussing and fussing at the nursing staff.

"Bree!" Pain welled up in his chest looking at her bruised face and arms. She had a bloody bandage on the side of her forehead and two on her calf and shin. Her eyes were bloodshot and her cheeks puffy with dried tears.

"May-cee-ohhh," she wailed. He hugged her tightly rocking her into his chest.

"Mr.?" a nurse asked.

He looked at her. "Grant."

"Your sister is in shock. She was robbed, we think. Brought in from Featherstone Town Center. No purse. No phone. Bruised. Not beaten, thankfully. The police are en route. She doesn't seem to remember much and she doesn't want to talk to the police."

"Okay. Thank you. I got her. We will take her home."

"She really needs to stay and talk to police."

"That's fine," he replied.

"Okay. We will leave you." The nurses exited and Nikki entered. Bree looked up from Maceo's chest.

"Niiiiik-keeeeeee," she whined stretching her arms out for her embrace.

"Awwwwww, Bree-wee." Nikki cradled her, rubbing her back and patting the side of her face. "What happened, babe?"

212

"I dunno." She raised her head slightly. "I was robbed. Dude came outta nowhere. Snatched my purse. My bags. And took off. He had a gun, pressed at my back. I thought he was gonna kill me." She boohooed and Nikki consoled her with loving arms. Maceo watched the love radiate between his two favorite women, his heart thankful for them, but he had to interrupt with the hard question. "Bree." She slowly turned her head to observe his countenance for the first time since they arrived. She resisted eye contact. "Did you take that money from Hiram?"

"I knew you were gonna think that, Mace." She buried her head in Nikki's bosom.

"Uh-huh." Maceo vigorously rubbed his cue ball head with frustration. "Gotdammit, Bree. You have no idea what you have done."

"What? I was robbed."

"Right. Who da fuck you think robbed you?"

"I don't know," she retorted sitting up on the hospital bed. Nikki sat beside her.

"Bree-wee, Hiram got his money back, sis." She patted Bree's thigh tenderly. Bree's jaw dropped, her swollen eyes blinking rapidly.

"Yeah. You got it," Maceo growled. "Now, you see? You see this shit? Now whatchu think I'm gonna do?"

"Aaaahhhhhhh...aarrrgghh," she wailed, slamming her head onto Nikki's shoulder. Nikki kept rubbing her thigh.

"It's gonna be okay, sis." She balled more intensely, her shoulders jerking up and down in agony.

"Nik, take care of her. I will see you back at my place."

Nikki glared at him sternly. "Maceo..." her voice was filled with warning.

"Nik, that's it. No discussion, boo. I'm out." She lowered her eyes, acquiescing to her husband's mandate. He kissed her lips, rubbed Bree's back, and left the hospital.

❤ ❤ ❤

Wednesday, 11:30 p.m.

Hiram rose from the bar stool at Nina's, his favorite watering hole.
"Aight, B. I'm gone."
"You cool, bruh?" the bartender asked the mildly inebriated, deeply troubled publisher. The stalker, the bodyguards, the cyber security team, and the envelope were heavy on his mind. Missing the comfort of Kendali's uninhibited womanly pleasures aggravated his depression.
"Yeah. I'm aight. Be easy, my man."
"You too."
Hiram strode to his Range Rover, fumbled for his truck key, and surveyed the dimly lit parking lot. All was quiet amongst the cars of Nina's patrons. He located his keys from his suit jacket pocket and hit the remote start button. Suddenly, a figure appeared in the distance. He reached for his gun and remembered that he put it in the glove box before he went into Nina's. *Shit!*
The silhouette of a man called out, drawing his own gun from its holster, "Hold on, there, my man. Hold up. Wait on it." The gunman aimed directly at Hiram's head.
Hiram raised his arms, dropping his suit jacket and truck key.
"I'm unarmed. I don't want no trouble. My wallet is in my right pocket. Truck key is right here on the ground."
"Don't nobody want your truck, nigga."

214

Hiram recognized the voice. "Maceo?"

"Yeah, nigga." Hiram lowered his arms. "No. Hands up, Hiram."

"Mace, are you serious? You just gon' shoot me? Right here? Right now? Just like this?"

"Naw. I ain't come for that. I hope. But I saw you draw."

"Right. Draw nothing. My heat is in the truck."

Maceo glanced at the SUV. "So you say."

"Bruh, what the fuck? I just came out for a drink. Check me out." Hiram turned around slowly, arms still raised. Maceo walked up on him quickly and patted him down. He kept his finger on the trigger. "I told you. I'm unarmed."

"Aight. I ain't know. I got this toast on me. I saw you draw." Maceo searched Hiram once more to be sure. "Thought I was leavin' this shit alone with the book publishing, man. Here I am, right back in street mode with a lynch mob attitude." Maceo shoved him. "You had Bree worked over? Took ya' money back?"

"Worked over? What?"

"Yeah. She's in the hospital."

"Hospital?" Hiram shook his head in disbelief.

"Yeah, hospital nigga. I oughta shoot ya' ass right now."

"Go ahead. You will probably be doing the world a favor." Maceo stepped back, surprised by Hiram's response. "What? You suicidal or something, nigga?" he asked with perplexed brow.

"Naw, bruh. Just tired. I got a lot bigger problems than Bree and the hospital. Is she alright?"

"No. But she will be. She's more in shock than anything. A few bruises." Maceo relaxed and put his gun on safety. "But I know you responsible witcha grimy ass."

"Look, man-"

"Don't try to lie Hiram. Just fix it. I don't wanna have to kill you, nigga."

"You ain't the only one know his way around a gun, Maceo."

"Oh, I know ya' ass. For real. You got these muthafuckas fooled. Like you some kinda silver spoon in ya' mouf type nigga. From a family of politicians, lawyers, doctors, and over-achievers. I know y'all the biggest gangsters out here. That's why I'm tellin' you what I'm tellin' you. Fix it, Hiram! Fix it fast!" Maceo started toward his truck. Hiram leaned on the Range Rover with its engine purring.

"Fuck you, Mace. For real."

"Yeah, whatever, nigga," he yelled over his shoulder waving his .45 in the air.

Hiram hopped in his driver's seat and dialed Crispus.

"Yo-yo!"

"Nigga! This was supposed to be clean. No muss, no fuss. A fuckin' untraceable grab and go!"

"What's up? What's goin' on?"

"Bree got hurt. She's in the hospital. Now Maceo is out for blood. My blood!"

"Gottdammit! I knew I should have waited. My usual guy was booked. I used another dude. Fuck! Gotdamn millennials. Shit!"

"I oughta take this outta your pay. Cuz I gotta make this right. I didn't want her hurt. And it was supposed to look random and untraceable."

"I know, man. Look, let me take care of it."

"No. Don't worry about it. I will handle it. Just get rid of that dumb muthafucka on ya' payroll. Keep him outta my muthafuckin' business."

"It's already done."

"Good. I'm gone."

"Peace, bruh." Hiram raced from Nina's parking lot. A deep craving for Kendali's gourmet loving flooded his soul, but Georgette's standard fare would have to suffice.

Chapter Twelve
Flies, Fires, & Fucks

Monday/Tuesday Midnight Morning Wee Hours

*Ha! Did they honestly think the cyber security specialist was
gonna stop me? Certified absurdity. I will have her. She is for
me. So, I will alter my movement and that is okay. Take your
servers back; all that I need is in my possession. And I can still
follow, Her Graceful Majesty. They don't know that I cloned her
new phone. They have no idea who I am.*

Naked, drenched in moonlight beaming in from the windows,
beads of sweat twinkling on his body like the stars, he kneeled
on the prie dieu and commenced his praying ritual for the love of
his life, Her Majestic Grace, Kendali. Seventeen candles burning
around the room filled the homemade temple with vanilla
lavender fragrance. He prayed that God would rip her from
Hiram's hold.

*He is so beneath you, my love. He does not deserve the sweet
taste of your flesh, pure honey on the tongue. He has corrupted
your purity and he must be dealt with. Everyone around you has
sullied your soul. Except for Dre, maybe. He seems a good guy,
but he has no clue what to do with you.*

He paused and lit a vanilla candle, then dipped his fingertips in a
small teacup of lavender oil. He anointed his forehead and
continued praying.

I am glad you are recovering from the ghostwriting exposure. I didn't want to hurt you. I don't even like Bree, but I know she envies you, Grace Amazing. You are an enviable force. I was so angry with you. You are still with Dre and you give yourself to the poisonous clutches of Hiram Rivers! The scoundrel of all scoundrels! How could you?! This discovery almost destroyed my passion for you, but alas! My love is too strong to be annihilated by your obvious insanity, a temporary, curable disposition. My need for you is too powerful to be decimated by Hiram's ravenous desire to control and contaminate everything in his grasp.

He frothed at the mouth and squeezed his hands tightly together, cracking his knuckles. He stood and stretched his arms out in front of the life size poster of Kendali, his thick phallus mildly erect, saluting the night and the goddess, Grace. Humming *Amazing Grace*, he ended his prayer, in the same way he always did.

In time, you will be mine. With Grace.

Wednesday, 10:00 a.m.

"Will that be all, Georgette?"
"Yes. That's it for now."
Tiyanna saw her proposal one sheet on top of Georgette's pile of tasks resting in the center of her desk. "What do you think of my idea?"

219

Georgette wrinkled her brow and her nose with perplexity. "Come again?"

"For Kendali's final release? The video shoot theme?" Tiyanna reminded.

"Oh, yeah. We'll see. Not sure if it will work. But we'll see."

"You know I really wanna transition into the marketing department and focus on promotions."

"I do know. And I am going to take care of you. I told you this. I haven't forgotten." She rolled her chair away from her computer screen, toward the messy pile of papers, mostly contracts and other legal documents.

"Okay. Thanks, Georgette. I really appreciate it."

"You are very welcome."

Tiyanna turned to leave, passing Kendali who was entering Georgette's office.

"Hey, Tiy."

"Hi, Kendali." Tiyanna closed the door behind her.

"Hey, Georgie."

Georgette smirked and rolled her eyes slowly, batting her lashes rapidly. "Gurrrrrrl...What the hell you got on these niggas?" Georgette stretched out in her office chair and propped her feet on her desk. Kendali plopped in the cushy armchair, grinning.

"Calls still comin' in?"

"Hell yeah. Mo is goin' crazy. And so is AJ."

"Why y'all got Mo fielding calls?"

"Because it's heavy duties callin'. Damn near heads of state and shit. Executives." She walked over to her wet bar and poured herself a smoothie from the blender. "Care for a green drink?"

"No, I'm good. I had my oatmeal."

"Hiram got sick of 'em and you know controversy is not my

area. He went to his right hand, of course."

"Of course. Poor Mo," Kendali lamented, smoothing out the wrinkles of her cobalt blue linen sundress.

"Yes. Poor Mo." Georgette tasted the cucumber melon spinach smoothie and sat at her desk. "Mmmm, good." She placed the beer mug of green goodness on a coaster and asked again, "Kendali, what do you have on these kneegrows?"

"Girl, nothing that no one else would have on them, if you are paying attention. Like I said on the show, it's all happening right in front of your face."

"Hmmm. I may need me a sneak peek. I ain't know you were throwin' down like that."

"Yeah. It's about time. People should know what they are celebrating in these celebrities. It's a sleazy, grimy business. And we all need to get clear."

"I hear you, Sista Souljah!" Georgette pumped her fist in the air and Kendali chuckled. "Okay. Did you wanna chat about anything specific?"

"Not really." Kendali shook her head. "How long we gonna be under cyber surveillance? I still can't believe they took our phones."

Georgette sighed. "I don't know how much longer. We should have an update soon."

"And I am so tired of having a bodyguard. I mean, Black is cool, but I wanna get back to normal."

"I know. Patience, Grace. Patience."

If only Georgette knew that Kendali was asking because she wanted to fuck her husband more freely. She despised herself from time to time for the transgression since Georgette treated her like a sister. Sometimes she imagined that Georgette knew of their affair and just didn't care.

221

"Yes, patience." Kendali started to rise from her chair. Georgette paused her exit, handing her Tiyanna's one sheet proposal. "Hold on. Take this with you. Look it over. Let me know if you like."

Kendali skimmed the sheet and stomped her feet on the floor joyfully. "You know I love it! A video shoot theme for my release? Georgie, you know we goin' out with a bang! I'm so excited!"

"I am too."

"Okay. I will review the details and get back to you." She wiggled her hips enthusiastically to the door.

"I am so glad you like, Grace."

"I love!" She blew her a kiss and left.

"Tiy Tiy!" Kendali greeted the cute face girl seated outside Mrs. Rivers' office. "Look what Georgette has planned for my release!" She gave Tiyanna the document, flying it into her hand like a paper plane.

"Uh-huh." Tiyanna fanned the paper nonchalantly, giving it back to Kendali after barely a glance. "Mmmph. Nice."

"It's gonna be a blast!"

"Yeah, it is." Tiyanna covered her anger with a phony smile. "Enjoy your day, girl."

"You too." Kendali continued to her office and Tiyanna feverishly pulled her phone from her bag.

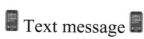 Text message

Tiyanna: This bitch needs to be laid down. I fuckin' hayte her !!!!!!!!

Darla: What now?

Tiyanna: I just gave this bitch the idea for Kendali's finale release party. She passed it off to Kendali as HER IDEA! BIIIIITCH!!!!!!

Darla: I told you to stop fuckin' with her. She's a thief. And she doesn't have your back and she is not going to look out for you.

Tiyanna:

Darla: Chin up, buttercup! It's going to be okay. I told you. You should move in with mommy and start your business.

Tiyanna: I don't want to do that.

Darla: okay. well, keep sitting there dealing with the liars, lovers, and thieves.

Tiyanna: aaaargh! whatever

Darla: ijs

Tiyanna: I feel homicidal. like I seriously wanna kill this bitch

Darla: Tiy. Quit it. Pull yourself together, sis. You know you jive psychotic.

Tiyanna: I am serious.

Darla: I know! That's why I am telling you to leave it alone. She probably got a serious condition. Kleptomania. It's real.

Tiyanna: I heard of that. But I always think rich white women

Darla: Well she a rich Black woman. So, hey

Tiyanna: You think she klepto? Wow. What you think wrong with her?

Darla: No telling. She married to Hiram. That money. That business. All that corporate madness. Just everything. You never know what's goin' on with people. But you, sweet sister, need to get out of it.

Tiyanna: Fine. But she still needs to be erased. You probably right. I need to start my own.

Darla: Eggszacklee! Love you, sis

Wednesday, 12 Noon

"You don't eat lunch?" Crispus looked around Hiram's office hoping he had some sort of inviting spread for them to partake. "You should be 500 hundreds pounds with that appetite." Hiram bristled at Crispus' hunger.

"I burn up a lot of calories in this work. And I jog. So...But it *is* lunchtime." Crispus raised an eyebrow with a sheepish half smile. He still felt disappointing sadness because of the Bree incident. The contractor's name was deleted from his phone for good.

"Damn, Crispus! I just need you to focus on this meeting. Tell me what's goin' on. We are ready for closure. Wrap this thing up."

Crispus dropped his messenger bag on the floor, took a seat at the office work table, and commenced setting up his work station. Hiram called Rica and told her to order KD's for lunch.

"I appreciate you, bruh. KD's always hits the spot."

"It's nothing, man. And you gotta understand my frustration. Lot on my mind." Hiram sat in the chair next to his fixer and put his tablet on the table.

"I know. But rest easy. We good."

"You think?"

"I know." Crispus organized Toussaint's investigative reports on the work table. "Now, for the most part these are for your records. Toussaint will email all of this to you eventually. It's a lot of tech jargon that reads like Greek, so we focus on the summaries."

"Good. What's the final word?"

"You *were* hacked. By whom, we are uncertain. We traced the hacker to a concentrated area in West Village. It's a needle in a haystack kind of thing, but we did get a photo of who we think the hacker was."

"Word?"

"Yeah." Crispus slid a surveillance camera photo in front of Hiram. Hiram studied the picture of a man entering the coffee shop, Common Grounds, dressed in all black, with a baseball cap pulled down on his head. His face was not visible. "I know there isn't much there. But you have any idea who it could be?"

"Can't see him. Why do you think this is the hacker?"

"Toussaint and his folks traced a few hacks to the shop. For the most part, hacker guy kept himself inside the haystack, but it seems for some reason, on a few occasions, he may have used Common Grounds wi-fi, or hacked their servers. May have connected to some kind of satellite signal around the shop for whatever he was doing."

"Hmmm. Kendali frequents Common Grounds. A lot of us in the industry go there. Black owned. Discounts. Good service. Excellent coffee. And they stay open late." Hiram studied the photo. "I can't see nothing. We can conclude he is a Black man."

"Yeah. And not much more. But Toussaint did say he is probably taller. Maybe six foot one. With a solid build."

"Hmmm. Okay."

"And he is smart. Well-versed in cyber technology. So, it is not a definitive conclusion, but a conclusion nonetheless. And he isn't following Kendali anymore. Is she getting gifts? Any more flowers?"

"Naw. Nothing."

"Yeah. He abandoned that stalker plan. He knew we were onto him after the chase. But he got a lot of dirt on y'all. Anything on those servers, he has it. That is, whatever info he wants."

"Wow." Hiram thought about his mysterious envelope. "Whatever he wants?"

"Yeah. Including this." Crispus placed a black folder on the table. Hiram opened the folder and leafed through the pages. He released a heavy sigh and rolled his eyes up to the ceiling.

"Yeah. You need to fix that, bruh. Toussaint did you a favor and cleaned up the tracks of your code, but you need to make this right."

"Yeah. Okay." Hiram replied.

"I'm serious Hiram. This is not good. If ole boy hacker has this, he can prove-"

"I know. I know. I get it."

"Don't take this lightly, bruh. If anything does come out, it will look better if you have already fixed it."

"I said I get it, bruh. I get it."

"Where did you learn this? You been taking computer courses?"

"Naw, no course. White dude showed me a while back. Tech geek. Made a lotta money in apps. I sold him a commercial building. He still has his HQ in that building. He taught me how to do it."

"Maaaaaaaan, you better-"

"Bruh, I got it. I'ma handle it."

"Okay. Meanwhile, Toussaint is trashing the old phones. It's better to start over he says. The replacement phones he thinks should be trashed and another round of new phones ordered. Kendali's phone was definitely hacked and everyone at Dominion that she communicates with. Toussaint is dismantling your databases and setting up fresh servers with all new cyber security packages. The latest and greatest state of the art software. You may need to add him to your payroll for a little while."

"How long?"

"A year, maybe. Gives him ample time to set everything up and monitor its efficiency."

"I can live with that. But this hacker dude. What's next?"

"Honestly, Hiram, this is a wait and see. *You* have to think about who it could be. Go back over your enemy lists. You and Kendali. You all know better than we do who wants to cause you trouble. It's somebody y'all know. And I am still sticking with the hacker and the stalker being the same dude. I'm certain."

"Yeah. Yeah. Okay." Hiram was displeased with the overall outcome. He wanted this dude found and silenced. Forever. "I need you to stay on this, Cee. You need to find this guy and shut him up. Destroy the evidence of all of this. And shut this nigga up. Permanently."

"Well, I need y'all to give up those enemies. I will keep my eye on the string of suspects I have from Kendali, but you never gave me anything."

"No, I didn't."

"Right. You gotta give me some leads. And see who else is on Kendali's list."

"Yeah. Her list has grown since this Vixen Notebook Myesha Morgan interview."

"See? This is what I'm saying. Who wants to destroy y'all. And the hacker dude may be a hired hand. Could be working for someone. Keep that in mind."

"Well, you are still on this case. And I need you *ON IT!*"

"I gotchu. Give me some leads. I will monitor Tasir, Isaac, Emory, and Dre."

"Isaac? You think he's a strong lead?"

"Well, he didn't tell his current girlfriend about his thing with Kendali."

"Yeah, so?"

"Well, why wouldn't he tell Nikki? I mean it's just a past relationship. Why not say?

"There could be a lotta reasons. That don't make him a stalker."

"That is absolutely true. But there could be a lotta reasons why, that *does* make him the stalker. You see?"

"Hmmm, yeah. I do see" Hiram rubbed his goatee, hoping that Isaac was the culprit. He would be easy to kill.

"Meanwhile, get your stories together in case hacker dude wants to go public with your malfeasance. You know how to tell stories. Fortunately, that is what y'all do. Write stories."

"Yeah. We do. We do know how to spin a tale."

///

Monday, 4:00 p.m.

"Gurrrrl...Now, is really not the best time." Monique pulled her long, straight locks into a bun at the nape of her neck."

"I understand. Go ahead. We can talk later." Monique detected a sadness in Priscilla's voice. She had to check in.

"Okay. Wait. Are you crying, babe?"

"Yeah-sss." Priscilla sobbed, drying her tears with Bounty paper towels, hugging the roll, stretched out across her bed. Monique rubbed her temples and situated herself on her office couch, feet on the coffee table, latte close by to listen to Priscilla's woes. Priscilla was the owner, operator of Prose Nose Editing and Writing Services, Dominion's first and foremost editing contractor. Her company handled eighty five percent of Dominion's business. "Okay, sista girl. Go ahead."

"Gurrrrrl…she just cussed and cussed and cussed. And you know I don't even play that. But gurl…" Priscilla slurred.

"Are you drunk?"

"Probably," she replied taking another gulp of Hennessy.

"Lawd Jesus. Okay. Who are we talkin' about?"

"Princess J."

"Okay, this gon' be real extra."

"Yes, extra. She is big mad. Talkin' about suin' Dominion. She cussed Hiram DA FUCK out."

"When? He didn't tell me about this? What happened?"

"It just went down today. Bottomline: she attended a writers retreat. Everyone there is a published author. Different types of fiction. They are there to exchange ideas, information, helpful tips. You know, typical retreat."

"Yeah. Okay."

"Anyway, they do writing prompts, writing critiques and ultimately it seems she kept getting a lot of negative feedback from various writers. She got mad about it and showed out. Told the people they was haters. But the organization's directors are award winning urban fiction novelists; they pulled her up to say, like, Yo, ma. You just need to take an English class or a writing class to tighten up your skills. They gave her the info on a hip-hop novelist who specializes in writing proper urban hood books with good English skills. She was hotttttttttttt."

"Damn." Monique lay her whole body flat on the sofa.

"They gave her several critiques from industry professionals and they all told her the same thing."

"Wowwww."

"She blames me. Told me I'm supposed to be a muthafuckin' editor and I ain't editing shit but shit."

"Whaaat?"

"I just asked her not to post anything on social media. Hiram asked her too. She said she wouldn't."

"Damn. You believe her?"

"I don't know. We will see. She say she didn't know the different grades of editing. I told her we don't do developmental editing."

Monique sipped her latte. "Hmmm. She threatened a lawsuit? Based on what?"

"I didn't understand all the legal talk she was spewing. I just apologized over and over and over again. She didn't hear me though."

"You do the best you can. I don't think you owe an apology."

"Yeah. We do. We all do. We know we are just crankin' out books. We know this. We all pretending, Mo."

"Well, I just thought we were giving it our best shot. I thought everybody was doing a good job."

"Yeah. But am I? Am I doing my best?"

"We do what we do. This is a niche market. Niche audience. Don't trip. We will handle it."

"I just can't take anymore right now. I have too many health challenges to withstand these legal threats. And oh my god. You read The Kaleidoscope?"

"You know I did."

"Direct attack on me. I'm just so tired, Mo." Priscilla blew her nose.

"Don't worry about lil' Miss Butterfly and her lil' blog. We will handle it. And Princess J is a gnat. She always has been. I told

Hiram not to sign her messy ass. So, the fly, the gnat, and any other flies. They're just bugs. We will swat them."

"I hear you, but she blames us for not being nominated for a Platinum Quill."

"Yeah. Cuz Princess J really thought she was gonna be nominated. I told her in a nice way not to get her hopes up, but she didn't get it."

"Oh gawwwd." Priscilla blubbered, drinking her last swig of Hennessy.

"Priscilla, stop. Pull yourself together. We got this. Trust, it's a small thing. I been puttin' out fires all day. This is not a fire." Monique sat up. "I told you, issa gnat! Issa fly!" she said in a little girl cartoon voice.

Priscilla chuckled. "Okay, Mo."

"This will pass. Don't worry. Stop drinking. Take your meds and go to bed."

"Okay. I will."

"I will check on you later."

"Thanks, Mo."

"And stop drinking."

"I will. I promise."

"Alright. Rest up, sweetie."

"Bye, Mo."

Monique buried herself in the cushions of the couch wishing an escape hatch would miraculously appear. She imagined that she could toss a disc on the floor like they did in cartoons and jump through, disappearing forever. Long deep breaths were her salve in the moment. Her cold latte proved ineffective. The day had been fire after fire and she still had to confront Hiram. Her conversation with Thaddeus, earlier in the day, played in her head:

"Yeah, Mo. Ya' boy don't wanna take my calls. But since you his do-girl…"

"Do-girl? Hold up, nigga. Wait."

"Nigga? Yeah, I gotcha nigga?"

"Wait. Who is this anyway?"

"It's Thad."

"Hold on. What's goin' on, Thaddeus?" Mo liked Thaddeus. Dope pen game. Damn good writer. Visionary. And passionate as hell.

"Look, Mo. No disrespect, but Hiram is not taking my calls. Having Rica hand me off to his lil' accounting whores."

"Tell me what's up."

"I want the actual printout of sales from Muse. And I am entitled to this info."

"Yes, you are."

"I know. But I am pretty sure Hiram is a thief. Hiram betta run me my muthafuckin' dough, Mo. I ain't nun of his lil' idolizing eatin' out his ass whores."

"Thad. No worries. I got it. He will call you."

"Yeah, he betta. Or he gon' find out how real the Black Blood Gang is. It ain't just a book. Cuz I will eat his ass alive."

"Lawd, Thad. I gotchu. No worries."

"Aight. Peace."

"Bye, Thad."

And if that wasn't enough, Lesli Lyn wrote a scathing blog that included some of Dominions top selling writers. Empowered by Maya Walker Bambara's acknowledgement, Lesli wrote more brutally honest blogs. Here tell, The Kaleidoscope readership skyrocketed after Maya's interview. Monique hated Lesli. She was a writer of superior skill, no doubt, no question. She just wished she would shut the hell up. Just shut up about the industry. She always had something to say. Monique engaged in a bit of self-torture rereading Lesli's blog, still lounging on her sofa, deciding how she was going to approach Hiram about the day's episodes. It was her third read:

Beloved Butterflies

I greet you in silky, soft-winged peace.

When I tell you that reading some of these books is like experiencing Groundhog Day over and over, and over, you'd better believe it. The rampant and reckless repetition of the same word in a sentence is unnecessary. Why are we repeatedly repeating ourselves? I just read the following in a book by one of urban fiction's most popular authors, Princess J (Dominion Publishing): "I opened the door to the store and walked inside the store." Store, and then store again. Really?

Here is another example from another fairly popular author at Dominion, Felicity Sparks:
"The sun beamed through the window as she stared out the window."
Window, then window again. Huh? I really want to cuss right here, but I refrain.

These sentences *are* grammatically correct, yet terribly written. Repetition of words in a sentence like this is a no-no for writers and authors who have any respect for the craft. Why is the author repeating the obvious? We know where you are and where you're going. It's ridiculous and aggravating. Readers, rebel! Do not accept authors weighing you down with poorly written work, dumbing down your brain and numbing your desire for good writing.

How in the entire hell are these editors and publishers letting this slide? Are we strictly running content mills now? Is the new creed for the craft, dollars before diligence? Dollars before details, development, and dedication? All quantity, no quality? How serious are we about what we scribe with our quills? No one is above taking a course or a class to enhance their skill set. Including me. Here is a website that offers a variety of assistance:

www.stepyapengameup.com

It's Double L~ Silky, Soft, & Signing Off...Float On 🦋

"Aaargh!" Monique yelled at the air. "She couldn't leave the names out?! Uggghh! I don't think she's ever named names!" She closed her eyes and took a deep breath. "But then again, maybe she has. But not like this." Monique reasoned her thoughts, recollections, and emotions aloud.

And of course, to be sure that her head would throb until she went to sleep, there were endless phone calls from music industry people threatening court orders and lawsuits. The response to *The Vixen Notebook* interview solidified a hectic hell raiser kind of day. "Lemme go in here and talk to this nigga."

Hiram looked up from his magazine when Monique entered his office. His door was ajar.

"Mo, Whatcha know!"

"Don't 'Mo whatcha know' me, nigga."

"Awwww, shit. What I do now?"

"First. I am siiiiiick of fielding these finale phone calls. What the fuck are these music niggas into?"

"You already know."

"No, really I don't. And I don't wanna know. They are up in arms about what this girl is gonna write in this book."

"It's a sick, sad world, Mo."

"Honestly, what does Kendali have on these people?"

"No tellin'. Entertainment industry is...in the words of Pac, 'hectic and sleazy'."

"Well, they don't wanna talk to me anyway. They lookin' for you with threats of cease and desist, and lawsuits."

"Don't worry about that. Schwiner, Smith, and Rosenberg will handle that. That's what good Jewish lawyers are for. Stop trippin'."

"Well, if there is nothing to trip about, I am sending them to you."

"That's cool."

"And that fuckin' Lesli Lyn. I am sooo tired of her fuckin' ass. You read her blog from a few days ago?"

"No. I heard about it though."

"I mean she is naming names now. Copying and pasting from our authors' books. Quality versus quantity. On and on chastising us for our work."

"Ha! Who cares?! I love it."

"What?"

"I told you before, Mo. I watch Muse like a broker watches the stock ticker. Every time she writes about us, our numbers go up. And with Muse Unlimited subscription service, that's still money in our account. While revenue dropped in paperbacks and ebooks, Muse Unlimited, is really unlimited when it comes to revenue. Everybody hates it, but we were never paid for a reader browsing or skimming a book. But now, cha-ching for every page turned. It all evens out. So let her talk. Let her write. It's money in the bank for us."

"Yeah, I hear you. But fuck her! I am so over her ass."

"But she is one of your favorites. Butterfly Brooks. You love her."

"I do. No compare on her skill set. She is the truth. But I just wish she would shut the fuck up and go write a fuckin' book. That on and on about how awful we are. I hated to see her go, but I am glad that she left. Shit."

"Mo, worry about something else."

"Okay, Mr. Cha-chinger. I just got off the phone with Thad. What the fuck is really goin' on, Hiram? He says he has been trying to talk money with you. Get copies of his Muse reports."

"Yeah."

"So, why aren't you giving them to him? What's goin' on in accounting?

"Nothing is going on in accounting."

"Hiram, don't fuck with me. He said you a thief. Are you stealing?"

"Stealing? Mo, you know me. I am no thief."

"Yeah. But are you stealing? Be straight with me, Hiram Rivers."

"I have a fund."

"A fund?" Monique was stunned. Her face inflamed. "What kind of fuckin' fund?"

"A fund for incidentals and empire building. Like the church building fund."

"You tellin' me you stealin' from our people, Hiram?"

"Would you quit using that word. I am not stealing."

236

"Who knows about the fund?"

"Nobody."

"Muthafuck…" she mumbled, her voice trailing off in disgusted amazement. "Ain't this some shit. I guess that's why you CEO AND CFO. You fuckin' skimmin', Hiram?"

"Look, Mo. They don't know what to do with the money. Go buy some more dumb shit they can't afford."

"But that's their money to fuck up. Not yours. What are you funding, your next Range Rover?"

"No, I am not. It's a fund for building. I am exploring investment possibilities for Dominion."

"Possibilities?" Monique felt herself suspended in animation, formless, massless, and weightless with anger. "Hiram, these people need their money. They have children. Kids in college. Kids that need books. Uniforms. Dance lessons. Field trips. Braces."

"Mo, we not talkin' about you. You and Vaughn take good care of your four. Don't try to play me like I am taking from babies' mouths. These wanna-be red bottom bitches ain't even bottom bitches, wasting their money on knock-off Prada bags and shit."

"But it is theirs to waste! Not yours! Gotdammit, Hiram! You are disgusting!"

"Mo, chill out. It ain't that serious. They not even missin' it."

"Oh, but Thaddeus Kane is. And him, you betta call back because he said you gonna find out how real the Black Blood Gang is. He said he will eat you alive. And I believe him because I feel like I could take a chunk outta ya skull right now!"

"Dang, Mo. C'mon. Stoppit, Ma!"

"No, you stop it. You a muthafuckin' thief." Her bone straight locks seemed to hiss like the snakes of Medusa's crown as she shook her head and rolled her neck violently. "This is it! The final straw! I cannot do this anymore. I am outta here."

"There you go with that shit."

"I am. I mean it. Fuck you, Hiram Rivers. Fuck Dominion. Fuck it all!!!"

"Oh fuck me? Fine. Fuck me then. Get da fuck on!" He leapt from his chair and made a sweeping motion with his arm.

"I am!"

"You'll be back!" he yelled behind her, imitating Al Pacino's *Scarface* accent.

"Don't count on it, nigga." She slammed the door, venom dripping from her strands of coal black hair and holding back acidic tears of pain and disappointment. She felt an indescribable sadness and a deep longing to talk to her husband, Vaughn. His hands would begin her healing and she couldn't wait!

Hiram wanted to flip his desk over, but he didn't. Mo was always right. He had to talk to Thad and make everything whole. He dumped the contents of the folder from Crispus with all the binary records of his skim coding. He had to write a story just in case the stalker/hacker came forth about his 'fund'. But he still had to process the mysterious envelope, maybe write a story for that too. He thought he would have received a blackmail offer by now, but nothing at all. No calls, no notes, no demands. And he had to restitute the Bree thing. His mind spun a thousand thoughts per minute. He was good at covering his true feelings and emotions. At the core of his being he was sad, afraid, and exhausted. Mo, got that part right- fuck it all!

🔥🔥🔥

238

Chapter Thirteen
Delicacies and Discoveries

Monday, 6:00 p.m.

It was quiet at Dominion HQ when Hiram called Thaddeus Kane. He relaxed on the rug that lay in front of his leather sofa talking to his former author.

"Thad, nobody is trying to hustle you. I am saying it takes time to pull the records. As big as Muse is, their accounting systems are antiquated. Dinosaurs in our midst."

"I don't give a fuck about dinosaurs and shit. I want my money. I know I have not received all of my royalties."

"I don't even understand what makes you say that."

"Don't worry about what makes me say that. Cough up my dough, nigga."

"Yeah, yeah. Aight. When I get around to it." Hiram balked at Thad's uproarious demeanor.

"Fuck that. I ain't playin' witchu, Hiram. I ain't no hoe. I ain't never been a hoe. And ain't gon' be no hoe!"

"Yo, bring dat back. I told you. I will look into it and take care of it."

Thaddeus scoffed sardonically. "Yeah. Y'all tried to carry that brother. The L-seven. But he knew what was up. He knew all the time. And y'all tried to play him crazy. Cast him out of the industry. Made him a pariah. Yeah. That square knew the game all along. But I ain't no square. Ya' betta run me my money, nigga."

"Who the fuck you talkin' about?"
"The square dude. Used to do ya' I.T. The computer dude. Wrote a couple books for y'all."

"You mean Max?"

"Yeah. That's him. Max. He wasn't such an L-seven after all."

Hiram was having an epiphany. Thaddeus went on ranting and raving about his royalties, his books, and squares coming full circle, but Hiram tuned him out. He was totally consumed by his own thoughts and reflections of Max, and their history. Max's profile blundered through his mind. Thaddeus sounded like an intermittent cell phone signal in Hiram's ear.

"Do you hear me? Is you listenin', nigga?!"

"Yeah, yeah, bruh. I hear you. I gotchu. I'ma handle it," Hiram responded nonchalantly.

"When? I want my money right the fuck now, Hiram. And I want my money on point from here on out. I'm onto ya' ass. I'm watching you."

"Right, right. Yeah. I know. Don't worry about it. You will have your money within a week. It's already done." He hung up the phone, Thaddeus' angry voice trailing off. He rose from the floor, poured himself a shot of tequila from his wet bar, and sat at his desk looking at the folder from Crispus. He studied the pages of Toussaint's findings, all of the skim code, the investigative conclusions, and technology summaries. He opened his mysterious envelope again and read the emails between him and Khai, between him and Kendali. Reading the emails made his dick throb and incited a deep craving for their gourmet loving. All of the language of the emails was encrypted but clearly someone could figure out the meaning of the conversations since Max deciphered their code. All this time, the hacker/stalker was Max. Maxmillian Gray, Computer Big Head. Brilliant mind. Decent writer. He penned three cyberspace espionage spy dramas for Dominion and they actually sold very well and were still selling. Hiram never considered him a suspect. He never crossed his mind until Thaddeus gave him his a-ha moment. It was Max all along. He had the tech knowledge and he definitely had a vendetta against Hiram. Their relationship ended on an ugly high note. Max was fuming that day, the day Hiram postponed the release of his final book, *The Obsidian Phoenix*. Hiram recalled the final conflict.

"What the fuck you trying to pull, Hiram?" Max stormed into his office, his head ringing with anger.
"Maaan. Ain't no pull. I just think we should wait."
"Wait? No. You are playing games. You know I am ready to close out this contract with the books and the I.T. work. Why are you fuckin' with me?" Max knew why; Hiram was trying to hold him up from his other ventures, namely The Myesha Morgan Show. It seemed that Hiram despised her. Max didn't know why, but ever since he informed Hiram that he was beginning a new

contract with Myesha, their relationship shifted for the worse.
He acted coolly polite toward Max.
"Max. I am not fuckin' with you. I just think there will be a better
time to release the book."
Max's nostrils flared upward, the edges of his nose seemed to
curl back onto his cheeks, like he was morphing into a werewolf.
Hiram didn't see the pounce coming, swift and fast like some
paranormal creature from an ancient time. Max was all over him
in a nanosecond. They fought a brutal fight. Rica walked in on
the commotion and screamed bloody murder.
"Oh my gawd!! Help! Somebody! Oh my gawd! They fightin'!"
She called for security. It took about six employees to pull and
keep them apart. Security escorted Max to the elevator, as he
shouted maledictions upon Hiram's head.
"You will pay for this Hiram! You will pay! You are evil! You
are a thief! You are a robber! Everybody watch out for this
fuckin' asshole! He is not who you think he is! Mark my words!
You all will see! He is the spawn of hell!" Shortly thereafter,
Hiram created a campaign to project Max as a delusional
psychopath, with A.J.'s guidance. Of course, A.J. had no idea
why Hiram had been diligently picking her brain about
marketing techniques after the skirmish. With A.J.'s sound
advice, Hiram crafted and issued a series of memos to Dominion
staff and published a short piece in the company newsletter that
depicted him as the understanding hero and Max as the crazed
lunatic tech nerd, mad about a book.

Hiram closed up his shop and headed for his truck. He texted
Kendali and Khai:
📱 Text Message 📱
Hiram: "Gourmet play?"

242

Kendali: Oooo. When?

Khai: I'm always down.

Hiram: 8pm?

Khai: I will be waiting.

Kendali: I am there

Hiram: Good ♥ I really need it.

Kendali: I know. Me too

Then, he called Crispus.

"Hiram!"

"Brohhhhh!"

"What's up, my main man? How is everything?"

"I have been thinking about what you said and I got two more possibilities on our culprit. But one, I am ninety-five percent sure he is the one."

"Okay. Gimme whatcha got."

"Thaddeus Kane. Used to be signed with me. With Dominion. And Maxmillian Gray. Also former author with us. But he was our main tech guy before he wrote books for me."

"A tech guy?"

"Yeah, man. Brilliant mind. I don't know why I didn't think of him before. I just haven't thought of him period. He is the one. I'm sure of it. But we gotta consider Thaddeus too, especially since he had a mild kinda thing for Georgette back in the gap."

"Is that right?"

"Yeah, that's right. But Max, I am sure it's him. Still, run up on Thad."

"Sho' ya' right. Sho' ya' right."

"Max is it. I know it. I hope I don't have to lay this nigga down."

"Well, lemme talk to him before you pull ya' guns out."

"Yeah, Cee. But he gotta lotta info, bruh. Lotta info on me. That's *my* business. *Mine* alone."

"I already told you. Write your story. Or get somebody to write it for you."

"You mean *stories*."

"*Storeez?*"

"Yeah."

"Well, you betta get ta' writin', my brother. I will work my end. You work yours."

"No doubt."

"Peace, bruh."

"Peace." The gourmet play was going to be right on time, to relax, relate, and release.

Monday 8:00 p.m.

"She said she is on her way?" Khai inquired as he decreased the oven temperature for their main course.

"Yeah. About ten minutes away." Hiram swallowed his second tequila shot of the night and rubbed Khai's shoulder. He took a seat at the cooking island and ate a jalapeno sausage and cheese popper in his mouth.

"Damn, Hiram. They are jalapenos. The whole thing in your mouth at one time?"

"You won't be sayin' that in a lil' while." Hiram smiled and Khai blushed. "I'm stressed, man. I think we figured out who the stalker was. Is."

"Word? Who?"

"Max. Maxmillian Gray."

Khai cocked his to the side, thinking. "The author I.T. guy?"

"That's the one."

"Get da fuck outta here?! No way."

"Naw. I'm sure it's him."

"How do you know?" Khai asked as he tossed salad greens in his homemade vinaigrette.

"Don't know absolutely, but I am ninety-nine percent sure. Thad clued me in. In a conversation today."

"Oh- kaaay..." Khai needed clarity.

"He made me remember that Max hates me. He threatened me and he has the tech know-how to hack me. Hack us." Hiram devoured another popper. "Damn these things are good."

"Yeah. That's makin' him look pretty guilty." Khai ground pepper from his hand- carved grinder into the mixed greens. "But why stalk Kendali? And not you?"

"Not real clear on that part, but I am sure it's his fuckin' ass. We gon' see. I just hope I don't have to lay this muthafucka down."

"Yeah, bro. Don't even say it."

Hiram's phone dinged.

Text message
Kendali: I'm here.
Hiram: Cool.

"She's outside," Hiram informed.

"Alright. I am setting us up in the dining room."

Hiram opened the entry door and Kendali waltzed her wide hips into the foyer, her arms filled with flowers and a shopping bag containing several bottles of wine. Hiram took the bag and tongued her down squeezing her ass while they savored long overdue lip lock.

245

"Damn, I miss you, girl."

"I miss you too, lovey." His heart dropped into his belly pumping him full of butterflies, cascading down to his knees turning them into jello. He was always melted by her force, simmering in her feminine fire.

"Mmmm, smells so good," Kendali remarked. She followed Hiram into Khai's state of the art gourmet chef's kitchen, replete with two double ovens, a ten burner cooking island, massive light gray stained wooden cabinets, and an industrial size fridge and freezer. "Hey, Khai Pie." Kendali planted a big, juicy kiss on Khai's lips.

"What's up, mamacita? You lookin' delicious as usual." Khai admired Kendali's yellow and green flower printed strapless dress, just touching her knee, showing off her graceful calves.

"Awww, thanks, babes." She gave Khai the flowers while Hiram returned to his seat and his poppers.

"You are such a class act," Khai said, smelling the flower bouquets. She kissed him again. "That lip gloss tastes so good." He pulled two vases from a lower cabinet.

"Why he gettin' extra kisses?" Hiram poured himself another tequila shot.

"Hiram quit," Kendali rebutted sitting on the stool next to him. "I haven't seen Khai in a while."

"We were at the supper club a few weeks ago. You saw him then," Hiram retorted, half smiling, half smirking, with jealousy at the corners of his mouth. He loved Kendali; he loved Khai, but he was the grand puba, period.

"Boy, stop," she said slapping his arm and then burying her head on his shoulder. He touched her head with his own and Khai smiled.

"Dinner is served, family." Khai raised his arms and waved them toward the dining room. The table setting was beautiful, all black and silver china and tableware. Kendali's colorful wildflower bouquets were the perfect color-pop compliment to the arrangement. Khai inherited the cherry oak dining room set from his great- grandmother, which included a china closet and buffet that he always used for guests and very important clients. Tonight, there were chafing dishes filled with crab stuffed salmon, grilled asparagus, fingerling potatoes, lemon pudding- his signature condiment for the salmon, green salad tossed in his famous vinaigrette, and warm mixed berry cobbler. Kendali and Hiram salivated at the delicious sight.

"Khai, you are so gifted." Kendali kissed his cheek.

"So true, bro. You put your all in everything you make, each and every time." Hiram kissed Khai on the opposite cheek.

"I have to. It's what I came to do."

They served themselves and enjoyed the delectables. They talked about KD's, Kendali's PQ award, and the Dominion in-house drama.

"So, tell me why you think it's Max again," Kendali inquired. Butterflies settled in the bottom of her belly, wings flitting against her flesh. As far as she knew, no one knew about her and Max's brief affair that she abruptly ended when she felt herself falling into his sweetness. Max was the kind of guy every girl dreamed of, certified husband material. He was a hopeless romantic, loyal, kind, strong-willed, very smart, cultured, caring, responsible, stable, and swinging long, strong, donkey kong dick for days. And while girls dream of Max as the perfect partner, many know they do not deserve his type, for they are too damaged to embrace the fullness of such a beautiful soul. Few are as conscientious as Kendali, who walked away from him before she decimated his spirit, leaving him in ruins for the deserving good woman to struggle with his resurrection.

"I know it's him. He fits the bill. Hates me. Threatened me. Just not quite sure why he would stalk you and not me. But I think he figured us out."

"As in he knows about me and you seeing each other?" Kendali sipped her moscato while Khai listened intently finishing his potatoes.

"Yeah." Hiram swallowed a big gulp of water. "*And* I think he knows about all of us, the *three* of us." They sat motionless, as the entire room seemed to freeze, contemplating the new information.

Khai spoke first. "What do we need to do?"

Hiram replied, "Nothing right now."

"Nothing? Dammit, Hiram. That's your answer for everything. You are just too fuckin' cavalier about shit." Kendali guzzled her wine nervously. In her head, she played out a rekindling with Max as an unappealing last resort solution to keeping him quiet.

"Panic and worry breed dumb, desperate decisions, sloppiness, and bullshit," he rebutted.

Khai rose from the table and gathered his dishes. "What does he have on us? How do you know he knows?"

"I got an envelope. A mystery drop with our coded communication."

"See? That's why I hate that internet bullshit. Nothin' but the fuckin' devil." Khai stormed into the kitchen.

Kendali stacked her plate and utensils with Hiram's and scurried behind Khai.

"It's not the internet, Khai. It's people. It's people using the internet for their devilish purposes."

Hiram joined them. "Look y'all. It's just some emails. I am already on it. I am writing the story in case he decides to go public. I'm just hoping I don't have to lay the nigga down."

"On the real." Khai rinsed the dishes and Kendali loaded the dishwasher. "He don't know who he fuckin' wit. My ass might be a punk, but I ain't no punk ass."

"Can y'all not talk about killing this man, please?" Kendali shuddered at the thought of Max being killed because of their truncated love affair.

"Let's not talk about it at all. I didn't tell y'all this for you to worry. It's FYI. That's it. Carry on with your lives as usual. I got this."

That was enough for Kendali. Hiram never failed her. "Okay, babes," she affirmed.

Khai, on the other hand, wondered. In his mind, he sensed a missing piece of the story. He made a mental post-it and stuck it at the base of his brain.

"Aight, bruh. If you say so."

"I do say so." Hiram toasted his lovers with his last drop of wine. They went into Khai's master bath and indulged a hot steamy shower with each other, taking turns kissing, touching and squeezing. Kendali's pussy streamed sweet nectar as each of them sucked on a breast and Khai played with her clit while Hiram squeezed her butt. Khai deep-throated his frat brother, simultaneously intensifying his massage of Kendali's love button. She resisted the orgasm, letting pleasure build as she watched her two favorite men tongue each other down. Hiram jacked Khai's dick and the warm water heightened the passions of them all. They exited the shower, lifted Kendali off of her feet, and raised her onto their shoulders, one buttock on Hiram's right shoulder and the other buttock on Khai's left shoulder. It

249

was a royal posture for she was their Queen of The Night. They laid her down tenderly on Khai's round California king size bed and devoured her, taking turns eating and fingering her pussy, kissing each other until she squirted in ecstasy. She curled up on a pillow and propped another between her legs while she watched Hiram and Khai make love to each other, heavily petting, squeezing, and rubbing each other's bodies into a steamy frenzy. Khai sucked Hiram's dick voraciously right before climax leaving him aching with anticipation. Hiram returned the fellatio until Khai was ready to release his love juice into the air and he stroked his friend to the other side of his pleasure. Khai purred and Kendali creamed at the sight of the orgasmic aftermath. Hiram blew her a kiss, reached into Khai's silver 'love box' located on the nightstand, grabbed two condoms, and tossed them on the bed. He mounted Kendali pushing her legs so that her knees tapped her shoulders with every thrust. He fucked her wildly, his dick pressing into her g-spot. She moaned and Khai kissed her face, then her mouth, and finally her nipples. A loving finger stroke of Hiram's anus forced him to bust his nut all over Kendali. He collapsed onto her warm, juicy body heaving like a lumberjack who had been chopping wood for a ten-hour shift. Khai took his turn with her Royal Grace and Hiram lay next to them gazing at the ceiling in orgasmic recovery. Khai fucked her while she lay on her side, toying with her clit, bringing her to her second squirt. He sprayed her ass with his loving cum and dropped onto the bed beside her. She lay quietly between her two lovers overly satisfied, reflecting on the first time they had a gourmet session:

They had dinner at Khai's about 3 years after she signed with Dominion for she and Hiram did not begin their affair immediately. When the rumors of their fling dissipated is when they actually began to rendezvous. Before then, they fucked a few times, but it was quick, fleeting moments, like test fucks. Kendali never asked Hiram how he concluded that she would participate in a threesome. She didn't even know herself. She had attended plenty of orgies during her hip hop vixen tenure, but she managed to steer clear of superfluous number of bisexual ones. After they dined, the three of them moved to the living area and relaxed on Khai's supersized sectional sofa. Old 90's hip hop videos played on the 65 inch TV screen, some of them starring Kendali. She fascinated them with tales of the behind the scenes action describing the personalities of the rappers, directors, and other video girls. They sat in silence for a while and then Khai rubbed Hiram's thigh. Initially, Kendali was disturbed. Though drunk, her moral senses were completely sober. Hiram answered her surprise with a passionate kiss and a deep caress of her pussy. Khai licked Hiram's neck. Her eyes widened, alarmed by his gesture. Her awestruck expression prompted Hiram to reassure her.

"It's okay, Kenni. I love you. And Khai adores you."

Khai winked at her, massaged Hiram's back, and slowly unzipped his pants while Kendali gazed at Khai's lustful eyes. He was so beautiful, and equally handsome. She felt a rush being in between two gorgeous Black men arousing her desires. Her craving for erotic quench intensified, with every gentle finger stroke of her pussy from Hiram in syncopated rhythm with Khai's stroke of Hiram's staff. Hiram sucked on her ears and her neck while Khai found her lips and kissed her wildly. Her vagina creamed. To her amazement, she embraced the ecstasy delivered by the moment. She was astonished that repulsion nor disgust was anywhere in her spirit, even while she felt Khai and Hiram

251

gyrating in their homoerotic longing, Khai rubbing Hiram's ass and Hiram pressing himself deeper into Khai's torso. Khai kept kissing her while he stroked Hiram into a brick hard state. He pulled his pants down and the gourmet love session, their eclectic erotic delicacy, was born.

Wednesday 11:00 a.m.

Crispus decided that a phone conversation with Thad would suffice, for Max was the more likely culprit. He looked around his office located in the house adjacent to his residence; it was a duplex that he bought years ago, one of several properties he owned throughout Seminole City. Taking inventory of the general untidiness reminded him that he needed to call the cleaning lady. He arranged his Dominion folders and notes in front of him and called Thad, leaning back in his creaky office chair.

"This is Thad."

"Yes. Thaddeus Kane. This is Adams, Crispus Adams. I work-"

"I know who you are. No need for the introduction. Your Hiram's personal fixer. If you ain't callin' me to tell me the bank transfer is on the way, I ain't got no rap for you."

"No, I am not calling about a bank transfer. I need to ask you about your relationship with Hiram. And Kendali Grace."

"Ha! Hoo~hooo!" He laughed a hearty, infectious, unique laughter. "You already know about my relationship with Hiram cuz he already told you. As for Kendali, I have no issues with her. Why? What's goin' on?"

"Just gathering intel since she has a new book coming out. We are taking extra precautions. The subject matter is controversial, so we are checking out her history. Hiram's history with people and so forth."

"Uh-huh. I heard the rumors she got somethin' goin on. She was seen with a bodyguard. But whatever, man. Anything else? I have a meeting soon."

"What do you know about computers?"

"Computers? Ha! I know how to pay somebody to carry out computer tasks. Ain't really my bag. You finished?"

"Just one more question." He etched a few notes on his pad. "Are you having an affair with Georgette Rivers?"

And there was his laughter again delivered even more heartily.

"An affair with Georgette? Hiram has been married, in an affair, with my would-be wife, Georgette all these years. She was mine first!"

"Oh yeah?"

"Yeah. Why you askin' me that?"

"Just askin'."

"Look here, ahk. If you think I'm tryin' to do Hiram sumpthin', think again. If I wanted him done, he'd be done. I want my money right. That's all. And I ain't got nothin' to do with Kendali. She ain't even on my dial plate, yam' dig?"

"I dig. I appreciate you, my man."

"Good. I'm gone. Peace."

"Peace, bro."

Crispus agreed with Hiram: Thaddeus proved a lot less likely culprit. He didn't have the feel of a stalker and definitely not a hacker. He called the cleaning lady, made her an envelope for her services, grabbed his briefcase, and dashed out the door. He planned to catch Max going to or coming from lunch at Myesha Morgan's studio.

The day was warm and easy like most days in Seminole City, perfect weather year round. It truly was God's country. Crispus felt a soothing calm as he eased down the tree lined boulevard toward the studio.

He spotted Max pulling into a parking space returning from lunch, about two rows away from him on the lot. He stepped from his truck and waited for Max to emerge. Max rose from his ride glancing around, but failed to notice the fixer walking in his direction. Max strode toward the main entrance. Crispus called him gaiting more swiftly.

"Max? Maxmillian Gray?"

Max halted his journey. "Yeah. Who wants to know?"

The two men were eye to eye. "I'm Crispus. Crispus Adams. I work for Dominion Publishing."

"No, you don't. You work for Hiram."

"Well, one in the same."

"Uh, technically, they are not. But okay." Max eyeballed Crispus head to toe, resting his elbow on his forearm, thinking and tapping his temple. "What do you want?" he asked curtly.

"Just wanted to ask you about Kendali Grace."

Crispus watched as Max's facial expression shifted from stoic, cold, and confrontational to angry, enchanted delight. Max chastised himself in his head, knowing he failed to cover his feelings. He forced his emotions into the bottom of his feet and pressed his heels upon them, rocking as he answered, "Okay. What about her?"

"What is your relationship like?"

254

"I helped her with some writing tips. Office chat. We and some other authors used to stay late from time to time, the few of us that are local. That's it." The lies came so easily, as he envisioned Kendali makin' it clap for him in one of the conference rooms.

"Okay. Now you and Hiram…"

"I don't discuss Hiram Rivers."

"But you did threaten him, didn't you?"

"Wait. What is this about anyway?"

"We are just doing some routine intel because her book is so controversial."

"Yeah right. Okay. We are done." He turned to enter the main doors.

"But Max. Hold on."

"No. No hold on. I said all I am gonna say." He disappeared into the studio and Crispus returned to his vehicle. He sat in the passenger seat so he would have more room to review his data and make his list of possibilities:

Thad-very weak

Emory- weak

Isaac- medium strong

Dre- large Strong

Tasir- super STRONG

Max- STRONGEST

He underlined Max's name multiple times until the line became the color of blood, a deep, rich, dark crimson. "I think we gotchu, Maxmillian Gray."

Chapter Fourteen
Discussions & Repercussions

Friday 3:00 p.m.

Mustafa leafed through the envelopes that he'd retrieved from his PO box. They were from fans and foes. He was used to the influx of differing opinions and feelings about his honest, uncut, expressive viewpoints. It was important to him to have raw engagement with his listeners, readers, and patrons. To Mustafa, it was a passionate element of the struggle.

"Business over bullshit." A powerful tag for a powerful brand. A powerful man. Those three words were easy to say, but the depth of their simplicity, meant the world to those who understood their weight. Years ago at a publishers conference, a reporter asked him to explain the slogan. He gave a strong, concise answer "The business is the truth," he began as he leaned closer to the mic. "And how you feel about the truth when it doesn't favor your views and feelings, now that, my sistah, is the bullshit."

He tossed the letters aside and turned his attention to his computer screen. "What will I be dealing with today when I go live?" Shaking his head he noticed that the majority of his emails were addressing a remark that he made regarding strippers and authors. "Really?!" he laughed. "This is *exactly* the bullshit I was talking about. Sensitive ass people in they feelings. Did they even understand what I said?" He clicked the Zing Live icon and cleared his throat.

Zing Live - Mustafa
"Peace, Love, and Blessings, Black Family. How y'all doin' out

there in the world? I know some of you are good, some in the middle, and some are not so well, especially the ones messaging me and emailing me about my strip club comment I made a while back. Let me clear the air so that I can move on to more important matters. I addressed those who had an issue with whether or not Kendali Grace has a ghostwriter. I talked about a couple things and I suggested that those of you who can't write and used to strip, should return to stripping or take some writing classes. Strippers. Writers. I love 'em both. Period. And for the record, I have no beef with strippers. I love me some Amber Alise. She's nice with the pen and the pole, but don't get it twisted. All of y'all can't do that shit. For real. It ain't for everybody. If stripping is your forte, then strip yo' ass off cuz I'm lovin' ya'. If writing is your forte, then write yo' ass off. But don't get off of the pole without a strong command of the English language and try to pawn off your supposed writing as collegiate level scholarship. Fuck that. Shit. Some of you would feel the same way if these authors started dancing and couldn't dance worth a shit. Y'all would say them bitches in da way. I know you would. See, the problem is that some of you have inspiration confused with occupation. Know your strengths and weaknesses and don't get in your feelings about this shit. If you don't want nobody in the way fuckin' up yo' strip game, don't get in the way and fuck up nobody's pen game. Y'all out here tarnishing the craft for no reason. Too fuckin' sensitive, but you writin' these insensitive ass books. Shit sounding like Dr. Seuss on mollies. Cut that shit out. Y'all need to go back to the beginning. Invest in a 'see-n-say', or a 'speak-n-spell'. Instead of pulling those g-strings outta ya hindparts, pull that string on the see-n-say. Get back to basics. For real. And as usual, business over bullshit. Peace."

257

Zing Live End

He closed his laptop and walked out of his office pleased with his short broadcast.

Friday 7:00 p.m.

"I hear you left Dominion and that you're looking for some financing," Maceo said to Monique as he stirred his cocktail. "Say it ain't so." They enjoyed the sunset view from his loft's balcony.

"Yes. It's true." Monique swallowed chardonnay from her glass.

"Damn. How you out here lookin' for financing and ya girl Georgette drivin' a Ferrari?"

"Well, she earned her Ferrari."

"Yeah, but y'all in business together, right?"

Monique sat silently.

"Aintchu?" She didn't respond. "I mean, I can finance you."

"I'm sure you can."

"I told you to come over here a long time ago. Help us build and reach a higher plateau and I will finance whatever you want. I believe in you and deeply respect your skillset, Mo. And we're looking to expand into these foreign markets. A lot of y'all don't realize how much these far easterners love our culture. We gettin' ready to blow all the way up."

"Yeah. Okay." Monique was stunned by his proposition and his plans. She maintained a straight face. She couldn't believe she was unemployed. Not in a million years did she think that she'd be in such an odd predicament. Her inner voice was still cussing at Hiram.

"Why are you resisting the help you need?"

"I'm not resisting. Just listening."

"Haven't you wasted enough of your loyalty in places where it's not appreciated?"

"What are you sayin', Maceo?"

"You know what I'm sayin', Monique. You far from slow. A lil naïve. Goofy even. But slow, no way. You know what's up and I guess you stayed so long because you were comfortable or you felt like you owed them somethin', but you don't owe them nothin'. You paid them in sweat. They owe you now. But your naiveté or loyalty, whatever you wanna call it, won't let you make a move on the truth."

"If it wasn't for Hiram, I wouldn't have had the opportunity."

"And it's because of Hiram that you're seeking other opportunities and funding. Listen, you don't owe them jack shit, ma. You brought the polish, the professionalism, the poise that separates Dominion from the rest. We need some of that at Gutta Butta, baby."

"I hear you, Mace. I just can't make a decision on that at this moment."

"Why not? I am telling you. You owe no one. You only owe yourself. Period. I will give you anything you want. I will even double your salary." Maceo's offer to Monique was getting more lucrative by the minute.

She gazed upon the horizon, the sun passing the baton to the moon leaving the clouds emblazoned with her orange glow. Orange cloud sunsets always made life seem hopeful to Monique. She made almost every life changing decision under orange-streaked clouds. Maceo's offer was tempting, but he was known to delve into a shady deal here and there. For the most part, he was a stand-up guy, supposedly, but rumors abounded.

"No pressure, babe. Just think about it. When you ready, I'm here."

"Okay. I am definitely considering Gutta Butta. Especially since I don't have a job now."

"What?"

"Yeah. I left Dominion." She gulped the rest of her wine.

"Well, let's refill your glass and get some dinner. This is a celebration, ma!" He excitedly led her from the balcony to the beautifully arranged buffet in his dining area. Crab legs, grilled lobster tail, corn relish, baked potatoes, and asparagus made her mouth water. She had one granola bar all day.

"A celebration you say?"

"Definitely, Mo. You comin' to GB, dammit!" He cast his million dollar grin and Monique chuckled at his magic words and ways.

"That is highly possible, Maceo." He pulled out her chair and she sat.

"I will make your plate, sis."

"Yes, Maceo. I need this. It's been a long day."

"I know. Let's eat!" He prepared their plates from the buffet. Monique texted her husband Vaughn, giving him the highlights of her conversation with Maceo.

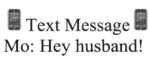 Text Message

Mo: Hey husband!
Vaughn: Nique! My Love.
Mo: Meeting is good. Maceo wants me at GB
Vaughn: Of course he does. You are the best
Mo: You always know how to make me blush
Vaughn: Just doin' my job
Mo: I'm torn. Not sure how to proceed.

Vaughn: Go with your gut

Mo: I just don't want to feel like I am betraying them. They helped me so much.

Vaughn: And you did more than help them

Mo: That's what Mace said. I don't owe them anything

Vaughn: He's right, Nique. Let's talk when you get home. I love you.

Mo: LU2

♥♥♥

Saturday 2:00 p.m.

The Nappy Vine wine tasting event was hosted every year for the past eight years by Bradford's cousin. Nappy Vine, the name of her vineyard and wine brand, was the only black-owned and operated vineyard in the region.

"This white wine is the shit, Brad." Toni had finished her third glass of custom pinot noir.

"You tryna get drunk, huh?" Bradford asked.

"No. Just tipsy. That's all. Doing my part to support black business. Don't hate on me, bro." Toni finished her last cup of wine and tossed the cup in the trash.

"Well, I don't know about y'all, but I ordered a case of it already. It didn't take me but a couple of sips to know that I was going to buy," Lesli added. "With all of the drama that's been going on, I need the whole damn vineyard."

"Turn up, dammit!" Toni shouted.

Lesli laughed. "You're drunk."

"Hey, sis. Don't even trip. You'll get through it. You always do. You're strong," Bradford stated with encouragement.

"Thanks, Brad. Trust me when I tell you that I had no idea that all of this madness would be coming my way. And the PQ event is right around the corner. I don't need any more distractions right now."

"Speaking of," Bradford began. "Is Kendali still receiving the award? Do you think it'll stir up more controversy if she receives it?"

Toni responded, "Well, the award is a people's choice award and the people love her. Kendali can do no wrong."

"Yeah, I get that, Toni," Bradford stated. "But what precedent are you setting for the judging and awarding of authors in the future? What rules are in play?"

"I see your point, Brad, but as I said, it's the people's choice. She's popular. She's beautiful. She's fine. And apparently she can write her ass off. Ghostwriter or not, Kendali Grace is the shit right now. We should just ride that wave smoothly. And as far as rules, qualifications, merits and credentials go, I will be making some changes in the future. I had no idea that a ghostwriter would cause so much uproar. At the end of the day who gives a shit. Whoever's name is on the book, that's who wrote it, as far as I'm concerned."

"I hear you, Toni, but I disagree on the ghostwriting. If you're a writer, then write. Period." Lesli toasted her comment with a swig of wine.

"I don't disagree, L-Double. But I have to remain neutral, mostly. Just for the sake of my position with the PQ. You are a writer and journalist. You can say what you want and get away with it. Truly, we don't need all the madness. And the drama. And the bullshit. The ghostwriting fiasco, we don't need. This could discredit us. The PQ. All of us. As the head of PQ, neutrality is key for me, you see?" Toni tied her locks into a ponytail.

Lesli sighed. "I understand and respect that. I do. And I'll do my all to bite my tongue until after The PQ, but I can't promise you that I won't bring it up again. Unless..."

Toni wrinkled her brow. "Unless what?"

"Unless you promise to change the rules for next year."

"I gotchu like I gotchu," Toni replied. "Consider it done."

Bradford added sternly, "And this is why the Isis platform is so important. To build a new literary empire based on merits. Standards. Based on the profound love and appreciation for the craft. We should leave all of that less than regal activity for the minions to fight and destroy each other over. We're too dignified for the bullshit. We squash the bullshit or ignore it. Never dance in it."

"Isis?" Toni questioned. "Why call it Isis?"

"Because we are going to resurrect the craft and restore it to its natural state. Like Isis did after Set murdered Osiris and cut his body up into parts and scattered them. Osiris represents the craft. Writing. Authorship. Pure authorship. Set. Set represents the opposition to the craft and all that it means. All that it stands for."

"Give it up, black man," Toni sang.

Bradford continued. "We have to build that foundation. We must resurrect black ink from its imminent death. From its brutal slaughter. Its dismemberment. Like Osiris' body parts were and scattered, so are the positive, necessary, and beneficial characters of writing. No dignity or a lack of. No love or a lack of. The list goes on and on. And if you don't see that we're in a dire state, look at a lot of the book covers. Ain't nobody on them covers smiling. No one looks happy. Fuck what a person writes when those types of images are involved. You might forget what you

263

hear and what you read, but you can never forget what you see. And this sad shit is being promoted worldwide as the face of urban lit. We're popular as hell as a whole for all of the wrong reasons. Isis is going to change that. Isis is going to put urban lit back together again. All of the kings. All of the queens. That's my living and dying promise."

Toni and Lesli sang in unison, "Amen."

🍷 🍷 🍷

Chapter Fifteen
Hot Butterflies

Sunday 3:00 p.m.

"You doin' better, ma?"

"Haaay, Mace." Bree opened her front door nice and wide for Maceo's brotherly wellness call. He gave her an edible arrangement and a bag from Deucey's. "Awwww, you are my brother."

"And you are my sister." He found a comfortable spot in her living room on her super-size sectional, cluttered with her tablet, of course, a few journals, a bag of gummy bears, several autographed copies of her Just Enough For The City series, and a few hair clips. She continued down the narrow hallway to the kitchen to make herself a plate, her mouth-watering from the aromas of Deucey's catfish and homemade bread.

She called out to Maceo, "You want a sandwich, Mace?"

"You can make me a small one."

"Extra hot sauce only?"

"You know it." Maceo scrolled through his emails and text messages. He had a lot of Platinum Quill Expo emails, mostly from his accounting team. His authors were finalizing their vending tables, their per diem, and hotel accommodations. Gutta Butta had a block of suites reserved for their team at The Sioux, the swankiest hotel in Seminole City and a boatload of GB paraphernalia to give away. Bree brought out a tray with their sandwiches and fruit and sat beside Maceo on the sofa.

She bit into her sandwich. "Mmmm. I was so hungry. This was right on time."

Maceo concurred. "Ain't nothin' like Deucey's." Maceo savored his fish and enjoyed the quiet with Bree, Sade's Promise LP serenading their lunch from Spotify. He looked at her bruised forehead, which was healing nicely. "You still attending the PQ?"

"Damn straight," she replied sucking down her peach tea.

"Aight, ma. I ain't know if you had the wind knocked outcha wings. You got the lil' bruise on your head. So I ain't know if you wanted to go out publicly or what. You know how vain you women can be."

"Ain't nuthin' a lil' makeup won't cover up."

Maceo noticed the biggest bouquet of flowers standing out from the other get-well arrangements covering her coffee table. "Who are all these flowers from?"

"I honestly don't know. Except for the biggest one. I don't know how people find things out, but they heard I was 'ill'," she said, making air quotes with her fingers.

"Word?"

"Yeah."

"And the biggest one is from?"

"Your boy, Rivers."

"Yeah. He know what's up. Is that all he sent?"

"No. I got an envelope. By messenger."

"Uh-huh. That's right. Trying not to kill his ass."

"You threatened him or something?"

"No threats. Just encouraging words. A brotherly conversation."

"So, he really had me robbed?" Bree dropped her sandwich on the plate, her appetite dissipating and being replaced by queasiness.

"Bree, didn't I tell you to stay away from that muthafucka?" She put her plate on the floor and cast her eyes at the window, upon the trees sitting majestically on the front lawn. She desperately desired Maceo to shut the fuck up. "You hear me, Bree?" She didn't respond. "Aight. I guess our lunch is over. I just wanted to check on you." Maceo started to rise from the couch, Bree's words paused him.

"Yes, Maceo. You told me. I didn't listen. I fucked up." Her tears of regret dropped slowly onto her chest. Maceo pulled her close to him hugging and comforting her. She wept, talking intermittently through her tears. "I was so scared. I kept thinking about my children. About my mama and my daddy. You. Nikki. The boys."

"I know. You gon' be okay."

"I thought he was gonna kill me. I can still feel the gun in my back. I mean I feel it, Mace. I'm not sleeping well...I mean...I-I-I..."

He looked into her eyes, cradling her by her forearms. "Bree. I am not gonna lie to you. You will never be the same after this kind of incident. You are forever changed. But you gotta stay positive. Accept the negative. Be smarter. Stay up. You will get through it. You will feel better. In time. But for now, just use the energy to write your next best seller." He smiled at her. "And let that other shit go. Just let go. Spread your wings wider and keep flying. Just keep flying. Dig, ma?"

"I do. I dig, brother."

Sunday 5:00 p.m.

You see, Your Majestic Grace. The ghostwriting scandal did not affect you. Not at all. You are still getting the big award. You are so deserving. It doesn't matter to me if AJ helps you. It's still your story and it's your story that inspires her to write your books so well. This does not taint your royalness, your purity. Now that thing with Hiram. Aaaaaaaaarrrgh! That could have tainted you. But alas! I know you are temporarily insane, allowing him to do unspeakables with you. And to you. With Khai. My God! What has he done to you?!

He kneeled on the prie dieu and folded his hands.

But it is okay. Because I will purify you. Sanctify you. When you allow me to know the fullness of your love. I know it is the eighth wonder of the world. To lay between your thighs with your heart wrapping around my own, healing me of this longing for you. I crave you and all your sensual possibilities in indescribable ways. My soul screeches like a wild banshee wishing you were with me.

He prayed quietly, humming Amazing Grace, while his ten inches of python steel rose to deliver the sermon, a sermon of his sexuality that he stroked with lavender vanilla lotion. He stroked his penis until it ached, imagining penetrating the object of his love and affection, Kendali Grace. Feeling the heat of her passions.

Aaaah, Your Grace. I cannot wait to give this to you. To you. And you alone. I can't wait to see how you respond to my passion for you. We will fall in love.

His entire body was on fire. He jerked and stroked his dick until he fainted from the release of the orgasmic pressure. He awoke hours later, naked, dried semen on the floor and his hand smooth with lotion. He looked around the room, candles flickering, illuminating the image of Kendali's life size poster.

"I know you are here with me," he mumbled. He crawled to the prie dieu, kneeled and closed his ceremony the same way he always did:

In time...you will be mine...With Grace.

Sunday 7:00 p.m.

Kendali sat on the edge of her bed, dreading the result of the home pregnancy test. She had not taken a test in many years but she had certainly taken her share when she first starting having sex. Her mildly man-crazy, preoccupied, unavailable mother didn't teach her much about her sexuality. She gave her pads when she started her menses and condoms when she turned sixteen. That was it. She learned about her femininity from older women in the acting business and a few men who wanted to explore her, not just fuck her. The elder sisters taught her natural birth control by monitoring the menstruation cycle and herbal supplements and preached the gospel against pharmaceutical birth control methods. But before she was able to apply her education to her reality, she had a few pregnancy scares and one abortion. She wasn't so sure that she ever wanted children. She was a nurturer, but was uncertain that she possessed the level of nurturing required for motherhood. She played with her toes, massaged her knees, and sucked in several deep breaths. She went to the bathroom counter. Two lines.
"Fuuuuuuuuuuuuuuuck!" She slammed her body against the bathroom wall, craning her neck, facing the ceiling. "Aaaaaah, shit!" She pulled another test from its packaging and followed the instructions. She waited. Two more lines. "Goddammit!" Her face and neck burned with anxiety. She perused her image in the mirror, sliding her hands down her body, turning sideways to look at her profile and visualize her belly filled with a baby. For about thirty seconds she was enamored with the idea. After thirty

seconds, she snapped to her reality, returned to the side of her bed, and changed the name of the baby maker to "Baby Fahvah" in her phone, for there was only one who had been consistently ejaculating inside her womb, 'accidentally on purpose'. She sent him a text.

📱 Text Message 📱
Kendali: I'm pregnant.
BF: wow! its mine?
Kendali: Of course.
BF: how you know?
Kendali: Are you trying to insult me?
BF: No. Ijs.
Kendali: Contrary to popular belief, I don't just go around letting everybody just cum up in me. Only you.
BF: Really? Why am I so special?
Kendali: I dunno. I just love you. I adore you.
BF: and I love you. We're having a baby.
Kendali: what? I'm not keeping it.
BF: Yes you are!! You not killin my baby!
Kendali: It's not even a baby yet.
BF: Don't kill our child.
Kendali: You trippin. I'm not ready to be a mother. and there's just too much swirling. I'm just launching my career. This PQ is gonna take me some other places.
BF: I know this. I gotchu on the career but you not killin my baby. Don't be so fuckin selfish.
Kendali: Look. I don't even wanna talk about it anymore.
BF: Yeah. We are going to talk though. Don't kill our baby
Kendali: It's my body. I make the decision.
BF: Then what the fuck you tell me for

Kendali: I dunno. I should have kept it to myself. I had no idea you would want a baby.

BF: With you, why not? Yeah, I do.

Kendali: You don't think we have enough going on in our lives? Enough people, places, and things? Too many relationships, commitments, responsibilities, careers, families? How do we make room for a whole child?

BF: We can do it. Don't decide yet. You just found out. Just wait for a minute. Just wait. Let's think about it.

Kendali: Fine. We'll think about it.

Chapter Sixteen
'Twas The Night Before Auspice

Friday 4:00 p.m.

Over the last couple days, Kendali and Dre were able to find
some peace and resolution inside a comfortable friendly space,
enough for Dre to serve as her escort to the PQ. They strolled
Sequoia Boulevard, shopping for a new tux for Dre to
complement Kendali's dress. The city was abuzz with the
activity of authors, readers, and publishers from all over the
nation meeting for one big weekend to celebrate the Black
literary arts. Hotels were booked, traffic was heavy, shops and
restaurants were packed, and cyber servers were on full tilt with
social media jumping.
"Okay, babe. I think we got everything." Kendali wrapped her
arm around Dre's forearm, stroking his wrist with her long,
freshly French-manicured fingernails.
"You think so?" He looked up and down the boulevard.
"Yeah. We go to Meena's, pick up my dress and we are good."
"Okay."
They walked to Aminah's shop, Goddess Garments, and entered
the crowded boutique. There were mostly out-of-towners buying
accessories and a few who ordered custom made dresses from
Aminah. To accommodate the Platinum Quill attendees, extra
seamstresses and customer service agents were hired. She
emerged from the fitting room in the rear just in time to lay eyes
on Kendali.
"Meena!"
"Kendali Grace! It's so good to see you, girl." They gave each
other a lingering bear hug. "You know you are all bagged up and

ready to go." She turned to one of her cashiers. "Bring out Kendali's dress for me." She squeezed Kendali's hand. "You excited? Nervous?"

"You know I am." Kendali sighed and patted her heart "Oh. This is my love, my sweet, Dre. Andre Walker. This is Aminah Akeem. Mustafa's better half."

"Good to meet you, love." He shook her hand.

"Nice to meet you too." The cashier returned with Kendali's garment bag and gave it to Aminah. "Thank you, sis." She gave a humble bow and walked away.

"Here you are." Aminah's mocha face and matching eyes beamed chocolate sunshine upon Kendali's glowing countenance. "You are going to look like you just landed from heaven," Aminah said referring to Kendali's all-white ensemble.

"Yesssssss! You are the best," she said, giving Dre the bag and hugging Aminah around her neck. Aminah kissed her cheek. "Congratulations, Kendali. I will see you at the gala."

"Thanks, love."

The couple exited the shop and Aminah mingled with her customers. She stayed open until 10pm Thursday, Friday, and Saturday of the PQ weekend and was closed on Sunday, which was the day of the award gala. She made dresses for all the who's who of the industry, Kendali, Georgette, Monique, Lesli Lyn, Shante, Latoya, Bree, and of course, Nikki Pearl. They all came in to pick up their dresses and accessories, readying themselves to show off their style, grace, and beauty. Sometimes, she felt her gift of needle and thread kept them from killing her husband. In spite of how bad he talked about them, they still came to her for their couture. She surmised that they, like she, understood Mustafa. Even though he was abrupt and abrasive with his tongue, he really did love his people, all of them. After the last item was bagged, she left the boutique, leaving her two most trusted shop keepers to close up. She was exhausted and looking forward to Mustafa's loving, soothing touch.

👗 👗 👗

Zing Post – The Sauce Mobb

Bree McDee (post): This is a sweet strawberry sauce made with the freshest organic strawberries. 🍓 We know for sure that Kendali gets the PQ award for outstanding contribution to the literary arts. I know we have had our issues but I have to say, congrats, @Kendali Grace. All the best! 🍫

Reactions: 609 Comments: 132 Shares: 98

Maria Robbins: That was sweet. 😊
Jessica Laws: Yeah. It was.
Delilah Newton: Awwwww 🐻
Kendali Grace: Thanks, babes. I appreciate it. xoxo
Fiona Washington: Now that's good in the sisterhood.
Eddie Love: Yeah. yall need to come together
Carl Stewart: 💯 One Love

Zing Post - Tea Thyme

Latoya Tea Mitchell (post): The PQ is always so much fun. How many of yall going? And which authors are you looking forward to seeing? I want to see the fashions! 😁😍 We know Kendali G. is gonna be fiyah 🔥

Malika Ess: Yes! Kendali is sooooo purdee! 😍 And stylish! Love her! 🖤

Faye Fite: And I think most of them shop at my favorite boutique, Goddess Garments aka Gigi's! 👗👠👗👜🏰 I love Aminah! 😊🖤

Ashanti Simmons: Bree is my favorite, no doubt! Her pen game is pure fye. 🔥✒️

Celeste Moore: I hope to meet Thaddeus Kane. He is so fuckin' sexy! 😍😍😍 Damn! I hope my husband not trollin me 😁

Cabria Davis: He is sexy, sis. 😊 I want to meet Amber Alise. She just seems like she cool people. 😊 I am not going for the whole weekend. Aren't they live streaming this year?

Pamela Hunter: I love them all, really. Live stream, I don't know. I didn't hear that.

Latoya Tea Mitchell: Yes, some portions will be streamed live. So for those who cannot attend, subscribe to Platinum Quill' TubeNation channel and you can watch in real time. 😁

Shaunte Turner (post): My favorite part of the PQ is the award gala. The food is always so good. KD's is doing the food this year...again. I know it's gonna be sooo good. Anybody ever been to KD's? What's your favorite menu item? I love his piña colada cheesecake explosion. You know his cheesecakes are super famous and he ships to the forty eight contiguous states. If you have never had, you gotta try one.

Crystal Alexis: Omg! That is too hard, sis. I love everything at KD's. Me and my family eat there whenever we are in town. But I do love KD's meat loaf. It is melt in your mouth herb goodness.

Samantha Swain: That meatloaf be on point. But I am going with the lamb chops with that lamb jam. To die for.

Latoya Pierce: I'm going with the banana pudding.

Gina Fife: The seafood mac and cheese. Definitely! The only place I know that doesn't skimp on the seafood.

Shirley Storm Jones: I cannot get enough of the garlic parmesan fries. Yummy!

Zing Live – Mustafa's Office

Peace, Love, and Blessings, Black Family. I was asked to offer prayer for the PQ Awards Gala. I am so honored. Shout out to Toni G! One love, sis.

So, y'all here selling books, signing contracts, giveaways pens, pencils, candy, and t-shirts. Of course, there had to be some drama. A scuffle here. A scuffle there, but y'all know Toni G. don't play that. And I'm tellin' y'all you gon' get banned for your wanna be boss bully behavior. Trust!

I can't family believe it, family. Fights amongst authors, readers, fans, and even so- called publishers. I have to ask this question, with conviction, from the depths of my soul. What is the color of your pen? What is the hue of the ink that drips from your quills? Is it the color of our people, black and powerful? Is it the color of pink, love and happiness? Is it the color of green, prosperity and fertility? No, Black family. Your quills drip the color red. A bloody red that's spilling all over the pages of mediocre mediums where it's accepted and praised, but not given honest appraisal.

Enabling and encouraging bullying, bossing, and bullshit. And bloodletting. Your quills spill hate and hate-mongering. It is red ink. Blood red ink. Your pens write robbing, raping, pillaging, torture, savagery, killing, and murdering without rhyme or reason. Red ink. You are writing these things into existence. Red ink. Can we write loving, healing, curing, elevating, and empowering into existence? Red ink. Can we write our beautiful history, our magnificent royalty? Red ink. Are we so unaware of the power of our pens? Red ink. Can we use our divine gift of the word for a greater good? Red ink. Do we not see that we are wading in this blood that we author? Red ink. Do we see that we are bleeding, bleeding all over the pages? Red ink. We are all responsible for this slaughter; we scribe it all on our own. Know that the blood of our ancestors is on our heads and the blood of our children is on our hands. I'm out. And as always, business over bullshit. See you at the banquet table. Peace

Zing Live End

Reactions: 547 Comments: 220 Shares: 1238

Zaire B.: Wow.

Geneen Sunbeam: Dang! Not much to say after that. #speechless

Stacy Egerton: Okay. Red ink. smh

Liah Harris: Ashe-o! #blackpower

Courtney Claiborne: Hmmm.

Gary Wimbush: Live and let live. Mustafa preaches too much.

Xavier Samuels: @Gary Wimbush Then get the fuck off his page if you don't want to hear him. Fuckin' asshole.

Gary Wimbush: Shut da fuck up!

Rita Hayes: See. This is exactly what he is talking about. The blood on our heads and our hands. Just everybody be quiet and let it sink in. Just be still.

Nailah J.: Yes, sis. Let the ink... sink. Shhhh...

Zing Live-End

Chapter Seventeen
Bye Bye Butterfly

Sunday 5:00 p.m.

The G. W. Carter Arboretum had its natural beauty and elegance enhanced for the evening's event. The already fragrant and colorful flowers were lightly adorned by the presence of swallowtail butterflies. Tables were draped with black and white tablecloths with glistening silverware and sparkling crystal. The anticipation of the evening's events generated a warm kind of electric in the cool air.

"It's funny," Hiram began as he surveyed the attendees entering the dining area. "Negros always seem to miss *every* event on the schedule except the meals," he continued as he stood next to Georgette. "If I could present that award then haul ass up outta here, I would."

"Baby, cut it out. You know that you love these events," Georgette said as she gestured for the waiter to refill her third glass of chardonnay. "You've always found some of your best authors here. It's one of your favorite hunting grounds."

"Yeah. When everything is following the schedule. Dinner should've been served 30 minutes ago. Shit is ridiculous."

"Well, at least you get to present the PQ award to Kendali. It gives Dominion, you, more exposure. This should kill all of that ghostwriting mess too. Especially with the award being based on merits that can't be discredited."

"Yeah, Gee, cuz I'm ready for that shit to die."

"Well, baby, today just might be the day that all of this ends. No matter what people may say, the Platinum Quill award validates her." Georgette straightened her husband's black and white bowtie.

In the garden, standing next to a life-sized statue of George Washington Carver, was a gathering that social media gossip and phone cameras would have died to capture. Bree McDee, Monique Ellis, and Shante Turner were talking and drinking champagne. It had been a while since the three had been together in the same place and space sharing laughs, memories, and good vibes.

"Girl, you are wearing that damn dress," Shante said as she took in Bree's evening wear. "Are you sure that you're not receiving the PQ award tonight? Because you're definitely dressed for it."

"Please," Bree began. "You know good and damn well that I wasn't stepping out without showing out." She stood and slowly turned around showing off her hot pink gown and five inch heels. "You like? Huh? You like?" she asked holding her champagne glass high. "Drip, drip, bitches!" she sang.

"You're a trip, Bree," Monique started as she sipped on her glass of sparkling bubbly. "I'm just glad that we made it to this night. I'm so tired of hearing all of this shit about who wrote what, how, and with whom. Kendali didn't. Kendali did. Ridiculousness on another level. I swear we gotta do better."

"Well, Mo, she is an author under your publishing house," Shante stated. "You should be happy for her."

"I *am* happy for her and I'm no longer with Dominion. So, that would be Hiram's publishing house."

"Wait. I didn't know that you had left Dominion," Bree remarked. "Damn. I'm supposed to be your girl."

"You are," Monique started as she placed her glass on the table. "The shit is crazy at Dominion, but Kendali is my girl. I'm glad that she's getting the award."

"Psssh," Bree sighed as she rolled her eyes. "Whatever."

"Well, I really don't care one way or the other. Who the hell cares if she has a ghostwriter? There are way bigger problems for us to deal with than that," Shante expressed.

As the ladies continued chatting and drinking, they were approached by Lesli Lyn and AJ West, working the room. Lesli had AJ float with her, assisting with logistics.

"Bree, Shante. Monique. Good to see you. Are you enjoying yourselves?" she asked.

"I suppose," Bree responded. "These damn heels are killing my feet."

"But you look soooooo good in them," Lesli stated with admiration.

"If you have a bucket and a mop, you can catch some of the drip, sistah." The champagne high had Bree feeling herself.

Lesli shook her head. "No thanks, not my cup," she smoothed out with a grin.

"What *is* your cup?" Monique asked.

"What do you mean?" Lesli inquired.

"I mean," Monique continued. "You piss people off with that blog of yours. We know you have had threats, hate mail. I just wanna know. What's your cup? Why incite? Why not write more and say less?"

"Because," Lesli explained. "I say what needs to be said. That's why. Because there's a freedom of speech. That's why. Because no one else is going to. That's why. Because I'm a writer. A journalist. One who's concerned and is invested in the public's interest."

"I'll just say this. With regards to everything you just said, and I love you and your work, but you're being messy, tacky, and desperate," Monique said.

"Tacky? Really? Wow. But your thug, boss, kingpin, bully books are full of class? Okay."

"Not my books anymore. So, whatever," she retorted and walked away.

AJ watched Monique saunter to the cash bar. "Wow. She really left Dominion. I ain't know for sure. Of course, there are always rumors."

"That's what she said." Lesli sighed. "Maybe it's time for you to come over to Meade now." Lesli brushed AJ's forearm lovingly.

"Yeah, maybe. Dominion bridge is falling down."

"Uh-huh." Lesli turned to Shante and Bree. "Enjoy the night, ladies!" They held up their wine glasses and nodded. She grabbed AJ's hand. "Let's go find Titus."

Near the fountain amid the salt and pepper anemones stood the soon-to-be celebrated Kendali Grace. She looked amazing in her gleaming white mini dress with matching lace brocade over skirt. Tonight was her big night and she was excited. She watched Georgette and Hiram interact from a distance and she felt a little jealous. She wanted desperately to ride the thrill of the entire night with Hiram. The anticipation. The dedication. The presentation. The celebration. She felt that Georgette wasn't worthy or deserving of the true depth of Hiram because she knew him like no one else did. She held his many secrets.

"Dali, you okay?" Dre asked.

"I'm fine," she replied as she snapped out of her fantasy. Kendali appreciated Dre coming along with her. He was always supportive during her ups and downs. Tonight, she didn't want to look lonely, pitiful, single, and unloved. Those points would not be added to the negative talk that she was already receiving in the social media news and gossip outlets. On this evening of acknowledgement and redemption, Dre came to her rescue because he was always a friend.

"You looked like you were someplace else. Nervous, huh?" he asked as he took in the elegant surroundings.

"Yeah. A little. I wish that I could just get this award and be on my way. The less time I'm onstage, the less time people have to stare and gossip."

"I get it, Dali, but fuck deez muthafuckas. This award solidifies you as the shit. To hell with everyone else's side talk. This award deads all of dat bullshit. So, you go up there with your head held high when you accept. And speak your truth when you give your speech."

Kendali's heart warmed as her soul began to ease from the tension. "I love you, Dre." She planted a tender kiss upon his lips. "I wish that…"

Dre stopped her mid-sentence. "You don't have to say or explain anything tonight, Dali. We can talk about that some other time. Tonight you need to be turning up," he said as he raised his champagne glass and handed Kendali her glass. "You're the star tonight."

Kendali smiled as she took in Dre's remedy from the madness. "You damn right. I'm Kendali Grace, bitches!" She and Dre laughed as they mock toasted the evening and Kendali's mental and emotional recharge. Hiram watched from below, but his eyes weren't the only ones fixed on the literary star.

The evening was quickly evolving into the magic that it was intended to be. The who's who of the industry were slowly filling the venue. Indigenous Soul was on stage playing light tunes suitable for the ambience. People had gathered in scattered pockets all over the arboretum.

283

Congregating near a beautiful man-made waterfall, Malachi Green and his wife Salima were in the company of Mustafa and Aminah Akeem.

"My God," Salima began. "I haven't been to one of these events in ages. Each event is always as elegant as the last one. I'm impressed with what Toni's done here. The butterflies. The fragrance of the flowers. It's all so beautiful," she continued.

"It is," Aminah added. "I could live here in peace and quiet with all of these butterflies."

"What about Mustafa?" Malachi asked.

Aminah responded, "Malachi, I said, and I reiterate, peace and quiet."

They all laughed.

"Yeah, and given some time I'll turn these butterflies into winged revolutionaries," Mustafa added.

Malachi chimed in. "I'm with that."

"We need to calm the chaos," Mustafa continued.

Aminah squeezed her husband's hand. "Uh-uh, baby. Not tonight. Tranquility is the vibe."

The friends erupted in more laughter.

"Hold up, baby. Gimme a second here," Mustafa pled. "Think about it. Look at all of these butterflies flying around here in harmony. No predators in this immediate environment. Their peace, it isn't fabricated. It just is. Their nature. Without compulsion. They evolve from what some will call ugly, as larvae and cocoons, to beautiful, colorful winged creatures. What stage are our people in amongst all of this chaos? Where's our peace?"

Mustafa's lightweight speech prompted silent reflection. "Now, while y'all marinate on that, I am going to see what I can see." He kissed Aminah and left the table.

In the black and white marble-tiled lobby, stood Bradford and Maceo.

"This is some bullshit, you know?" Bradford began.

"What? Kendali receiving the PQ award?" Maceo asked.

Bradford laughed. "Nah, bro. I'm talking about how long it's taking them to get that food right. What the hell is Khai cooking back there? Some elephants? Damn."

"Yeah. I had enough of the shrimp puffs and salmon bites. Time for the main course."

"Precisely." Brad swigged his cognac. "At least the liquor is flowing," Brad commented referring to the free wine and cash bar that was customary for every PQ gala.

Maceo raised his glass to Brad's observation while he watched Kendali walk around with Dre on her arm working the room.

"And this is some bullshit. On so many levels. Scandals and all."

"What? You mean Kendali?"

"Yeah. I can't believe the bullshit in this industry. I always tell Nikki, this industry is worse than the streets."

"Tell me about it. And it didn't just start. You know my father worked in publishing for many years, magazines and such. There was foolishness going on then, but instead of us eradicating it, we have nurtured it. Elevated it. We are supposed to do more than our forefathers, be greater. We have definitely lost our way."

"So true, bro. So true. What we gon' do?"

"Well, me and some of the brethren got some things cooking. With the guidance of our learned elders, we about to make a big change."

"You mean Isis?"

"Damn! How you know?"

"I used to be the connect. Once a connect, always a connect. Dig?"

Brad laughed. "You need to come on in with us, man"

"Let's talk about it. Show me what y'all doin'."

"Cool. I will call you next week."

"Bet." Maceo swallowed the rest of his wine and placed the glass on the high table. He saw Nikki at the lobby's far end arguing with Isaac. "Hold on, Brad. I will be back." Maceo strode quickly toward the discrepancy.

"Why you here with this nigga?"

"Maceo is my husband, Isaac."

"I don't give a fuck. You my fuckin' woman."

"Not any more. If I ever was."

"If you ever were? If you ever were? You wasn't sayin' that when that nigga was locked up and I was dickin' you down. Holdin' you down. Helpin' you with Black Pearl."

"You want me to write you a check for your services?"

"What?! You fuckin' bitch."

"Isaac. Please. Just let it go. Keep stalkin' Kendali."

'Fuuuck! I told you that I am over Kendali. That was way back when. And I never stalked her. You wouldn't even let me explain." Isaac's voice echoed in the high ceiling acoustics of the lobby. Nikki and Isaac were so caught up in their argument, they did not see Maceo approaching.

"Yo, you need to pipe that down," Maceo bellowed jumping in front of Nikki. He palmed her hip and with one smooth strong motion, pushed her directly behind him.

"Maceo, it's-"

"Hush, Pearl!"

Isaac pulled his gun from his waist, stepped back two paces, and aimed straight at Maceo's forehead.

Maceo raised his arms. "You ain't even got the heart for that, nigga. Now put your toy away."

"You don't know me, Mace. You think you do, but you don't."

"I practically raised you, ahk. Now put the gun away. I don't want no trouble. I just want you to stay out of my wife's face." Nikki leaned on his back, aroused by Maceo guarding and protecting her as nectar dripped onto her panties. Bradford rushed to the commotion and Mustafa ran behind him.

Mustafa spoke, "Look here brothers. This is not who we came to be." He looked at Isaac. "Ike, c'mon man."

Isaac started to put his gun away and Mustafa asked, "Will you give it to me. Just let me hold it for the night."

Isaac reluctantly handed over his gun, an absolute sucka move in the streets. "ONLY because it's you, Brother Akeem. Only because it's you." Mustafa accepted the gun. Isaac gritted his teeth and spat his words at Maceo, "You got saved today, muthafucka." Maceo leapt toward Isaac and punched him in his jaw. Isaac stumbled backward holding his face. He rushed Maceo and they tumbled to the floor, rumbling , an elegant tuxedoed ball of confusion.

"Would you two please!" Nikki screamed as Mustafa and Bradford used all their might pulling the two brutes apart. Mustafa held Isaac as heaved large amounts of air in and out of his mouth. "Fuck you, nigga."

"Go get your own wife, muthafucka." Maceo shouted as Bradford restrained him against the wall. With apologetic eyes glimmering at Isaac, Nikki pulled a handkerchief from her purse and gave it him so he could wipe the blood dripping from his lips. He blew her a kiss that only the two of them saw. For her, it was the final kiss goodbye; for him it was a kiss of hope.

She glided to her husband's side, softly pecking the places where she knew bruises were forming. Regretting that her lack of patience, trust, and courage were the cause of the bloody scene, she caressed his right hook. A spiritual evolution was upon her, prompting a vow to cease scolding herself for the broken relationship with Maceo. It takes two to tango and everything was not her fault. They were *both* dancing the samba of love.

Moments later a familiar voice sounded from the speakers. "Okay, everyone. We're sorry for the delay, but now it's time to break bread," Khai announced. "So, if we can have our highly esteemed brother, Mustafa, to offer the blessing for the food, we can all get our stomachs right."

"Amen to that," a hungry attendee yelled from the crowd of patrons. The remark drew light laughter.

Mustafa proceeded toward the table where Khai stood and turned to face the guests.

"Black power, bruva!" Maceo shouted as he raised his fist.

Mustafa pumped a fist and responded, "Black pen power!" He adjusted the mic.

"Let's bow our heads please." He cleared his throat. "To The Most High: We thank you for this food that we're about to receive for the health, strength, and nourishment of our bodies. As it was issued from upon high with love and prepared in love, let us ingest this love and be full from it. Let us break bread and not hearts. We express infinite gratitude. Amen."

"Amen," the attendees shouted as some of them applauded lightly.

An hour into the feast, there was a tap on the mic followed by light feedback. The hostess cleared her throat. "Eh hemmm," she began with a smile. "Is this thing on?" Toni tugged at the sleeve of her tuxedo shirt as the attendees turned their attention to the stage. "Okay. So, let me first thank all of you for being here tonight. And thank Khai for blessing us with KD's best from his supper club's kitchen for a helluva lot of stacks," she joked. "So, I'ma be y'all Mommas tonight when I tell you to eat eeeeeeverything on the plate," Toni sang. The audience laughed. "On a serious note though, I love you and appreciate you, bro. Give a round of applause for Khai Draper and KD's Supper Club." The event guests complied. "And a round of applause for your beautiful selves, and Indigenous Soul for blessing us with their soulful sounds. Y'all the best. I swear."

Toni focused her sight on the star of the event, Kendali Grace. "Now, for the real reason that we're here, which is to celebrate a beautiful, gifted, and often controversial pensmith. She's a friend to me and many of you, but I feel it's appropriate for this award to be presented by someone who works closest with her. Someone who has been in the ink and paper trenches with her. So, Hiram Rivers, if you'd come up and do the honors."

Hiram ascended the stage as the audience clapped. Toni took a few steps aside and stood near the platform where the award was displayed. Hiram approached the podium dressed sharp and crisp, his walk, smooth and confident.

Hiram fixed his eyes on Kendali extending his right arm. "Kendali Grace," he began. "Tonight, we celebrate this beautiful and gifted icon and bestow upon her the honors, awards and accolades that she has earned. Rightfully earned. And anything that contradicts this is far from the truth." Dominion Publishing's CEO continued singing the praises of his top-selling author for another three minutes. Next, it was the moment of truth. "Kenni? Come up here! Kendali Grace everyone." The garden erupted with roaring applause as literary star walked up the marble steps to receive her christening. She was about to be made a boss.

Hiram adjusted the mic stand for Kendali and then stepped aside. She took a breath and silence fell upon the garden as they anticipated her next words. A stranger's eyes honed in on her from a distance.

"I don't know where to begin," Kendali started with a glowing smile of honest appreciation. Butterflies danced and swirled around her. She felt royal and magical. "I am honored even amongst the controversy," she said as she lifted the diamond and platinum plaque. "I earned this." The butterflies fluttered around her.

The attendees applauded.

At that moment a sharp, piercing whisper was heard. It lasted for a split second. The butterflies' serene dance was disrupted into chaotic scatter. There was confusion. Yelling. Screaming. All watched in bewilderment as the beautiful Platinum Quill award recipient fell back onto the marble floor, her award shattering into shards of broken glass and broken dreams.

Hiram rushed to her aid thinking that she'd fainted. As he got closer to his wounded lover, he saw the blood flowing from her chest. "She's been shot!" Hiram yelled. "Dial 911! Now!!!"

Some of the guests began a rapid exodus of the garden. Others looked around for the shooter while some took cover. Kendali's closest friends and colleagues rushed the stage to help their fallen star.

"What the fuck?" Hiram shouted as he removed his jacket. He placed it under Kendali's head and his hand over her bleeding heart. "Somebody get me some fucking towels! Something! Shit!"

His eyes welled with tears as he watched the blood mix with the glass on the floor. He looked into her eyes as he rocked her and squeezed her hand. "Kenni, hold on, baby girl. You gon' be alright. Just hold on. Help is on the way."

Georgette and others watched from the sidelines as Hiram did all that he could to save Kendali. They watched the attempt to save Kendali's life, but Mrs. Rivers caught a hint of something else. Kendali began reaching for Hiram. She tried to speak.

"Hir...Hiii... Hiram," she coughed staining his white shirt with crimson.

"Where's the fucking ambulance?" Dre shouted as he rushed to the stage with a tablecloth. "Dali, baby! Dali!" he said rushing to her side. Hiram placed the tablecloth over her fatal wound as tears fell onto his cheeks. He knew that there was nothing else that could be done. Only he knew that in that moment.

Kendali began fading away. "Dali? Hold on, baby. Please hold on! Help is on the way. Hold on."

An odd cool wind swept the stage as a bloody-handed Hiram and others witnessed the last breath of life leave Kendali's body. The sirens could be heard in the distance, but the aid and the rescue had come too late. Kendali Grace had written her final chapter on the evening of receiving her greatest honor. She fell before the eyes of friends, lovers, fans, and foes without giving proper thanks. Not even a wave or a wink, or a warm kiss goodbye.

TO BE CONTINUED

Join The Kaleidoscope
For discussions, giveaways, and special events!
https://www.facebook.com/groups/thebutterflykaleidoscope/

Visit my website for sneak peeks, gift books, and The
Kaleidoscope Shop!
www.ButterflyBrooks.com

9 781730 842832